# The George Story

## Callie Ann Atkinson

Spellbound Publishing House, LLC

Spellbound Publishing House, LLC

Austin, TX | www.spellbound-publishing.com

First edition: November 2024

The publisher is not responsible for websites (or their content) that are not owned by the publisher.

Identifiers:

LCCN: XXXXXXXXXX (coming soon)

ISBN 979-8-89123-082-8 (paperback)

ISBN 979-8-89123-083-5 (ebook)

# Contents

*In memory of Gramps, whose stories were the beginning of this adventure into the past.*

# Trigger Warning List

At Spellbound Publishing House, we are committed to providing an inclusive and safe reading environment for all our audiences. We understand that certain topics may be distressing or triggering to some readers. Below is a comprehensive list of potential triggers that may appear in *The George Story*.

- Physical and wartime violence

- Suicide

- Historical racial terms

# Author's Note To Readers

Memories can haunt us. Sometimes, they can send us on journeys we never fully expected on which to go. For me, this novel has been one of those journeys. It all began as stories; tales told to me by my grandfather of my great-great-great uncle George Atkinson. They were the kinds of stories that are nearly unbelievable, told through the hazy memory of an elder. These oral memories landed in my mind and mellowed, then grew, and I followed the pathways they had unknowingly created in my mind. I began to put the stories down on the page.

The stories took me deep into the history of the Civil War up through the turn of the twentieth century and the history of my family. Through newspaper clippings I learned of the places George lived and worked, and many of the stories told by my grandfather were corroborated by columns in these newspapers. This then sent me on a physical journey; following in the footsteps of George, I traveled through Colorado, New Mexico, and Arizona, my dad accompanying me on this quest of history, family history. We found artifacts of George's life, signs of the life he lived still visible on the landscape, even as time tried to erase them. From a small, open-latch brick house in Black Hawk; to the ruins of a large stone building in Chase Gulch that was once the masonry; to the fine lines of John's own handwriting; to a photo of Governor Evans' Denver mansion built with Atkinson brick...to the presence of ghosts on the bluff at Sand Creek, in the surrounding sagebrush, the flat, winding creek bed, and the rolling hills of prairie; and finally to George's grave in Tucson, found so easily it was almost frightening. Above the stone grew a beautiful tree that somehow felt more important than the stone. It felt right, perfect even, and I imagined the tree being planted by his family in lieu of writing on the stone. What better way to remember someone? Perhaps even a better way than a novel, but his story pulled at my fingertips, at my mind, and my heart. It needed to be told.

The journey took us to the Santa Cruz Valley in Arizona, and there I felt closer to George than ever before, watching the mountains turn the purple of prickly pear at sunset and soften in a mist at sunrise, hearing the click of a roadrunner's call like the click of a tongue, feeling the bark of mesquite and being surprised that it is rough in spite of the glossy appearance. Knowing that he must have seen and heard and felt these things, as well, brought me closer to him. Evidence of his life came unexpectedly into my hands through finding his name in a local history book, discovering his name in museum displays, unearthing shards of brick where the hotel he built had once stood, being gifted a whole brick by the museum curator, walking along the Santa Cruz River and knowing George's livestock once grazed there. Every new discovery came with a personal thrill: this was my ancestor, and I had proof in my hands that he had *lived*. And so, I came home with a notebook full of stories and history, ready to be woven together to form this novel, and pieces of brick made by George's own hands, serving as both inspiration and remembrances.

In this novel, I wanted to share the history I learned through my traveling research, as well as to tell George's story, giving both a wide, historical point of view through an intermittent historical narrator, and a closer, personal point of view of the places and times in which George lived. It was important to me to present pieces of this time from an objective viewpoint, zooming in slowly from this initially distant, historian's point of view before moving closer to see history through George's eyes, showing how the events of the past can be seen and interpreted by different perspectives. The objective, historical point of view is given through a prologue and in interludes within the novel, from which the narrative shifts into a closer view of this time in history. This is a work of fiction, but I hope that it also sheds some light on the historical facts woven throughout; historical memories that shouldn't be forgotten.

# Prologue

The streets of Black Hawk were cut into hillsides, the houses balanced on stone wall foundations, stair-stepping toward the sky. The town is surrounded by mountain slopes and weaves through gulches that turn gold in the afternoons; alpine-glow the people there call it. It sifts through the branches of supple aspens and perfumed firs, disappearing into rocky mineral soil. What began as a stroke of luck, gold found in 1859, becomes a bustling center that boasts homes of politicians and military men, drawing people by the hundreds, and in 1864 Black Hawk officially becomes an incorporated town of Colorado Territory. Some come for the mines, others for the business opportunities a newly sprung mining town affords, still more come for the scenery: "Neither pen, pictures, or photographs do justice to the scenery," they like to say.

Then, gold and silver mines make Black Hawk the place to be. People settle into their homes with what feels like permanence, though deep down they know it won't be. The scenery changes: trees disappear and are replaced by shanties and sluice boxes, skip wagons and narrow-gauge mine railways, mine shafts and trestles. Ovando Hollister writes in *The Mines of Colorado*, "The bordering hills were densely wooded when the mines were discovered, but the trees were small, and few now remain within five or six miles around." Change. Prosperity.

Black Hawk becomes so prosperous, Territorial Governor John Evans makes it his home, building a mansion on the eastern side of the canyon. It faces Chase Gulch, the slopes grassy and pockmarked with mines. The mansion is spacious, being two-stories tall, and has a roofed porch along the front; here Mrs. Evans entertains with lemonade in a cut-glass pitcher and tea-cakes on china from her mother. The porch railings and the trimare whitewashed, the rest of the house painted blue, with filigree curving and curling like ivy along each eave.

Evans builds his house beside the house of businessman Peter Merchant, investor Tyler M. Clinton, and entrepreneur John Atkinson; the street is one of grandeur and stature. Some say that Black Hawk will rival Denver, but it is remote, insular in that it is tucked away in Clear Creek Canyon. Soon the townspeople feel miles away from safety, as tales of Indian warriors gathering and attacking settlements slip into every shaft line of the town.

With the urging of citizens, and unable to see how he can protect the people of his territory without some kind of military group, Evans raises a private militia, issuing:

*Executive Department, Colorado Territory, United States of America.*

*To all unto whom these presents shall come, Greeting: Knowye that, reposing special confidence in the patriotism, integrity and ability of C. M. Tyler of Black Hawk C.T. & John Evans Governor of the Territory of Colorado, in pursuance of and by authority vested in me, do hereby appoint and commission him Captain of the 'Tyler Rangers' Colorado Volunteer Militia Cavalry. And I do authorize, empower, and require him to execute and fulfill the duties of the office, according to law; and to have and to hold said office, with all the rights, authorities, privileges and emblem(?) thereunto appertaining, for and during two years. In testimony whereof, I have hereinto set my hand and caused to be affixed the Great Seal of the Territory. Done at Denver, this eighteenth day of August in the year of our Lord, one thousand eight hundred and sixty-four. Jno. Evans.*[1]

Clinton M. Tyler agrees to it all, even though he has nomilitary background. He is an investor, a businessman, but he has visions of a safe place to bring up his children. He has always been a dreamer, taking on partnerships in mines and sawmills throughout the mountains and gulches from Black Hawk to Nederland to Boulder. Being captain of a volunteer militia is away to try something new, to show what he can do, and prove that maybe he is more than a businessman: he can protect his family just as well as any frontiersman. And so he becomes the captain of volunteers who receive no compensation, provided only with a blanket and a few food rations that will last barely half of the time they are in commission. These men will serve purely by conviction and will be called Tyler's Rangers. They will be nearly forgotten.

[1] Italics directly quoted from original document.

# Chapter 1

From the sitting room of the small brick house at 102 Horn St., Black Hawk, Colorado, George Atkinson could stand at the window and look across the spire of the Methodist church into the gulch where the brickyard breathed. It had been in that brickyard that the bricks of this humble house had been formed. The house was built in the English style, with an interlocking brick design that created a curvature to the structure and gave it elegance. It was the last house on the street, which rose steadily to the end, the houses all on one side. In contrast to the brick house in which George now stood, the other houses were only clapboard, with wide porches and filigree along the roofline. The street was on the edge of town with a view of the rest of it spilling down the canyon and the surrounding hillsides of rock and shrubby evergreens.

In the early morning of August 19th, 1864, George pressed his forehead against the window frame and stared into the predawn light. He could just make out the church spire, and he fixed his eyes on it, thinking he'd say a prayer. In the window glass, his reflection looked back at him, dark blonde hair brushed back from his forehead to reveal deep-set eyes. His face, with the beginnings of a mustache above the decisive line of his mouth, still had the roundness of youth, but the bones of his cheeks were visible and the curve of jawline squared at his chin.

"We can finally do something for our country," Jack had said when he'd pressed the flyer calling for volunteers to join Tyler's Rangers and quell Indian uprisings into George's hand. Jack was eager to join the fighting and every day brought news of another battle: the Battle of the Wilderness, of Port Walthall Junction, of Cold Harbor, of Fort Pillow, of Atlanta, the siege of Petersburg, the Battle of Mobile Bay. With each one, George wondered if his childhood friends were there. Which side were they fighting on? Jack said they had cheated or been cheated out of the chance to prove themselves, their manhood, their loyalty, living so far west of it all, but George wasn't so sure. The right and the wrong of it all, the urgency blurred with distance. Who could say on which side they'd have fought if they'd been there in the thick of things? Jack's certainty of the Union being right, being justified, frightened George in a way he couldn't describe, almost as if he and Jack would have been on opposite sides.

This was different, though, a different kind of fight. At least, that's what he thought as he watched the mist rise from the canyon. He'd heard the stories of mutilated families, read the accounts of the Hungate massacre that had flooded the papers all summer, his stomach clenching at the thought of the young couple and their two babies murdered along Box Elder Creek. The papers said Indians were responsible. This would be what the rangers would put an end to, the recruiting poster promised. By volunteering, he'd be protecting his loved ones, the new life they'd made. Somehow this decision was clearer, but maybe it was just because of the proximity. Still, he could see a purpose: to keep those he loved from harm, and yes, maybe he could prove to his father he was every bit a man as Jack. He could be strong and do what had to be done. Here was a chance to prove that. He'd take it. The house behind him was quiet, peaceful, and blissfully unaware of the decision George had made.

The town clock began to strike the hour and George counted each chime. "One, two, three, four, five." His voice was just below a whisper, and as the last chime echoed down the canyon, he continued, "In the name of Jesus Christ, Amen."

"Amen," a voice behind him repeated, his father's voice low and gruff with morning disuse. He stood in the doorway, already dressed for the day, his shirt buttoned and tucked with a precision learned in the British army. Fastening his sleeves tightly around his wrists, John stepped into the room and came to look out the window, his thinner, slightly taller reflection joining George's own. "And what are we praying for?" he asked.

George shook his head, as if he didn't have an answer, and he wasn't really certain that he did. But then he said, "I've decided." He paused, clearing his throat. "I've decided to volunteer."

John laid his hand on George's shoulder and gave it a squeeze. "Good," he said, "it is the right decision." His voice was filled with a surety that George did not share, and he couldn't help quietly saying, "I'm not sure it is."

"Of course it is." A commanding edge sharpened John's voice, and George recognized it as the voice he used when giving orders that were not to be disobeyed. "It will make you a man."

George hoped his father was right. He wanted to be the man his father wanted him to be, needed to be, and there was an expectation that he and his brothers would serve their country, as John had served his as a young man in Britain, and again as a mature man in Colorado on the Denver Home Guard. George remembered the meticulous way John would straighten the collar of his guard uniform and level his hat brim, the sergeant insignia embroidered in gold on the band, before stepping out the door for patrol.

John squeezed George's shoulder again. "Make me proud, son," he said, and the weight of the words settled across George. He drew in a deep breath, silently promising he would as he nodded, unable to voice the promise aloud.

"I'm here to volunteer," George told Clinton Tyler later that morning in front of the Methodist church. The church's newly acquired stained glass reflected the colors of the coming autumn on the browning grasses around the coarse, wooden front steps.

"You understand there is no compensation?" Tyler asked, and George nodded. "You'll be provided with a bedroll and food rations for a month. You need your own horse and any other supplies," Tyler continued, and again, George nodded. Tyler, a slight man of medium height, appraised George with sharply discerning eyes, his face stern, angular. He then gave a short nod and passed George a piece of paper. "Make your mark," Tyler said.

Holding the paper in his hands made George's heart pick up tempo, and for a moment he just stared at it, the words bleary and blotted as though the ink used had been lumpy and cold. The words cleared and George read, "I hereby swear to uphold the office of a private in the Colorado volunteer militia known as Tyler's Rangers for a total of 100 days, during which I will act to protect and serve The United States of America and the Territory of Colorado, under the command of Captain Clinton M. Tyler."

Under these words were scrawled a dozen or so names, most of which George knew, including the name of his brother Jack. He reached for the quill to sign his own name to the document, only to have his elbow jostled by someone coming up behind him. "Now hold on a minute, GW, don't go signing that without me," came the familiar voice of Jimmy Dobbs.

George turned with a smile and Jimmy leaned over the parchment to read the declaration, the curls of his brown hair falling over the fair, freckled skin of his forehead.

"You're joining up?" George said, asking the obvious question.

"Yep, it's been decided that I can't let everyone else protect my loved ones." The statement was serious, and George knew Jimmy meant it in all seriousness, but there was a sparkle in Jimmy's eyes that suggested he saw this as an adventure not to be missed. Jimmy took up the quill and signed his name, **James Dobbs.** He held the feather out to George, and George took it, the sight of Jimmy's name there setting him more at ease. He signed Geo. W. Atkinson. This was a job that needed doing, and when it was over they would come home to Black Hawk and settle back into the rhythms of the town.

"Glad to have you," Tyler said, gripping first Jimmy's then George's hand.

"Thank you," George said, unsure if that was the appropriate response. Before Tyler could engage him in any conversation, he ducked away and walked up the street. His body felt strangely light, while his heart felt like it had dropped to the bottom of his stomach, leaden. It was as though his body had separated in two, and half of him watched while the other half felt. Jimmy caught up with him and fell into step.

"Lucky ain't we," Jimmy said, "that we get to ride and camp out under the stars for the next one hundred days."

"I guess that's one way to look at it," George responded. His throat felt tight and his words came out quietly.

"It's the only way to look at it." Jimmy smiled and poked George in the ribs with his elbow, as if knowing the uncertainties that swam in George's mind. Then he snatched the hat from George's head.

"Hey!" George jumped for the hat, but Jimmy grinned and ducked away, running down the street. George raced after him, the heels of his boots clacking on the boardwalk, and the gravity of volunteering fading away. "Jimmy, give it back," he shouted.

"It's just an old hat," Jimmy said, slowing and turning to face George. "Why would you want it back?"

Before George could answer, a pod of girls in bright calico came onto the street from the bakery, and Jimmy thrust the hat against George's chest, nearly hard enough to knock the wind out of him. Jimmy smoothed his hair and straightened his shirt, brushing bits of dust and grass away, before sauntering across the street toward the girls. George stood there, holding the brim of his hat, and watched as Jimmy swept his arm around one of the girls, planting a kiss on her blushing cheek. George knew the girl, Lizzie, only slightly, mainly through Jimmy's talk, and there had been times where he had been jealous that Jimmy had someone. Now though, a sudden sensation of relief slid over him. At least he wouldn't have to say goodbye to any sweetheart, grateful now that he hadn't asked Rosie McEllen to walk out with him. He'd thought about it often enough, almost asked a time or two, but something had always stayed him, as if he knew somehow he would be leaving Black Hawk. Still, as he watched Jimmy chat with ease, making the girls laugh and Lizzie's eyes shine, he wished he had at least the same bravado.

"See ya on the morrow, George!" Jimmy called, waving from across the street, before taking up Lizzie's hand and walking on down the way.

Rosie broke away from the other girls and came toward George, smiling. She bounced on her toes as she walked, making her dark curls spring. George wanted to back away, run, but he'd stood too long, and now he'd have to talk to her. He forced a smile. "Miss McEllen, how are you?"

"Well, thank you," Rosie answered. "Do you have the day off?"

"No, just a lunch break," George replied. "I should be heading back now." He made as if to turn, but he waited, not wanting to be rude.

"Go," Rosie said. She smiled, and George thought he caught some wistfulness in the look.

"I joined the new rangers," he said, "the ones Tyler is leading."

Rosie nodded. "Jimmy told us," she said, adding after a breath, "I knew you would."

"I didn't," George said. It felt good admitting it, admitting that he almost hadn't joined. With the admission came the realization that he really was going to leave this place, that he really was a ranger now.

"What man wouldn't? How else will the Indians know they cannot get away with massacre?" The color bloomed in Rosie's cheeks when George didn't answer. "My apologies. I'm afraid I crossed a line," she said.

George shook his head, but still didn't respond to her questions. Instead, he changed the subject, wanting to hold on to the illusion that he wasn't going into battle anytime soon. "Do you want some taffy?" George asked.

"I'd love some," Rosie said, taking his offered arm.

They walked back up the street without speaking. Swallows, glinting in the sun and flashing near-fluorescent teal on their shoulders, darted between the buildings and swooped to overhanging rocks on the canyon walls where they plastered their mud nests. In spring their white chests gleamed with newness, like the first snowfall, but now their feathers had dulled to an off-white that made George think of a handkerchief used too long. As he watched the swallows, with the warmth of Rosie's arm on his, he could almost forget he was leaving and that he had to somehow break this news to his family, to Sarah. But in the back of his mind Rosie's convictions floated, persistent and waiting for answers.

*Young George didn't remember much about his mother, but sometimes he could feel her. A warmth and softness like a wool blanket tucked up under his chin, a voice singing lullabies without any words, and glimpses of satin strands of blonde, or taffy brown, or maybe the color of cherry wood. Sometimes he thought he remembered bursting into giggles as the hair brushed across his face; that was all. George did, however, remember Sarah coming. She came when he was five and fit into the household like a foot into a warm slipper.*

*At seven George understood that Sarah was his stepmother; that his father had married her after his real mother died. "Do you love Father?" he asked. It was before they had moved west, and he was sitting on the edge of the table in the warm kitchen of the house in Peoria, Illinois. The table edges had been worn smooth by the years and felt nearly soft beneath his fingertips.*

*She ruffled his hair and laughed. "Of course."*

*"As much as my mother did?"*

*Sarah's eyes went soft, their blueness deepening. She handed him a cookie rich in raisins and nuts. "Your mother was a special woman," she said.*

*George bit into the chewy sweetness.*

*"I was just a girl when she was alive, so I didn't know her well." She paused, listening to hoofbeats in the yard, then nodded slightly, confirming she recognized*

*them.* "But I knew she was a special woman. You didn't have to know her well to know that. She loved you all."

*George finished his cookie as Sarah stepped to the window and pressed her hands on the sill.* "But yes," she said, "I love your father as much as I'm able." *Her voice became quieter, and when she looked back at George her face was flushed.* "Now," she said, "how about you fetch some water so I can get dinner going?"

Now, eleven years later, George stood in the doorway of the kitchen watching Sarah mix biscuits. Her dusty blonde hair, starting to gray around the edges, escaped from the tight bun at the base of her neck in long strands that fell across her sharp cheekbones. The veins on her hands were more visible now than they were when she married his father, but they moved with a gentleness that had always been there. They were hands that never hesitated to soothe, to pull someone close, to check for fever, to care for her family in every way that she could. George tried to remember what his mother looked like, but standing there watching Sarah, he realized that she really was his mother. The woman who gave birth to him was just a soft feeling in the back of his mind.

"Sarah?"

She looked up with a smile and pushed her hair off her face with the back of her hand. "Georgie boy, stick another log in the stove will you?"

"Mmhmm." He pushed a log into the flames and watched it catch fire.

"Something on your mind?" Sarah dropped sticky lumps of biscuit dough into a cast iron pan. The dough sizzled when it hit the hot melted butter.

George poked the fire. "I've joined Tyler's campaign."

Sarah paused, her hands above the bowl, dough sticking to them. "Your brother put you up to this?" she asked.

"No. No...maybe, I don't know," George said. He stood and shoved his hands into his pockets. "Only, I thought maybe it'd be something—something I could do for once."

The fire crackled. Sarah dropped the rest of the dough into the pan. She scraped the dough from her hands, cupped them around her mouth and called through the open door, "Skip." The white and brown dog bolted across the barnyard to her. She dumped the biscuit scrapings on the doorstep and watched him lick them up, one hand on her hip. She wasn't a tall woman; George had passed her in height by the time he was twelve, but she was sturdy, the kind of woman who could stand straight even in the force of a gale. Turning back, her chicory blue eyes flickered over George, and he felt as though she were reading his thoughts.

"I can't tell you not to go," she said, "but I wish you wouldn't." The cast iron clattered as she shoved it into the oven. "War doesn't make a man. Kindness does."

"How long will you be gone?" Aurora, George's young sister, asked, sitting on the rail of the corral as George groomed his gelding after dinner. He hadn't bothered to tie the horse, letting him continue to eat hay beside the half dozen other horses while being brushed. The sun had sunk low, nearly disappeared behind the ridge. There was the chill of alpine summer evenings sneaking up the sleeves of his jacket. Aurora wrapped her skirts tightly around her ankles and pulled her shawl close, arms crossed.

"One hundred days," George answered.

Aurora frowned. "That's a long time."

"Not that long."

"Long enough." Aurora sighed. "Wish I was going."

"No you don't."

"How do you know?" Aurora's voice took on an indignant tone of a younger sibling being told they were too little.

George shrugged. "I just know," he said. A fly landed on his gelding's back and the gelding rippled his skin and then shook, dust clouding into the air. George took a step back, waiting for the dust to settle before returning to grooming the horse's sleek sides.

"Heya," Tib, one of George's younger brothers, said, climbing the fence to sit beside Aurora. He brushed his lank brown hair out of his eyes and bit into an apple. At the crunch, the family cart mare raised her head and nickered, making Tib, Aurora, and George laugh. The mare tipped her ears forward and eagerly stepped to the fence. Tib took another bite of the apple and then offered the rest to the mare. She took it from him with her lips.

"Won't you get tired of riding after a hundred days?" Tib asked.

George shrugged. "I like riding," he said. It was the truth; he loved the way it felt to ride long miles on horseback, the way the wind burned his face when moving at a gallop, the way each movement of the horse seemed to become his own. If he was looking forward to anything about being a ranger, it was being on horseback for days on end.

"I'd get tired of it." Tib pulled another apple from his pocket and shined it on his shoulder, before biting into the crispness.

"Got any more of those?" George asked, giving his gelding a final brush and walking to the fence.

"Naw, this is my last." Tib took another bite and juice dribbled from the corner of his mouth.

George reached up and snatched the apple from him, taking a bite quickly. Tib kicked at George, but George was ready and moved out of the way easily. "Catch," he said and tossed the apple back toward his brother. Aurora caught it instead, taking a bite, too, before presenting it back to Tib. Tib took it, scowling at both his siblings. George smiled back at him and Aurora giggled, and an ache opened in George. He would miss these two. That was the part he wasn't looking forward to.

George saddled his lanky gelding the next day, tying his bedroll atop his saddlebag. The morning was warm even though the sky was filled with gray clouds. Chickens scratched in the corral, clucking to themselves, and the milk cow lowed softly to her calf. Along the edge of the barn, yarrow bloomed and alpine dandelions turned their bright yellow faces skyward. Sarah liked the wild flowers, tending them, cultivating them as if they had come from seeds across the continent.

George tried not to think about when he would be standing in this barnyard again. Beside him, Jack saddled his own horse, pulling the cinch sharply tight. Not only was Jack older, he was also taller than George by a good inch. His shoulders were slighter, sloping down where George's squared. He had dark brown hair that when the sun hit it just right glinted auburn; the night before Sarah had trimmed it close. "You should get a haircut, too," Jack had told George. "We're going to be gone awhile." George shook his head, stubbornness settling in. He'd already decided he'd let his hair, which in the light of day settled somewhere between brown and blonde in color, grow long and wild. It was a small bit of defiance against his brother.

Sarah tucked biscuit and jam sandwiches, made with the last of last year's chokecherry jam, into their saddlebags as they said their goodbyes. Their father, John, shook first Jack's hand, then George's. "Take care of yourselves," he said gruffly. George saw his father's eyes, which always seemed to mimic the color of the sky, moisten. He looked away before a tear could drop, hugging Sarah and his young sister and brothers, wishing for time to pause so he could stay in their warm arms for just a moment longer.

"We should go," Jack said, already settled in his saddle.

George looked back just before the farmstead passed from sight and saw his sister, Aurora, still waving, her hair bright red in the sun. He couldn't help but wonder when and if he'd ever see it again.

At the southern edge of town, miner's shacks lined the wagon tracks of the road, and the men who'd volunteered as rangers gathered, George and Jack and Jimmy amongst them. The air was cool still, not yet warmed by the late summer sun, but George was sweating as Captain Tyler rode up. Tyler guided his horse gently, settled deep in the saddle with the air of someone who had ridden long days before. It surprised George. To him Tyler was a businessman, someone who dealt in stocks and made investments from behind a desk; George hadn't expected him to be a horseman.

Tyler began to address the men, taking on his new role of commander as if pulling on an old, favorite jacket. "Good morning, men. I salute you for your courage in volunteering, though I expected no less of the men in Black Hawk. We are setting out on an important campaign, one that will protect those you love and help make this territory safe for settlers. Our job is to patrol the area surrounding Black Hawk for any hostile Indians. We will keep the mail and travel routes open at whatever cost." Tyler spoke with an ease that settled the nerves of those around him. He rode his horse up and down in front of the ranks of rangers as he spoke, looking directly at each of the men under his command. As he came in front of George, George didn't meet the stare; the directness made him shift in his saddle.

"At whatever cost," Tyler repeated, "do you all understand?"

George glanced quickly from side to side as the rangers responded to Tyler's question with a synchronized nod.

"Answer with confidence!" Tyler's voice rang clearly. "Do you all understand?"

"Yes, sir!" The rangers responded as one, and as his voice melded with theirs, George felt a sense of sudden comradeship. They were all in this together, for better or for worse.

"Let's ride!" Tyler turned his horse and headed at a lope down the road. The rangers fell in line behind him, riding two or three abreast. Some of the horses snorted, pulling at their bits in an attempt to race the other horses around them. George's horse pinned his ears and nipped at Jack's horse, catching only air as George tightened the reins. After a mile the horses leveled out, settling into a rhythmic and synchronous gait, a motion they would all, horses and riders, become quickly accustomed to.

As Tyler had said, the rangers rode the mail routes through the remainder of the summer and into fall, scouting the South Platte, to discourage Indian uprisings. They patrolled Bijou Creek, camping at Douglas Ranch, then on to Godfrey's, following the Platte River Road into O'Fallon's Bluffs. For weeks Indians were only seen in the distance, and at times George wondered if he was actually doing something worthwhile, or if he was just avoiding the real conflicts of the country. Were they fighting for the Union or the Confederates in their chase of Indians through an unaligned territory? He liked the evenings and the mornings at camp, though, when things were still except for fires snapping and smoke rising. He'd sit and watch the sun set or rise, sipping on bitter coffee that tasted more like dirt than anything else.

On one of those quiet mornings he was joined by Jimmy. "Never been much of one to watch the sunrise," Jimmy said, pouring himself a cup of the over-steeped coffee.

George smiled; he loved sunrises. "So why are you up to watch it now?"

Jimmy shrugged. "Can't seem to sleep any longer." He took a seat on a log and held the tin mug of coffee between both hands, the steam rising and condensing on his chin. "Sure is peaceful," he said after a while.

George nodded. "Why I like it."

Jimmy gave him a sideways glance. "Want me to leave?"

Chuckling, George shook his head. "No, nice to have the company."

"Good, 'cause you're stuck with me." And from then on the mornings were the two of them, sipping coffee, talking quietly about whatever came to mind, and waiting for the sun to break the horizon with light. Here it was that George came to appreciate just how good a friend Jimmy could be; he could raise the spirits of the lowest man. Jimmy never seemed to worry. He took everything as it came, declaring, "What fella wouldn't fight for the safety of his family?" Jimmy was as steadfast in his convictions as a compass pointing north, and his north was decidedly Lizzie.

"She's a peach," he said, grinning, accentuating the laugh lines already present at the corners of his russet lips, chapped from the wind and sun. His skin had tanned quickly in the long days of riding, and his brown hair curled over his ears and fell into his light green eyes. There was something about his appearance that made it seem as if he had quite literally sprung from the earth itself.

"She'll really wait for you?" George asked, thinking that the uncertainty of their lives could barely warrant asking a girl to wait, the wait possibly indefinite. What girl would agree to that?

"Yep. See, men leave, women stay, and if no one ever waited, our race would've died out a long time ago." Jimmy laughed, and George was sure it'd wake the whole camp.

He had a point, but George was glad all he had left behind him were Sarah and Aurora. That had been hard enough. If he'd had a girl, he never would have left. Unbidden, Rosie came to his mind along with thoughts of the walk they'd taken after he'd signed up. For a moment, he could still feel the warmth of her arm, the way her questions had struck him silent. He brushed the memory away.

"When this campaign is over, we're gonna get married," Jimmy continued. He held his coffee cup in both hands and gazed over the rim, as if gazing into his future.

"Thought you hadn't asked her?" George said. He looked at his friend with raised eyebrows and a half-smile.

"Near enough have, she's waiting for me, ain't she?" Jimmy grinned, looked away, and swigged coffee. "That stuff is the devil," he grimaced, and George chuckled.

"I think I've gotten used to it," George said almost regretfully, which made Jimmy guffaw.

His attention wasn't swayed for long, though, and soon he returned to Lizzie. "I figure I'll build us a little place out back of the smithy, she can keep up her seam-stressing, and I can work with my daddy. She gave me this watch." Jimmy snapped open his silver pocket watch and showed it to George. He had already shown it to him, but George didn't mind. There was something strangely sooth-ing about the way Jimmy rattled on about Lizzie, saying the same things he'd said the day before and the day before that. It made George believe that they would all make it back home without even a tale of a skirmish to tell, and that the campaign would stay peaceful and bloodless.

The rangers camped for the first week of September at the base of O'Fallon's Bluffs, named for Benjamin O'Fallon, a trader and teamster, who led Oregon Trail travelers through the twenty mile stretch of river breaks that were known to hide bands of Indians in their hidden folds. When standing on the top of a bluff, George could nearly believe that the ground was flat and unbroken for miles around. Then suddenly the flatness dropped off into a gully filled with gnarled junipers, their indigo berries frosted to a near gray by a chalky outer coating that could be rubbed off with a thumb and forefinger. At the bottom of these bluffs the rangers could tuck their camp out of the weather, for the most part. Wind blowing the right way could still reach the men as they tried to stay warm through the ever-cooling nights.

At night Jimmy liked to tell tales of places he'd heard about, and he'd get as caught up in these tellings as he did when he talked of Lizzie. Sometimes the tales were so elaborate that George knew Jimmy had to be exaggerating, but other times the tales sounded as real as the ground they sat on.

One night, George pulled a blanket around his shoulders to keep the wind from getting to him. "Feels like snow," he said. The other men around the fire didn't answer, not even Jack, but George knew they felt it, too. Jimmy came to the fire and hunkered beside George.

"Quiet 'round here," Jimmy said, then barely pausing for a breath, "heard of this place down south, that looks to be ruins of a city."

Jack, ever the cynic, shook his head. "Couldn't be a place like that." Jack never believed tales that bended toward the magical. Hard facts, unembellished, he believed. George remembered that even as children Jack questioned tales told at the hearth. Sarah used to tell of the god Lir on windy Illinois nights and then chilling Denver evenings when the boys were young. George loved the story, getting caught up in the idea of a god who could bring his children back to life, but only as swans. He remembered leaning forward to catch every word of the tale, and in his mind he could see his siblings doing the same, all except Jack.

*Jack rolled his eyes, one night saying, "There's obviously no way that could happen."*

*"And why not?" Sarah had challenged, her blue eyes steady on him.*

*"People can't be brought back to life," Jack said, matter-of-factly.*

*"What about Jesus?" Sarah asked.*

*"That's different."*

*"Oh? How?"*

*"It just is," Jack snapped, and George had giggled, knowing, even then, that an argument with Sarah was always one that was lost.*

Despite this, Jack had remained steadfast in his belief that if the teller hadn't seen it, it couldn't be true. He'd often make comments to this effect when Jimmy spun his tales. This never seemed to bother Jimmy. He skipped over Jack's words as if they were merely pebbles in the road.

Jimmy raised his eyebrows, making them disappear in his curls. "They say there's walls and rooms, several stories houses, all linked together, regular cities built of masoned stone. The city is built along cliffs, built into cliffs, built on cliffs, some buildings suspended above a canyon. They figure thousands of people lived there once."

Jack laughed, disbelief hanging on the edges of the sound. The fire crackled, sending sparks into the cold, dark sky. "You're full of beans, Jimmy," he said.

"It's the truth!" Jimmy insisted. "What you think, George?"

George took a slow, steady sip of coffee. It was hot, too hot for drinking really, and tasted of old socks and bacon grease. "Can't say I've heard of this place," he said, "but don't see why it can't be true." He wanted to believe in such a place, just like he wanted to believe in Sarah's myths. He couldn't fully explain it, but believing in these things seemed to make reality more, well, real, and somehow more bearable.

"There you go, Jack." Jimmy looked pleased. For a moment there was silence, as though their conversation had ended. Their breaths formed clouds of steam in front of them even with the warmth of the fire.

"He hasn't heard of it except from you, same as me," Jack said after a while.

"It's true though. The army has a map, some general mapped it. Some of the houses were circular, the doors low and arched, all seemin' to face in the same direction. Must have been a reason for that. Maybe it was to let the light in." He rubbed his hands together over the fire. His gray woolen gloves were worn, his fingers showing through the fraying yarn. "Do you s'pose it was some kind of ritual, or way to pray? Maybe they knelt there in their doorways, you know, like we do at an altar." Jimmy's imagination took root and grew. "S'pose the people were like us? S'pose they worshiped, watched sunrises, warmed themselves by a fire." Jimmy poked the fire with a stick, drawing in the ashes. "What ya think happened? Why ain't they still there? Where'd they go?" he mused, his voice sounding almost lazy.

Jack grinned at George across the fire. "He sure is full of questions. How'd he get in this campaign with a mind like that?"

George laughed. "Guess it takes all kinds," he said, trying to make light of it, but wanting to hear more. He found himself wondering where this place was, if there really were such a place. Those who'd lived there, would they have been ancestors of the Indians the rangers sought?

"Just think about it a minute," Jimmy said. "Shucks, if I'd spent the time and energy to build a city of stone, I'd sure as hell stick around. By gum I would. The rest of the world ain't much to see, least it ain't what it's made out to be. I say if you take the trouble to build a home, you better stick it out 'cause you never know when you'll get a chance to build another one."

Jack and George were silent. Something floated in George's coffee cup, a leaf maybe, or a fly. He watched the object spin in the hot liquid. Maybe the people had been forced out of their stone houses, set adrift on the prairies like the Irish that came in desperation to Black Hawk. The fire crackled, and a burst of sparks flew up. One landed on George's knee, burning a small hole in the coarse blue fabric of his uniform. He extinguished it with his fist, leaving yet another black smudge. Jack turned a glowing ember to black nothingness beneath his boot heel. He cleared his throat loudly. George glanced to see Jimmy staring into the fire, his face sheened with dancing colors of orange and red firelight. George felt a strange catch in his throat, as though somehow the colors dancing across Jimmy's face were a prophecy.

"Just think if there was such a place," Jimmy said, "a place built hundreds of years ago, by unknown people, built from stones they shaped, tall walls risin' into vast sky, risin' to a high, impossible height, room after room, wouldn't you wanna see it?"

# Chapter 2

As September drifted by, the company of rangers split in two, half staying at base camp, while the other half rode downriver. George and Jimmy were assigned to ride under the command of Robert Denton, while Jack stayed at camp under Captain Tyler. The bushes along the river were just turning a burnt orange, as if they had been scorched. The river ran clear and cold, autumn-like, and George thought of times he and his brothers stood calf-deep in water tossing lines into the current, waiting for a fish to strike. "We used to fish on days like these," he said.

"Catch much?" Jimmy asked.

"Sometimes." George shrugged.

Jimmy smiled, and George realized that his friend knew it wasn't always about the fish caught. One particular memory stood out from those many days spent fishing in Clear Creek. It had been a Saturday, and they had the day off from the masonry. He'd been fourteen, no, maybe fifteen, and he and Jack had raced each other to the creek, trying to leave Tib, their younger brother, behind.

*Tib shouted after them, and they grinned at each other, hitting the creek bank and splashing into the cold water. George sucked in his breath as the water numbed his feet and calves, and loosened his grip on his fishing rod. He cast the line out across the sparkling ripples, in near synchrony with Jack, as Tib arrived on the bank, breathless. Tib collapsed on the bank. "You shouldn't leave me behind like that," he groaned. "I'm gonna tell." The older brothers looked at each other, still grinning. They knew Tib would tell, but they also knew that they would not get in trouble.*

*"Come on, Tib," Jack said, "it's in good fun."*

*Tib's only response was another groan, which made George laugh. Then he asked, "Where's your pole?"*

*"Forgot it." Tib pouted, making both his brothers shake with laughter.*

*"Come on in," George said, "and I'll let you use mine a minute."*

*"Really?" Tib jumped up and splashed into the water, effectively scaring any nearby fish away.*

*"Aw, Tib," Jack scolded, and Tib glared, even as he reached for George's pole. George handed it over and stood back as Tib drew in the line and then cast it back out again. The rocks underfoot were slick with algae and rounded from the current. The boys had to grip with their toes to stay upright, which was harder to do as their feet became numbed.*

*"I think I've caught something!" Tib exclaimed. He stepped backward, pulling on the taut line; his foot slipped. Tib put out his arm, dropping the pole, in an attempt to catch himself; his hand missed the rock he was aiming for and he went down into the water with a splash and then a crack as the side of his head hit the rock his hand had missed. George stumbled forward, shouting for Jack. Together they pulled Tib out of the water, slapping his back until he sputtered out water. George felt as though his heart would never settle again. He saw his own fright mirrored in Jack's eyes as he looked at him over Tib's wet head. Blood dripped from Tib's temple. He coughed again and then opened his eyes. "I lost the fish," he moaned, and his brothers burst into relieved laughter.*

Halfway into the first day the rangers came upon a trail of hoof prints, half-moon scuffs in the dirt showing where horses had been moving at a trot.

"Unshod," Robert Denton said, but he may as well have said "Indians." George understood, and he side-glanced at Jimmy. From Jimmy's wide, furtive glance back George knew Jimmy did, too. George wished they hadn't found the tracks, but then as the company picked up the pace and his horse lengthened its strides beneath him, he got caught in the exhilaration of movement, his spirits lifting. Strange how the strides of a lope could make things different.

The company rounded a corner and were able to look down into the river drainage. Yellowing willows lined the bank and a dozen Indians watered their small, short-backed mustangs at the river's rushing edge. The Indians relaxed astride their ponies, their backs bare and tanned, ribbed in muscles, and their hair thicker and glossier than George had ever seen. One Indian placed a hand on his pony's rump and leaned back, scanning the sky, a familiar gesture of checking the weather, or looking for hawks, or just simply enjoying the moment. The ponies drank then lifted their heads, shaking their manes. Drops of water sparkled on their coats, on the painted yellow and black stripes and circles covering their rumps. George wondered what the markings meant, but the thought was fleeting. It was driven away by the rangers drawing arms and the whooping of the Indians, driving their ponies across the river in sudden awareness of the rangers' presence.

The ponies' strides were strong and light, a kind of athleticism that could only come from being raised on the rough terrain of sagebrush prairie. The rangers spurred their own horses into pursuit, George among them, caught again by the exhilaration of speed. The rangers rode thoroughbreds, horses of war, horses with long legs and long backs, bred for speed. George gave his mount his head and leaned over the whipping mane. He imagined outrunning them all, the long strides of his mount pulling him across the land and outstripping each Indian pony, leaving them all to breathe in the dust and sage in his wake. Water rose in misty clouds around them, drenching the horses' legs, chests, and sides, and soaking the rangers' pants until they clung tightly to their legs. They followed the Indians up a brushy hillside, curving around protruding rocks, and the Indians were fixed upon the bare backs of their ponies as if they'd grown there, leaning into each turn with the fluidity of water. The rangers' horses began to breathe sharply, but they kept going, cresting the ridge and dropping down the other side, the Indians already at the bottom. George felt his horse sink onto his haunches, digging his hooves deep into the dirt for stability. George urged him on, wanting to see the astonishment on everyone's faces when he won this race.

Suddenly, the horse in front of George slipped in the loose soil and stumbled so that George was forced to pull his own horse up. Lance, the ranger riding the stumbling horse, shortened his reins, trying to enforce balance on his mount, but it only threw it off-balance more. Its back legs tucked sideways and then it went down on its knees, jerking to a stop so abruptly that Lance was thrown from the saddle. But Lance's foot caught in the stirrup, so when the horse rolled it took Lance with him. Horse and ranger hit the bottom of the hill with a thump and a whoosh of air expelled from both sets of lungs. The horse thrashed, cutting at the brush with its hooves, and Lance tried to roll away, groaning.

George jumped from his horse, race forgotten in the urgency of a horse in trouble, and grabbed the bridle of the thrashing animal. "Shhh, shhh," George said, reaching to cover the horse's eyes. He'd learned this technique from his father. It'd been before they'd journeyed to Colorado, a crisp winter evening in Illinois. He'd gone out with his father to check the animals before nightfall; he remembered there was a skiff of snow on the ground and he'd tried to step in his father's footsteps, but his legs weren't nearly long enough, so he'd jumped from one to the other. He wanted to be just like his father.

*As they neared the barn, the sound of something thrashing met them, and John sprinted ahead. George hurried after him, running as fast as his little legs could carry him. In the paddock beside the barn, one of the brown plow horses lay on its side, struggling to get up and failing, its head slamming into the dirt and snow with every failed attempt. Blood spattered the ground around its legs, coming from cuts where wire fencing had the horse entangled. George watched as, without hesitation, his father bent beside the large horse's head and covered the rolling eyes with his hands. Fog from his own breath puffed out in front of George as the horse quieted and became still behind his father's hands.*

*"Come here, George," John commanded in a low, even voice, and George cautiously moved forward, stopping by his father's side. "Put your hands where mine are," John instructed.*

*George hesitated, looking at his hands, thinking that they were too small.*

*"Quick, now." John's voice was still low, but there was a sharpness to it that was not to be disobeyed.*

*George hunkered down and reached his hands out, placing them over his father's. Carefully John pulled his away, and George felt the soft bristles of the horse's eyelashes on his palms. He focused all his energy on the task, not noticing that his father had succeeded in clipping the wire and releasing the horse from its entrapments, until John placed a hand on his shoulder. "Okay, you can let him up," John said. "Stand back quickly, he may startle."*

Ever since then, George had been able to make a horse go quiet, and every time he placed his hands over a horse's eyes he thought of that first time, barely six years old, his hands just big enough to cover a draft horse's eyes in darkness. And here on the sagebrush slope it was no different, the memory coming unbidden as in the darkness behind George's hands the horse calmed. Jimmy was able to get close enough to pull the cinch loose, letting the saddle slip off and releasing the horse from its binding situation. George took his hands away from the horse's eyes and let the horse get to its feet. By then Robert Denton had turned back, along with the rest of the rangers, the Indians disappearing down the gulch. George couldn't see who, but one of the rangers fired a single shot after the dust kicked by the Indian ponies as if to say, "we could still come after you."

George held Lance's horse, letting the animal shake off the impact of the fall, before catching his own mount, who had come to a halt at a thick bunch of grass. He tied the two horses to a scrubby pine and went back to where Lance sat. Robert slid the saddle away, taking care to not pull on Lance's leg. George took the saddle from Robert, as Jimmy hunkered beside Lance. "Do you think you can stand?" Jimmy asked.

Lance shook his head, but then said, "I could try."

Jimmy took one of Lance's arms, Robert took the other, and they helped Lance to his feet. Lance cried out.

"You're not going anywhere," Robert said. Robert was brusque and efficient, giving orders to make camp, hobble the horses close, start a fire, and to take an inventory of supplies so that in the morning he could discern what the next steps for the company would be. The exhilaration of the chase drained from George and left him feeling tired, hollow even, but in the way of one now used to soldier duties, he set about making camp with the others. Everyone moved separately, and yet together, subconsciously aware that everything they did was for the good of the company and no single man alone.

Around the fire that night, Jimmy offered Lance his blanket. "Don't want you catchin' a chill on top of this," Jimmy said.

Lance nodded his gratitude and closed his eyes.

Morning came with an explosion of sparrow song and Lance no better. The fire had nearly gone out, and George shivered as he shifted his rifle in his lap. Glancing around the camp, he saw others stirring, and soon the camp was as alive as the sparrows fluttering in the bushes. Rangers ducked out of the dozens of small canvas tents that were clustered in a semblance of a circle where the ground was flattest. They pushed aside the flaps and stretched, many standing and blinking in the dawn light before moving to start fires, gather wood, get water, or any of the other mundane morning tasks. They moved both individually and collectively, each taking a task without question or hesitation. George left his post by the fire and gathered an armload of sticks. He blew the coals of the fire back to life. Jimmy came back from filling canteens at the river and put a pot of the water over the flames.

Over a breakfast of coffee and cornmeal mush, Robert laid out the plan. "We'll split into two parties," he explained. "Half will stay here, while the other half will go for help. If we can get a wagon in here, we should be able to get Lance out." Robert swirled his coffee and took a gulp. "There are only enough provisions for two days, so those of you staying must ration them carefully, and those of us going will only take enough to get through the day. We should make it back to base camp in two or three days, but hopefully will come across another camp before then."

George watched the group of rangers ride away, wondering how long it would be before he saw them riding back.

"There they go and here we stay," Jimmy said, then he glanced around at the others. "Who's in charge here now?" No one answered his question, but it wasn't really a question to be answered. The hierarchy would sort itself out by the end of the day.

By afternoon, the camp had settled into quietness, almost a laziness. The rangers lay on their bedrolls in front of the half dozen tents left clustered on the campsite and dozed or played cards, using the ground or the seat of a saddle as a table. Some men pulled out books that they hadn't parted with yet and read; others wrote letters home, hoping to post them at the O'Fallon Bluff Post Office after rejoining the rest of the company. The soft air of fall moved through the camp. It crept across George's skin as he cleaned his rifle and gave him goosebumps, not because it made him cold, though. The breeze reminded him of something, but he couldn't quite put his finger on it. It was like an illusive memory that left your hair on end as it slipped away before you grasped the fullness of it.

A ranger at the edge of camp jumped to sudden attention, and the rest of the camp followed, scattering cards and dropping papers and books in a scramble to lock and load rifles, as a man on a large sorrel horse came into view. The man brought his horse to a halt and pulled a white kerchief from his pocket. The rangers lowered their rifles as the man introduced himself as an Indian agent coming from Fort Laramie.

"You following those Indians heading downriver?" the agent asked.

"We were," Jimmy said, going on to explain how Lance's horse had fallen and the rest of the detachment had gone to get a wagon to get him back to base camp.

"They're friendly Indians," the agent said. "They stole five of my horses a few days ago. They're friendly."

"Stealing is a sign of friendliness?" George couldn't help asking.

"Yes." The agent dismounted without further explanation of how Indians could be friendly and thieves at the same time. It was one of those frontier rules that was never explained and only made sense to a select few. If stealing was friendly, how were they supposed to know which Indians were the savages they were mustered to quell and which ones weren't? He remembered the way the one Indian had leaned back to scan the sky. A gesture as friendly as a smile or a handshake between old acquaintances.

"Tether my horse?" the agent asked, putting the reins into George's hand. George nodded as the agent slapped dust from his hands and said brusquely, "Let's see what I can do to help you get to base camp."

Three weeks later an account of the accident appeared in *The Daily Mining Journal*. "Doodles" wrote in extensive detail, and poked fun at the "real militia," but his accounts were truthful and aimed to give those at home a taste of life as a ranger.

*This will give you some idea of the extent of our scouting, and the severity of the duties which our boys cheerfully perform in their desire to open this road for traffic, and to avenge the atrocities committed by the red-skins. The man (Lance) who was hurt is rapidly recovering. He received no injury except the shock and will be in the saddle again in a few days...The road is now perfectly safe and you may rely upon our keeping it so. If confidence could only be restored, there is no reason why mails and freight should not at once come through by the Omaha route. It appears to us with proper representations this might be done. There are at present no trains on the road. There is one camped at Cottonwood, and that starts for Denver, to-day.*[1]

Jack got a days old copy from the station master at the O'Fallon's Bluffs station as the rangers passed by on patrol, and Jimmy entertained the men by reading the account that evening in camp. There was something about seeing an account in the paper of their experiences that made George feel like what they were doing really was ensuring the safety of those they loved. Looking around the fire at the quiet faces of the other rangers, half-smiles on all of them, he knew he wasn't the only one who felt that way.

Jimmy folded the paper and set it over his knee, leaning forward to warm his hands above the fire. "So," he said, "which one of us is Doodles?"

The men glanced around at each other, and George tried to catch a clue in someone's eyes, but no one gave anything away, and Jimmy's question went unanswered.

"Ah, well," Jimmy shrugged, "guess it's better that we don't know, just in case he slips up and says somethin' he shouldn't."

A collective chuckle went around the fire, and as sparks drifted up into the now darkened sky, the rangers disappeared into their tents.

At the beginning of November the rangers were issued new horses, this time army horses, their own having grown tired. The tired mounts were corralled at the O'Fallon's Bluffs station to be taken back north once they had rested. Each ranger received ten dollars in army script for their old mount and chose a new mount from a herd of army branded horses of varying age and size. George felt a twinge

---

1. Italics directly quoted from *Daily Mining Journal*, Black Hawk City, Gilpin County, Colorado, Tuesday, 27 September, 1864.

in his heart as he let his old gelding loose, letting the halter fall off his face, trailing his fingers over the gelding's nose in a final gesture of thanks.

By the time George chose his new mount, the herd had dwindled to those passed over. So it was that George's choices were limited to a rangy black gelding with a scar down his right hind leg, a swaybacked gray mare, or a small bay, pigeon-toed gelding. He chose the black, even though he was a horse who had obviously seen more rangeland than riding. "Honest eyes, though," George said, adjusting the halter to fit the large head of the gelding. "I'll call him Abe."

"Hey, boys, better write the president, he's got an ugly beast as a namesake," Jimmy said, already saddling his new mount, a tall, fast-looking sorrel of thoroughbred heritage.

George stroked his new gelding's nose. "Pay him no mind," he said. He fed Abe the soft center of a piece of cornbread. The gelding worked it with his lips, crumbs dropping into the dirt. A little love, a little extra care, and George knew that he and Abe would become strong companions. He leaned forward to whisper this in the large black ears that flickered in time with the noises around them, and then looked up to see his brother sitting astride a large gray. Jack gave George a soft smile, and at first, George felt embarrassed, but then he caught his brother's eyes and saw a kind of understanding there. Gratitude flooded him, and he smiled at Jack in return.With the new mounts came a shift in the weather. The nights were colder, the days took longer to warm. Ice formed on the edges of the river where the rangers continued to camp, and brown leaves fell from the trees. With the chill, the rangers became restless, and George felt that they were just biding their time until their one hundred days were done.

One morning a rider came in with a letter for Captain Tyler. Tyler opened and read it while the rider waited for a reply, shifting from one foot to another, a finger looped through the ring of his horse's bit. His face impassive, Tyler folded the letter, put it into his pocket, and, calling to the rangers to break camp and saddle their mounts, he strode to his tent, disappearing inside. The rider glanced about and was about to swing back into his saddle when Tyler reappeared with a sheet of paper folded and sealed with candle wax. He handed it to the rider. "Send this reply to General Wynkoop upon your return to the station," Tyler said.

The rider nodded, shoved the paper into his jacket pocket, and leaped into the saddle as, simultaneously, his horse lunged to a gallop. George paused in rolling up his bedroll and watched the rider tear out of sight. He looked questioningly at Jack, who shrugged and bent to stuff his belongings into saddlebags.

As soon as the last tent was rolled, the last cinch pulled tight, and the last bridle strap buckled, Tyler stepped into his saddle and pulled his horse around to face the men all standing uncertainly by their horses.

"Mount up!" Tyler cried down the line of rangers. "We've got a long ride."

The rangers mounted and spurred their horses east at an even trot. Abe had an easy gait, despite his rangy appearance, and George settled into it, knowing he could ride it for a long time.

"Where are we heading?" George asked Jimmy, who rode beside him.

"No idea," Jimmy said.

For the past two weeks they had been hearing rumors of Sioux warriors terrorizing settlers, but the rangers hadn't seen any signs of anyone beside themselves and the mail carriers for going on ten days. Captain Tyler sent them out in pairs to scout the area every day to no avail. The Indians had disappeared in the sagebrush, and now the rangers were riding east again.

"It feels good to be going somewhere again," George said as Jack and Jimmy fell in on either side of him.

Jack grunted in agreement.

"But where is that somewhere?" Jimmy asked, and for the first time George saw a sober light in his eyes.

# Chapter 3

"To Sand Creek!" Chivington cried into the frosty pre-dawn outside the walls of Fort Lyons. His mustache twitched, ice visible on the edges of it, his sword drawn and extended in front of him. He spurred his horse forward and his cavalry, the Bloodless Third, fell in behind him. The cavalry horses pushed against each other. Snorts and whinnies filled the air, and then the pushing, the impatience, the noises stopped as the soldiers fell into place.

George felt uneasy as his company came into line. The rangers had fulfilled their one hundred days of service upon arrival at Fort Lyons and should have received their discharges. Many believed they would when they reached the fort, but instead the company had been greeted by Colonel Chivington, a zealous Methodist preacher who had taken a forceful command of the fort. His men, too, were about to be discharged and hadn't seen any action. They were restless and tired of being mocked as useless.

Chivington knew where Indians were camped along Sand Creek. "Indians," he said, "who are leaders of the Dog Soldiers." With his sword drawn, he'd asked Captain Tyler to join his march on the camp and bring the Indians to justice. Tyler had asked where General Wynkoop was, and Chivington spat, saying Wynkoop was no longer in charge of the fort, while brandishing his sword close enough to catch the tip on Tyler's shirt collar. Tyler had complied. George wondered if Tyler had agreed out of fear of the Colonel or out of the conviction that the Indian camp was hostile. If Chivington would draw a sword on a fellow soldier, what did he have in mind for the Indians? What were these Indians supposed to have done? Didn't justice mean a fair and unbiased trial? He had a feeling this was not what Chivington had in mind.

George's horse bumped against his brother's. Black against gray, black into gray, then just black. His horse matched pace with those around him. The rangers were riding across a wide prairie cloaked in snow in the company of the 3rd Colorado Cavalry, headed north. At first they followed a wagon track, but soon they took to cross-country travel, against drifting snow through which bunch grass poked, making the land look like a blanket held together by knots of thread. A bitter taste, like the green chokecherries he had eaten as a boy on a dare, settled on George's tongue. He felt as though he were carrying out a dare now, remembering the round, smooth cheeks of his brother when they were boys. He glanced at Jack's face and thought he saw that boy in the windburned skin. "Young soldiers make good soldiers," George remembered someone saying once. "Or scared ones," his father had answered.

"Hey, George." Jimmy rode up beside him. He grinned, easy as always, childhood still marking his eyes and lips. "Think we'll live through this?"

George shrugged. "I guess." He tried to sound at ease, too, but he heard someone mutter, "I don't like this," and the uneasiness within him persisted, like a cough.

"When we get back I'm gonna take me a nice hot bath," Jimmy said, "and then I'm gonna walk down the street and ask my Lizzie to marry me."

"Hope she doesn't turn you down," George said, concentrating hard on being cheerful. "Good thing you're taking a bath before and not after."

Jimmy laughed. "Christ, it's cold! I think my fingers dropped off miles ago and my feet certainly ain't been around the past couple of days."

"Quiet in the ranks!" Tyler barked.

Jimmy fell silent after one last grin at George. George managed a half-hearted smile back, but he didn't feel like smiling; the chance of seeing real action was too present in his mind. He'd been glad of the prospect of discharge and returning home, with just tales of chases through sagebrush and rocky gullies, skirmishes where the worst injuries were sprains and scrapes. The rangers had been a presence on the roads and he believed they'd established safe routes for travelers. There had been a sense of accomplishment. But now, everything felt upside down, and no one seemed to understand where they were going and why.

The morning faded into a gray afternoon and any gaiety that had existed in the men was smothered by the flurries and drifting snow. The prairie continued to stretch out before them, and George wondered if it ever ended. As far as he could see the land lay in waves of snow, only broken by where it met the gray sky. George tried to blow warmth into his fingers, but even his breath was made cold by the winter wind. He scanned the company. Everyone stared ahead, as though afraid to look at each other.

George saw Captain Silas Soule riding steadily on the edge of his company. Soule was young, the lines on his face not yet defined, his blonde hair yet to go gray. He had his coat buttoned all the way to his chin; the second to top button was loose, hanging on by a single thread, and the coat was beginning to fray at the edges. George knew Soule had been promoted to captain earlier in the year and had been stationed at Fort Lyons for several months. He was known as a man with staunch beliefs, a man who did things with the strength of those convictions, but something about the slope of his shoulders made George question the Captain's surety of this campaign, especially after the exchange he had heard the night before.

"They're peaceable," Soule had said.

"There's no such thing as a peaceable Indian," Chivington answered. Chivington had a strong jaw, accentuated by a neatly trimmed, gray mustache.

"Sand Creek camp is and you know it!" Soule insisted. "They don't want trouble."

"You just don't have the stomach for the army." Chivington spat into the dirty snow.

Now, Soule slowed his horse and said something to Tyler. Tyler nodded. They rode together, their horses matching pace, and George watched them. What were they discussing? What mission were they really riding out to execute? Soule glanced back at the company, his dark eyes clear and sad as they scanned the ranks of soldiers and rangers. George followed his glance, and saw everyone's shoulders hunched against the wind, their eyes cast downward.

As the cold seeped into George's body, any accomplishment he had felt fell away, leaving him with nothing but questions of what he was doing. What was the point? What were they really out here to do? Why did he enlist? How could he really be certain which Indians were capable of the savagery, had committed the savagery he had volunteered to protect against? Sarah had asked him if it was because of Jack that he had enlisted, and then he hadn't been sure, but now he knew that Jack was part of it. He hadn't wanted Jack to be the only one doing something for the country, the only one proving he was something, and he hadn't wanted Jack to go alone. Somehow it was better that two went instead of one, as if it doubled the chance of them coming back. And he hadn't wanted to disappoint his father. That was something that George knew he couldn't bear. John had once been a soldier in the British Army, and he carried a strong sense of duty from that time. He expected his sons to serve; it was what made them worthy of being men, of being his sons. All throughout his growing up years, George had felt this expectation, felt the responsibility, felt the fear of not being able to live up to it. He knew the disappointment that would stare out at him from John's eyes. So, yes, if he could do things over he would volunteer again. Still, at this exact moment, he would have given anything to turn Abe around and head home.

The snow came up higher on his black mount's chest. How far were they riding? How far could the horses go in this snow? George's toes were numb from cold as his boots filled with snow. His eyes stung, and as he blinked the ice from them, a mirage of home floated in front of him. He wanted to touch it, and his body ached. Jimmy shoved a flask into his hand. "This'll warm ya up," he said. The whiskey burned and the sun sank lower, but still they pressed on. Slowly the land in front of them began to change. Gentle hills broke the flatness of before, and on the horizon George thought he could make out some trees. He hoped so; trees would give them some relief from the continuous snow.

The horses were tired. The men were tired. No one talked. No one whispered. The only sound was the breeze in their ears and the strained breathing of their horses. It was quiet, like the quiet right before the sun breaks the horizon. George felt it, heard it, and tasted it. He remembered Jimmy's face a-sheen with firelight. "Brick walls into the sky." A prophecy, or maybe just an odd feeling to be discarded, forgotten. His horse snapped a twig in the snow, dull to his ears, but loud in the deafening silence. He tasted bitterness on his tongue.

They rode up a hill into a copse of bare-branched cottonwoods. Called to a halt, they waited uneasily for the next command. The ground in front of them sloped first gently, then steeply to a winding creek bed. Tepees dotted the bank amongst brown peach-leaf willows and desiccating saltbush stalks. The sun was now gone from the sky, and they waited. Soule's horse stamped with impatience, and Soule looked grim and old. George shifted in his saddle. Adventure traded for fear; fear a bitter, friendless companion. He looked at Jimmy, who stared into the village below them, no emotion breaking the surface. They waited and watched until the sun came to the eastern horizon.

Chivington raised his hand and his men snapped to attention. Tyler and Soule didn't make a move. The rangers shifted, confused. George and Jimmy exchanged glances, Jimmy's hands placed in readiness to urge his horse directly into a gallop as soon as Tyler gave the signal. The camp remained quiet, except for thin threads of smoke escaping through the tops of teepees, signaling the start of morning fires. George imagined kettles of water being hung over the flames, hands being held to the warmth, and for a moment he was back on the trail, somewhere between Peoria and Denver, warming his hands at the campfire behind their wagon, while Sarah mixed cornbread and rocked baby Evan on her hip. The memory puffed out just as quickly as it had come, and the command for attack was given.

Chivington dropped his hand sharply. "Charge!" he shouted. "Don't leave anyone alive!" He spurred his horse hard in the ribs, and the animal plunged down the slope. Chivington's men careened after him, both on horseback and on foot. Blue coats littered the snow-splashed ground as soldiers stripped them off to lighten their load. Battle cries filled the air. Soule's men moved forward in the rush and confusion. "Halt, Company, halt!" Soule screamed, his face red, his arm high in the air. His men hesitated. Most stopped, but a few went on by, following Chivington's company, too caught up in the cries to hear their commander.

Beside Soule's company, Tyler held his rangers at a halt. Abe pulled at the reins and George held him tight, even though he was just as confused. He didn't understand what they were doing here; were they merely an escort for the Bloodless Third? Had they come for some other purpose not yet told to them? A gunshot sounded. One single shot searing through all thoughts, all cries, the cold air magnifying the sound by a thousand. George's ears exploded, and he covered his head. Vaguely, he heard Tyler shout, "We have to stop him!" The rangers moved, racing down the hill, and George let Abe go with them. Shots splattered the ground. Soldier's battle cries. Screams. They were almost there, the rangers, and Tyler swept around the corner of Chivington's company. He turned his horse into the oncoming fray of soldiers. The rangers followed him, previous hesitation gone. All they knew was to mirror their leader. Side by side, George and Jimmy turned their horses into the wave of the 3rd Cavalry.

The oncoming soldiers didn't stop. They continued their charge into the village. Tyler stood in his stirrups, both arms in the air, high above his head. His commands to halt went unheard in the clanging din of shots and horses' hooves. Fires had started in the village, flames licking at tepee walls, tepees bursting in sprays of sparks and leaping flames. The village was firelight and into that light the soldiers streamed.

The pounding of horse hooves reverberated in George's ears, until all he wanted to do was let his horse run. So he did. Dropping the reins on Abe's neck, he allowed the gelding to turn with the flow of the stream of galloping horses on his own accord. George felt warmed by Abe's long strides as they struck the ground. Maybe he could get ahead of the other soldiers, somehow turn the tide if he just rode fast enough. He saw Jimmy still beside him, and, for a moment, their eyes locked. George thought to tell him they should turn back and turn back others with them, but another soldier came between them, and Jimmy disappeared in the swirling chaos. The village came closer, blurred by speed, but he made out a woman with a child clutched in her arms running between two burning teepees and a man with long gray braids standing as though lost as soldiers rushed in. This was no warrior encampment.

George's eyes stung from the smoke and speed as he reached down close to his horse's bit to pull the black gelding around. Before he could change directions, George's horse abruptly stumbled and fell, first forward, then to the side, sending George out of the saddle. Hitting the ground, he lay still, his breath gone. This was it; this was where it all ended, where he was going to die, and this thought made him feel cold once again. Abe's large black side heaved once, and, watching the final breath leave his horse, George's mind cleared. His horse had been shot, but he hadn't been. He pushed himself up to see where he was, finding himself on the edge of the village. Flames danced and hooves churned around him. He may not have been shot, but he'd soon be trampled if he didn't get out of the way.

Still shaky from the wind being knocked out of him, he crawled to his horse, his honest Abe. His chapped hands cracked open, leaving blood on the snow behind him, but they were too cold for him to feel any pain. He huddled against his dead horse, feeling the last of Abe's body warmth. Abe didn't deserve to die this way; why were they asked to put these innocent beasts in danger like this? He shifted to look at the long, black face of the horse that was his companion for too short a time. Abe's eyes stared, large and dark, into a sky gray with dawn, and George desperately tried to close the eyelids over their blankness. They wouldn't stay closed, though, and he turned away, pulling his pistol from his holster as if doing so would remedy it. He watched another horse fall and anger rushed over him. He pulled the trigger, sending a shot aimlessly across the prairie.

Tyler shouted, bellowed to his men, "Retreat to the ridge! Rangers retreat! Retreat to the ridge!"

To George his voice seemed far away, almost out of a dream. "Retreat!" The word hit him again, this time the meaning registering in his mind, and he turned to scramble up the slope which his horse had come down so easily. That's when he saw an Indian, no older than himself, facing him. The Indian held a long knife, poised to strike. George drew his pistol. The Indian stared, coolly, unblinking back at him, his eyes as deep and unfearing as Abe's had been. Minutes seemed to go by, hours even, as the two stared each other down, and George could hear his heart beating, wondering if the young man facing him could hear it, too. Then the Indian yelled, leaping forward, knife raised, and George pulled the trigger. But his hand shook, and he missed his mark. The Indian's knife grazed George's arm as the Indian fell to his knees, George's bullet having passed through his hand. Not waiting for the other man to stand or even to see if he could stand, George scrambled away.

The smell of crushed silver sagebrush was potent, and the sound of small arms fire rang in George's ears. He could taste the violence surrounding him. Fear was better. He could understand fear. He stumbled forward, back up the slope, alongside other rangers obeying the call to retreat. Most were on foot, a few still in the saddle. George saw the light-colored tail of Jack's horse go by. He reached for it and fell to his knees, his fingers brushing the end of the tail, his hand plunging against the frozen ground, bleeding again, leaking a color like embers. George pushed himself up and ran on.

They made the ridge. "I should never have tried," Tyler said, as though to himself. No one answered him. George's eyes mortared to the scene in front of him, stuck in a disbelieving horror that made him feel as if he were worlds away, perhaps in a bad dream. Blood froze on his arm, and seeing it there made him remember the young Indian. He scanned the creek valley below for the young man. He shouldn't have missed...no, he shouldn't have fired the shot. What had he been thinking? The rangers had been sent down to stop the other soldiers, not shoot Indians. He couldn't see the Indian he'd shot; he wasn't even certain where he had been, there was too much chaos below. Cavalry horses ran, crashing through tepees and fire rings. Fire engulfed all in its path. A girl stumbled, fell, and was still. Braves fell fighting. Red, fire red, blood red. A soldier slid from his horse, a pile of blue among crumpled brown that almost disappeared in the ground. Back to the earth; a full circle. Orange, sunrise orange, fire orange. An American flag, a white flag, snapping in the breeze in the middle of it all and they still fell, the soldiers giving no heed to either flag.

George felt as though he was watching from another world, another time, and there was no fear, no sadness, no anger...just nothingness. He couldn't turn away, couldn't speak, couldn't think. He stood and watched as though it had nothing to do with him, but an immense guilt fell on his shoulders as if to smother him. He didn't look when Jack came to stand beside him. The fire continued, and the sun broke bright over the horizon.

Wearily, the rangers made camp. It was early, only just after two. George watched Tyler pitch his tent with a force only anger could bring. Three rangers were dead, and they buried their bodies on the ridge; those who were wounded bandaged their own wounds. George wrapped his bleeding hands in strips torn from his blanket. Jack offered to help, but George didn't respond, intent on his hands. He heard conversations around him as if through a wall, muffled and hard to understand.

"Captain Tyler?" a skinny ranger by the name of Thomas Young said.

"Yes, Young?"

"All men accounted for except Jimmy Dobbs," Young told him. "He's missing."

Tyler's shoulders sagged. "Thank you, Young."

When George heard Jimmy's name, words around him became clearer. He stood still and again the scene of Jimmy at the campfire flashed through his mind. The flames then were the same as the flames that ate the tepees.

"George?" Jack looked closely at his brother. "You okay?"

George nodded and bent to tie a tent rope to a stake. It was Jack's tent, his own still down on the hillside, tied to the saddle on his dead black horse. He thought about Abe. He had liked him, an honest horse. He shivered and finally looked at his brother. Jack's shoulders were hunched; he looked up and met his brother's eyes. Neither one was all right. They saw it in each other and in their minds acknowledged it, but they didn't say anything. Words of comfort would be too empty, because they had no comfort to give.

George watched Tyler move restlessly around camp. He wondered if Tyler was thinking about Jimmy. Where was Jimmy, if he was still alive? He stared at the campfire and watched as the flames danced and parted like curtains on a stage. Blood and fire became one. Tepees glowed and people ran. Families just like the families the soldiers came from. They fell, tripping against the embers and lying still. Had the young Indian with the collected gaze found his way out of the chaos? Surely he had—he had to have. George kept thinking of how his father taught him to never leave an animal wounded, and here he'd left a man. He'd disappointed his father after all; he'd answered the need of his country, done what his father had wanted, had expected, and still managed to be a disappointment.

A pot of beans on the campfire boiled over, the juice hissing and sputtering against the heat like the rattles of a snake. George moved it in a painful, slow gesture, then scooped a spoon of beans onto a blue tin plate. Some of the beans clanked on the metal, not quite cooked, but George didn't care. He handed a plate to his brother. They ate. Rangers around them ate as well, consuming a meal of undercooked beans and stale hardtack. George wasn't hungry, probably none of them were, but eating was a routine they knew, so they did it, weighing their already weighted stomachs.

Young lost his dinner as soon as he had eaten it. George handed him an under-brewed cup of coffee. Young drank and lost it, too. Then he crawled into his tent, not bothering to wipe the drool from his beard and lips.

The sound of a single horse walking into camp alerted George, and he saw Jack's hand go to his side. George brightened a little as he recognized Jimmy, and moved with the other rangers to greet him, plates left forgotten by the fire, spilling their contents onto the frozen ground.

Jimmy slipped from his horse. He had a gash above his right eye. Blood, like firelight, washed down his cheek. His eyes swept over his fellow rangers, seemingly unseeing, not even pausing on George. He undid the cinch and pulled the saddle from his battered mount. The horse wandered toward the few other horses tethered to a high-line. George wanted to say something, but words disappeared from his mind like smoke into the night sky.

"I killed a baby," Jimmy said, his voice quiet and loud all at once. He let his saddle drop to the ground and stood, hands limp at his sides. His eyes stared, wide open like a dead man's. He dropped to the ground and hunched against his saddle. George stood, unable to move; no one else moved, either. The night was so quiet that George thought he could hear their hearts all beating slowly like a funeral procession. Someone finally turned and went to tell Tyler.

Jimmy rocked slightly back and forth. "He was so small. Only this big." He held his hands about a foot apart. "So small."

Someone, George wasn't sure who, draped a gray wool Army blanket across Jimmy's shoulders and said, "Take it easy, Jimmy."

Jack offered him some whiskey. Jimmy didn't seem to notice. "He was a pretty baby."

"I want you all ready to move early tomorrow morning," Tyler said, appearing for a moment, then disappearing again into his tent. The rangers heard him, but only a few acknowledged him with slight nods.

Jimmy looked up at his companions, catching George's eyes. George looked away. "He had brown eyes," Jimmy said.

"Shut up," someone said.

# Chapter 4

Jimmy's body swung as if in a stiff wind, but George had never felt air so still. Everything was breathless. Jimmy's boots tapped together with each swing, making the only noise in the dawn light. There was a skiff of fresh snow covering the grayness of the old, and as the sun rose, it made the ground sparkle. George kicked at the snow until it lost its luster.

"George," Jack's voice intruded into George's thoughts. His focus came back to the brown ears of the horse he rode across the expanse of snowdrifts back to Fort Lyons. In summer it could be done in a day with a good horse, but the horses the rangers rode were tired and the snow slowed them. As his horse's breath became increasingly labored, George thought three days of riding would be more likely. The horse he rode had belonged to Jimmy—the saddle, too; even though George's feet were in the stirrups, the saddle seemed empty to him.

"George," Jack said again.

"What?" George responded, his voice snapping like the air around them.

"Nothing, just checking."

Checking what? George thought, but he just gave a short nod. The brown horse stumbled. He pulled on the reins, jerking the horse's mouth, forcing the gelding to raise his head, whose steps continued to falter. George dug the horse with his spurs. The horse fought against the reins, trying to respond to the cue to move faster.

They rode into Fort Lyons the following night at what George guessed to be midnight. The fort was quiet, nearly empty with Chivington's and Soule's companies gone, and the man standing guard let them in without a word, just giving a single salute of acknowledgement of Captain Tyler. The men rode to the corrals and methodically unsaddled their horses, letting them loose in an empty corral. When George pulled the saddle from the brown horse's back, sores on the withers opened, leaking trickles of blood. The horse moved stoically away from George, his head low, his steps stiff. George watched him, almost turning to find some grain, but before his feet caught up to the thought he had pushed it away, leaving the gelding in the cold dark, and found his way to the barracks.

George lay on his back on a musty mattress. His pistol dug into his side, but he didn't move. Jack dropped his boots and gun belt on the floor, the sound loud, as if the pistol had fired, and George flinched. Jack moaned as he stretched out on his cot, then he cleared his throat. George waited for him to say something. The barracks creaked, and the cot on his other side remained empty. A horse whinnied and wasn't answered. Jack's breathing slowed to the even pace of sleep, and George lay listening to it. The sound reminded him of home, of sitting on the rug in front of the fire with Aurora leaning against him, Sarah in her rocker darning a sock, his father and Jack talking about masonry, Evan and Tib playing jacks on the floor, Aurora's head becoming heavier on his shoulder. He tried to hold on to the memory, but he could feel it slipping away. It had been too long since he had sat at the home hearth. He focused on Jack's breathing, trying to bring the memory and feeling back, but suddenly all he could hear was the rope Jimmy used rubbing the branch from which it hung.

Jimmy's horse had gone back to stand with the rest of the horses, one rein trailing in the snow, the other snapped off from him stepping on it. He flinched when Jack caught him and touched his shoulder. The hoof prints beneath Jimmy had barely been covered by the snowfall. He had spurred his horse out from under himself. There was no chance of following with the rope around his neck.

New mounts were issued to the rangers for their ride to Denver where their campaign would finally come to an end, and they could go back to their lives—if they possibly could. George stood along the fence, thinking that Jimmy should be standing next to him, Jimmy should be returning to his life as well. But the space beside him was cold and empty, and he watched alone as the mounts were run in. They were an odd assortment of plow-horses and Spanish ponies, gaunt in the ribs and above the eyes, but they moved with the ease of horses that were rested.

"Catch a horse, saddle up," Captain Tyler called down the row of rangers. "We've got a long ride afore nightfall."

George shoved his hands further into his pockets and hunched his shoulders against the chill of morning. The sun filtered coldly through a film of high gray clouds that would burn off by noon, but the sun would remain at a distance, barely warming the air. As the other rangers climbed the fence with ropes, George backed away; it felt strange to pick yet another horse, disloyal almost, and more than he was able to face with Abe's body left unburied along Sand Creek.

He bit back his emotions, trying to keep the memories of the previous day at bay, finally turning to the corral where their mounts of the days before huddled, their heads low and eyes glazed or half-closed, whorls of ice that had once been sweat matting their backs and chests. Jack's gray stood on the outside of the group, ribby and slack-jawed, but his back was straight and his legs still had muscle. A week of rest, and he'd be ready to go again. Jimmy's brown wasn't visible from where George stood. He knew, though, that the gelding would be worse off than Jack's and almost felt relief that he couldn't see him. Yet, he did want to, just once before they left.

"George!" Jack shouted, "Horse! Let's go!"

Jack flung a rope at his brother, on the other end an unconcerned chestnut mare. George led the mare to where he had dropped his saddle, throwing one final glance over his shoulder at the huddled horses. Jimmy's horse still wasn't visible. George tossed the saddle onto the mare's broad, plow-horse back and pulled the cinch. She flattened her ears, tossing her head and reaching around to nip at him. He moved out of the way of her teeth and didn't bother to scold her, tying his pack behind the saddle as quickly as his numb fingers could work, and then swung into the seat.

Jack came up beside him on a bald-faced bay. "Get yourself together," he said. His brow was furrowed and his unkempt mustache made his expression unforgiving.

Tyler shouted for the rangers to fall in, and before George could glance once more for the brown gelding, the company moved off, his mare awkwardly jogging between a trot and a lope to keep up with the speed of the horses around her. Her back hooves clipped against her front hooves with every other stride.

The hammer struck the nail, piercing through the leather tops of Jimmy's boots. The sound rang along the ridge like a bell striking the hour or telling of every other time a man's boots had been left to mark the place where he lay buried. The boots were worn, cracked across the tops, the soles thin and flapping open. George put Jimmy's watch in his pocket and walked away. No one looked back.

# Chapter 5

A wind blew down Black Hawk's main street as Tyler's rangers returned. George had dreamed about arriving on this street, picturing the sun on red bricks two and three stories high, white awnings reaching freshly painted into the street and covering plank sidewalks, where crowds assembled to cheer and welcome them home. He'd imagined the rangers smiling, himself smiling, eager to catch sight of loved ones. He'd imagined Jimmy grinning and riding tall, poised on the brink of asking Lizzie an important question.

Instead, here they were, gaunt, shoulders stooped, eyes bloodshot, with no crowds to greet them. George saw a ranger to his left manage a thin smile as slowly people began to appear out of the shops, brought by the noise eighty horses made on the street. George searched for his family, but instead he caught the eager eyes of Lizzie. Her features hadn't dimmed in his mind from having seen them nearly daily in the photograph Jimmy carried. A lump rose in his throat and the watch in his pocket became the weight of lead. He turned his horse down a side street, unable to face her. He rode back streets, letting the mare take her time and pick her way, letting her breathing slow from the final push to make Black Hawk before dark. George supposed he was violating a code by breaking from the others like that, but he was too tired to care and would be done with the rangers by nightfall, so it really didn't matter all that much, did it?

The rangers had parted ways with Chivington and the 3rd, who were now no longer bloodless, outside of Denver. It had been a silent parting, Tyler grimly saluting Chivington, Chivington eager to parade his men through the streets of Denver. They'd been raised to fight the Indians and now they had and they'd won. No one needed to know anything else.

"We were victorious," Chivington shouted, turning his company and leaving the rangers.

George shivered at the words, and in silence the rangers moved on, following the flow of Clear Creek into the mountains to the canyon where Black Hawk waited for their return.

When the house came into view, George pulled the mare to a halt. The house looked the same, or else he had forgotten what it looked like, so the image of it now replaced any previous memory. The brown shutters were closed, the flower boxes filled with snow, and smoke spiraled from the kitchen chimney. Sarah must be stoking the fire to cook dinner. George could imagine her arranging root vegetables around a rump roast, kneading dough together for dumplings, and setting a bowl of cold butter on the side of the stove to warm. He imagined Aurora coming in with a foaming bucket of fresh milk, laughing as it splashed on her shoes and Sarah gave her a soft side-glance.

The chestnut mare relaxed, her ears flickering loosely, her hip sloping gently to the left. George rubbed her neck and watched the spiraling smoke. Three hens came squawking around the corner of the barn, scattered by Spot running. Aurora came behind them, shaking her red hair as she smiled over her shoulder at a boy in a blue coat. Suddenly he felt uncertain, not sure what he would say to his father, to Aurora, to Sarah. The boy caught hold of Aurora's arm and she turned to face him, the milk in the bucket she held splashing into the snow. Spot came wiggling to her feet, lapping at the snow and bumping against their legs. George watched them laugh and the boy rub the dog's ears. He felt like an intruder; when had his sister gotten old enough for an admirer? He picked up the reins to turn the mare from the scene. She startled, having been woken from a doze. Her breath came out sharply, cloudy in the cold. George rode out of town, asking the mare to lope easily. He needed a moment alone, with just the sound of the mare's breath.

George tethered the mare beside Jack's horse at the hitching post in front of the house. He scratched her cheek for a moment. A wavering of heat had replaced the smoke coming from the kitchen chimney, showing the fire burning hot. He wondered what Jack was telling them about the campaign. He could see them all sitting down around the table already, his father asking Jack how many raids they quelled, how many skirmishes they were involved in, before saying, "You did right, son, by your country."

George took a deep breath, the deepest he had taken in a long time, and had a strange feeling that he had just begun to breathe again. The feeling lasted him to the door, but as soon as he put his hand on the latch and pushed the door open his chest tightened.

"George, there you are," Jack said. He smiled, but George could sense worry in his tone.

Aurora ran to him and threw her arms around his neck. "I missed you," she said into his jacket.

He kissed the top of her head, roughed Evan's and Tib's hair in a brotherly gesture that belied what he was really feeling, then shook his father's hand. John's face seemed thinner than George remembered, more angular, with more lines creasing his forehead. His hair was more gray, too, but his mustache was the same, still neatly trimmed, and the small white scar beneath his left eye was still visible. John didn't say anything, just gripped his son's hand tightly, but George thought he saw tears in the corners of his eyes, whether from joy that he had returned or pride in what he had done George couldn't be sure. But there was no disappointment in his eyes, and this gave George a small amount of relief. Sarah came through the kitchen door with the roasting pan. She hastily dropped it onto the table and hugged George, not bothering to check her tears. She touched the back of her hand to his forehead as if checking for a fever. "You're thin," she said, "are you well?"

"Better now," he answered with a forced smile.

She laughed. "Get on." She squeezed his arms, then wiped the tears from her face. "Hungry?" When she said this, she looked around the room as if including everyone in the question, but George knew it was mainly directed at him. He nodded.

"A real meal'll taste good, huh, Jack?" He caught Jack's eyes across the room, and something in them made George uneasy. Had Jack been saying something about him before he came in?

"It will," Jack said. He smiled. George felt pity in the smile. Ever since Jimmy's hanging he had felt pity from Jack.

John carved the roast and passed plates around. George's mouth filled with saliva; he hadn't realized just how hungry he was, and he held his hands tightly in his lap to keep himself from wolfing the food before grace was said. The grace hadn't lasted this long since he had been ten, coming in after playing all afternoon in the creek.

"Thank you for this food and the nourishment it brings to our bodies. Thank you for providing us with health and the warmth of home. Thank you for bringing my two sons home safely. Thank you for helping them with their work and showing them the way. Bless everyone sitting at this table and all our family and friends. Bless this country and may it be delivered from turmoil. By your word and your son, Amen." John spoke the grace slowly, in a low voice like a minister, drawing the amen out.

Everyone echoed the amen except for George. He wanted to say it, thinking it would make him feel as if he had come home, as if he had never left, but somehow the word got stuck in his throat. He coughed and picked up his fork. The roast fell apart in his mouth, buttery, and he closed his eyes to savor it. He could feel the richness of the broth enter his veins, and his muscles relaxed along with his thoughts. This was good, being home, savoring a home-cooked dinner, watching as Aurora cut her potatoes into small squares before eating them.

"Still the potatoes," he said, breaking the quiet that always seemed to descend when a meal first began.

Aurora laughed. Her laugh had become wider, as if encompassing a bigger world, and it almost surprised George; it had been so long since he had heard the sound.

"I hear you cleaned up the Indian trouble by Fort Lyons," John said. His voice was carefully neutral, like he knew how his son would respond, but maybe he was just innocent of what the real events of the days by Fort Lyons were.

George swallowed and ate another forkful before answering, "I guess."

"Told them about the braves we caught scaling telegraph poles," Jack said. He looked directly at George. George relaxed again.

"That's right," George said, remembering the two young braves they apprehended along Adobe Creek on their way across the territory to Fort Lyons. There was a scuffle, but the braves were only armed with knives, having left their other weapons on their sleek ponies grazing close by, so it didn't last long, and no one was hurt. They took the Indians into the nearest town, where they turned them over to local law. The Indians' faces remained stoic the entire time, and George admired their fortitude. He couldn't help but wonder what was going on under the surface, though, behind the black stripes painted over their strong cheekbones.

"Wish I could have gone with you," Evan said. "I'd give anything to hunt down Indian braves."

George shook his head. "It isn't a hero story." The words surprised him and must have surprised the rest of the table as well, for everyone focused on their plates.

"Was Captain Tyler a good commander?" John asked, breaking the silence that threatened to stretch into awkwardness.

"Good, good," George said, trying to regain his composure and unsure what his father really wanted to know.

"Men respected him?"

"Yes." George ate a carrot, hot and sweet, then added, "I did, I do."

"He's a good commander," Jack agreed, "knows how to keep men in line. Never had trouble with anyone and never had to raise his voice, never had to single a man out."

"Governor Evans knew what he was doing when he put him in charge." John's statement was matter-of-fact and sure. "Heard there was some disagreement, though, with another commander?"

Jack and George exchanged furtive glances, and George felt his bones closing in on themselves, making it hard to breathe. He'd known deep down that Sand Creek would be discussed, but tonight, the first night back, at the dinner table, he just couldn't. In his mind he pleaded Jack to answer, to make light of it for tonight. As if in response, Jack swallowed and then cleared his throat. "Well," he began.

"There are new kittens in the barn," Sarah interrupted, changing the subject with an easy and quiet manner.

"Cold for kittens," George said, grateful that the conversation had moved to things more sweet and innocent. These were the things he wanted to think about, not the Indians they pulled off of telegraph poles, not the long, cold rides through the snow, not attacks on villages, or broken horses, or broken soldiers, or the Indian boy with Abe's eyes. Kittens, kittens were all he wanted to occupy his mind.

"Yes, but the barn is warm, lots of straw. Of course, they were in the kitchen for a week. In a box behind the stove."

George felt a smile spread through his body. Sarah hadn't changed, not at all. He wanted to hug her for it and keep her this way forever. "How many?"

"Five. Two black, a calico, and two orange tabby. One of the blacks has a white splash under his arm."

"He's Ma's favorite," Aurora added, bouncing slightly in her seat. "He snuggles up under her chin every time she picks him up. The calico is sweeter though; she'll lick anyone's hand."

"And the calico is yours." Once George would have laughed as he said this, gently teasing his sister, but now he didn't even feel a laugh rising. Had he forgotten how to laugh? He smashed a potato under his fork and swirled it in the broth, as if it were his worrying thoughts.

After dinner, George went to stand in front of the wide window that looked up the gulch. It felt strange to be back here. Everything was the same, and yet he didn't know how to be in this space anymore. There was too much space, and too many people within that space that expected him to be who he had been.

A boot heel on the wooden floor alerted him to someone entering the room, and he turned to see his father. "It's a good view," John said, coming to stand beside his son.

George nodded. "I missed it," he said quietly, surprising himself with sharing the sentiment.

"It's good to have things to miss. It makes coming back that much better." John cleared his throat. "You served your country well, George."

George didn't answer. He didn't know what to say, and let his attention shift back to the land outside. The trees in the gulch were bare now of their leaves, and they reached stark branches into the dusk gray sky. He wanted to ask his father if he'd ever shot a man, but the words stuck in his throat. In some ways, he didn't want to admit that he had, he didn't want to have to talk about it, and yet part of him wanted to know how it felt to someone else.

John clapped him on the shoulder. "You served your country well," he said again, "and it's good to have you home."

Life in Black Hawk seemed to pick up where it had left off; both George and Jack went back to work at the masonry in Chase Gulch, where they had worked every day before leaving with Tyler's Rangers. The masonry was a large stone and brick building built alongside the creek, with three outbuildings for storing brick and supplies on the opposite bank. When coming up the gulch, the masonry always came into view as if it had suddenly sprung from the ground; the sandy color of the stone and reddish brick made it blend in with the surroundings. It made George think of Arthurian legends, the way it stood singularly, majestically almost, in the gulch with its rounded door frames, a dozen windows, and large chimney for the kiln jutting above the rest. George often ran the kiln fire, keeping it hot by pumping the bellows, so that the bricks Jack formed would bake quickly and not crack.

Now, just days after returning, George pressed the bellows of the kiln until the fire roared. His face grew hot and he stepped back, staring at the flames. They leaped high, licking at the air. He remembered how the flames had licked at the night sky while the rangers sat around campfires drinking the last sludges of coffee while Jimmy told his tales. *Walls into the sky.* He wondered if the people who built the city Jimmy talked about fired the stones they used. He had an urge to find Jimmy and ask him. Jimmy would know, or if he didn't he would make something up, and it would feel so much like the truth that no one would dare to question it. George closed his eyes, and in the darkness behind his eyelids he remembered that he couldn't ask Jimmy. He pressed the bellows again and listened to the fire crackle. It sounded like sagebrush under horse hooves or distant pistol shots. George's heart sped up, and his breath came irregularly.

"See your boys are back," a man said from the front of the masonry.

"Yes, glad to have them," John answered, an edge of pride in his voice.

"Busy times, busy times."

"The city is growing."

"About time. We might just catch up with California."

"Might, might not. A growing city'll always need brick."

George listened to the conversation, letting it push the sounds of the fire and the memories out of his mind. His father firmly believed that brick-making was essential to human existence and always had been fond of saying, "We'll always need bricks. Anything can be built with brick."

"That's true," the man said. "Let's hope it keeps growing."

"Even if it stops, we'll always need bricks," John said.

George caught Jack's eyes over the top of the kiln. Jack pushed bricks into the oven with a paddle like he was baking bread. "He hasn't changed," Jack mouthed.

"Come on back, talk to the boys," John said.

George wondered if they would always be "the boys" no matter how old they got. They had both long passed the age of boys; even Evan and Tib were hardly boys any longer.

"George, Jack, you remember Harry Burns, don't you?"

George nodded simultaneously with Jack saying, "Yes, how are you, Mr. Burns?" Jack shook hands with Harry.

"Quite well," Harry answered. "Good to see you, Jack, and George." He turned with his hand extended to George. George shook it. "Wanted to thank you both for what you did with Tyler's campaign," Harry said.

"Couldn't let our country down," Jack said, his tone light, casual, as if discussing weather or a church picnic.

"You put the Indians in line."

"We tried." Jack paused a moment to peek at the bricks being fired and motioned to George to wake up the fire. George was grateful to go back to the bellows, but he made sure not to turn his back on Harry, a gesture that would have been a slight. "We didn't see much action. It was quiet out there," Jack continued, and then like slipping a note under a door he turned the conversation. "How's Mrs. Burns? And your daughter, Emily, is it?"

The heat of the fire made sweat bead on George's forehead, and he wiped it away as Jack conversed lightly with Mr. Burns to the door. How could Jack fall back into everyday conversations so easily? Why did small talk seem so hard for George to face?

# Chapter 6

"Did you see the news?" Jack tossed the *Rocky Mountain News* onto the dining room table. Late afternoon light came in through the window, a kind of muted yellow that made the light purple, paisley wallpaper look nearly brown. George sat at the table drinking a cup of coffee before going to help Evan and Tib with the chores. He liked this part of the day, getting home from the masonry and having a moment of silence before the others flooded in.

George wasn't pleased with the interruption by Jack, but he turned the paper and read the headline: *Lieutenant Silas Soule Contests Ethics of Sand Creek*. He grabbed the paper. It read, *The case of the Sand Creek attack has moved to the Supreme Court. It is being taken under advisement that this attack was against the morals of the army and this country. Lieutenant Soule is ready to testify that Colonel Chivington was not acting under orders. The attack he ordered on a village of Indians camped along Sand Creek is being called a massacre, which is out of line for military duties.* George stopped reading as the words began to swirl in front of him.

"We were a part of this," he said quietly.

"We stayed on the ridge," Jack said, "and we did try to stop them."

"That doesn't matter."

"It does matter."

George shook his head. Not all of us stayed, he thought, and that makes us all responsible. And he had shot an Indian, a young man like himself. He'd wounded him and left him to die in pain. And Jimmy... The tightness in his chest grew. "Soule knew. Tyler knew." George couldn't stop staring at the headline of the paper, but he wasn't seeing the words. He saw the rangers lined along the ridge, holding back horses that danced, rearing and stamping in the gray snow. These were horses trained for war, and with every shot fired their blood ran hot and they yearned to run the slope. He saw the flags raised and flapping in the middle of the village, one the stars and stripes, the other white. George flung the paper across the room where it hit the doorframe flatly. Sarah stopped short in her entrance, one hand touching the wall to steady herself, the other hand pressed to her heart. The clock clicked as the hands counted the seconds going by.

Sarah bent and picked up the paper. Her eyes moved across the headline, then she looked up at George. "Georgie boy," she said, "come into the kitchen with me?" She inflected her words like a question, but she wasn't asking; she was demanding that he come into the kitchen with her.

Without a word, George followed her.

Sarah moved the kettle onto the stove and put a round piece of wood into the fire. "Talk about it?" she asked.

George pulled a chair out from the table, digging his fingernails into the wood, before pushing it back. It slammed against the table, making the bowls sitting atop it rattle together.

Sarah showed no surprise; she didn't even flinch. Instead she smoothed her apron over her stomach and then pinned wayward strands of hair back from her face, all the natural gestures of her day to day. "You're a good man, George, only doing what you thought was best. It's not your fault. None of it is."

"You don't know what happened," George said.

"Tell me." Sarah caught his eye, her own deeply blue with empathy. George looked away. He had a feeling that if he held them too long he'd cry, and he didn't want to cry; he wouldn't cry.

"Tyler ordered us to stay, we didn't attack, but the chaos..." He shoved his hands in his pockets, something he had started to do frequently, and went to the window. Outside the sky was crystalline blue and cloudless. A raven cut its wings across the clearness and landed in the top branches of a pine, one of the few tall ones left on the hillsides. George knew the raven would be letting out a call, guttural, almost like a low chuckle. He could hear the sound clearly in his mind.

Behind him, Sarah started peeling potatoes. The peels dropped onto the floor with a soft thwack and established a rhythm of sound that once would have been comforting, but that now he resisted. He didn't want to be comforted; he wanted to be sad. But even more than that, he wanted to be angry.

"It was easy to get caught up in it. I should have seen it. I didn't." George thought of the race down the hillside. There had been so many of them, so many horses running down that hill, so many soldiers on the horses' backs, so many rifles in the soldiers' arms. "My horse was killed there, you know."

The peeling stopped. "I didn't. I'm sorry." Sarah put her hand on his shoulder. George almost shrugged it off. It had been so long since someone had tried to comfort him that it felt strange, and not only did he not want comfort, he didn't feel he deserved it.

"It's fine. It's war, right?"

"Doesn't make it hurt less."

"Chores need doing." George made to leave the room, nearly running into his father at the door. He stood shifting from foot to foot, wanting to get past John, but not wanting to push by him. His face felt too hot, his heartbeat too fast, his chest too tight, the room around him too close.

"Excuse me," George said, his voice raspy.

"What happened?" John asked in a tone that demanded an answer, but he stepped to the side, and George ducked through the doorway. "George!" John called after him.

George kept walking, not slowing his step until he entered the barn. It was warm and musty and reminded him of his childhood, of playing pirates in the hayloft. The cows below were sea monsters and the cats were sailors, mewing around the mast, pulling open imaginary sails. An old grain sack served as a flag, hung out of the window. Jack insisted they paint crossbones on it. All they had was charcoal, so each time it rained they had to redraw the image.

Trying to hold on to that memory, to the innocence of it, George climbed the ladder into the loft and found the kittens. He sank into the straw and let them crawl into his lap. The calico licked his hand, just as Aurora had promised.

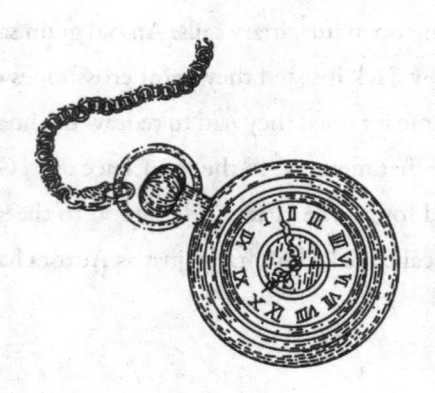

# Chapter 7

Winter days slipped into a rhythm as a new year came and began to blow by like the wind off the mountains. George stopped reading the paper. He wanted to be in a world unmarred by life outside Black Hawk, so why should he care what a court was saying about a case when he knew the truth? Whatever was ruled wouldn't change his life. He ate his meals hurriedly, leaving the table before Jack and his father could comment on what they had read or heard. At the masonry, he stayed by the kiln and did his best to avoid conversation with customers. In the heat of the fire he could forget the outside world and sink into his own mind, but his mind was so full of memories that it wasn't much quieter. He had this thought, though: maybe the heat of the kiln fire would melt his memories away.

George took the silver watch from his pocket and clicked it open. It was 5:20; still another twenty minutes before he could leave the masonry in good conscience. He put one last log on the fire, just to keep the room warm. Brick firing was done for the day, the order stacked along the furthermost wall until morning when he and Jack would load it onto the freight wagon. He hoped to take the wagon himself through the Black Hawk streets and up to Central City where there would soon be a Catholic Church sending spires into the clouds.

There was something in the damp March air that he wanted to be part of, as if he could catch the air between his fingers like a sheet on a clothesline, before pulling it to reveal another view behind it. March had never been his favorite month, but this year it held a secret.

John came in the back door with a bag of sand over his shoulder. "There's more in the wagon," he said, jerking his head at the door.

"Yes, sir," George said. Since his return, exchanges of this kind were the extent of his conversations with his father. They'd never talked as easily as Jack and John did, but George felt that there was a wall between him and John now that hadn't been there before. He wasn't sure who had built it or how to take it down, and part of him was afraid to try.

As George grasped a bag and flung it over his shoulder, he breathed in deeply. A musty smell met his nostrils that reminded him of Sarah's root cellar lined with jars of pickled and preserved vegetables and fruits and piles of potatoes packed in straw. As a boy back in Illinois, he'd hide there, sitting with his back against a barrel of salted meat, watching spiders crisscross their webs between the round, pine beams of the ceiling. One time Sarah found him there in the early days of her being part of the family.

*Sarah startled when she saw him, as she entered for a jar of pickled beets.*

*"Give a body some warning," she exclaimed, laughing at herself and lightly scolding him.*

*"Didn't mean to," George said. He got to his feet, feeling as if he had intruded where he shouldn't have. "I'll go."*

*"No, no, didn't know you were down here is all. Do stay." She put her hands on her hips, closed her eyes, and breathed in audibly. "Smells good, doesn't it? Smells like everything good and comforting. Sometimes I think I could just stay down here. And it's warm, too, even in winter."*

*George nodded. He reached into the potato pile beside him, rubbing the rough skin of one with his thumb until the dirt was brushed away and the potato became smooth.*

*"This must be what it's like to be a badger," Sarah said, "or an earthworm."*

*"I'd rather be a badger," George said.*

*Sarah opened her eyes and smiled at him. "Me, too." She put her hand out as if to tousle his hair, but then she stopped, letting her arm drop by her side. "Stay as long as you want," she said. She found the jar of beets and went to the door where she turned back. "It'll be our secret," she added, "and when you're ready, come into the kitchen. I have raisin cookies in the oven."*

"George, keep it moving," John said, breaking into George's memory. They stacked the sand beside the clay, tan beside red. The bags were dusty, letting off puffs like smoke. John coughed, a harsh, dry cough, and straightened his hands on his back.

"I'll get the last of them," George said.

"Thanks, son, then head off for the day. We'll start mixing tomorrow." John patted George twice on the shoulder, went to the front of the shop, and pulled out the books. He ran his finger down the orders, checking amounts and payments, writing notes in the margins. George didn't know how he kept all the numbers and names straight in his mind, and he wondered what his father wrote everyday when he checked the books. The bookkeeping felt private, as if it were John's journal. In all likelihood there wasn't anything secret written in the corners of the pages, but George never opened the ledgers, as if it'd be an intrusion into his father's mind.

As George entered with the final bag of sand, a woman's voice met his ears. With care he stacked the bag and glanced to see who it was. The woman was young, blonde hair bleached nearly white, her wide-set eyes dark and luminous, as if tears were ready to pour from them. Lizzie. George felt panic rise in his chest; he couldn't get a deep breath, and his ears began to ring. Lizzie's voice cut through the ringing as she introduced herself to his father.

"I'm Lizzie McMechen," she said, and, not waiting for John to reply, hurried on. "I heard your sons rode with Tyler and I—I wanted—wanted to ask, they did know Jimmy, didn't they? Uh, Jimmy Dobbs?" She fumbled with the button of her purse. "I—I have a—a picture." She succeeded in opening her purse, but George didn't wait to see if she found the photograph.

Shoving his hands as deep as he could into his pockets, he walked away from the masonry toward the Tivoli Brewery. His feet felt heavy, and his breathing came short and fast, but he walked quickly, his boots collecting the slick mud of the first thaw. He took the quiet back streets. Ever since returning, he had only been on the main street once when he dropped Sarah and Aurora by the dry-goods store. He didn't like people seeing him and asking questions. He was afraid of running into old friends. He was afraid of running into Lizzie. Back streets were safer, fewer chances of seeing someone he knew or who knew him, fewer windows in the backs of buildings where people could see him walk by.

The Tivoli Brewery was mostly brick. George remembered when they supplied the owner, Sigi, with it. Sigi had wanted bricks of different lengths. He said the building was an artistic project and wanted to make it a mosaic. In the end he had settled for mostly bricks of the same length, but he had succeeded in giving the doorway an arch which he had whitewashed so that it stood out against the rest of the brick like an eyebrow gone white before the hair. George pushed open the heavy wooden door clad in iron under this brow and entered the dimness of the brewery. He kept his eyes straight ahead to avoid conversations with any other early comers and took a stool at the bar.

"Give me a pint," George told the bartender, flipping a coin onto the bar. It turned over three times before landing heads up. A memory flickered into his mind of a time when his eyes were below the general store counter. Up, up went the silver, turning once, twice, disappearing from his sight as it landed. His father had smiled, his mustache twitching. "Heads," he'd said, as the storekeep cussed lightly at him. George stood on his tiptoes and his eyes rose to counter level. It was a whole other world on the polished top, pieces of paper forming houses, a stub of pencil like a stage stop, the silver edge of a coin as the town square. He had wanted to poke it and see if anything moved.

"Heads!" the bartender said now, as George's father had said then. The bartender swiped the coin off the bar and swirled a foaming mug of beer to George.

George let the beer slide down his throat in gulps, stealing away his memories. He had no regrets as he drained the last drop and asked for another.

In the dark he wandered home. The temperature had dropped below freezing again, and the mud of the day had a crust of ice that crunched and sank with each step. George liked the sound and stepped heavier to sharpen the noise. But it made each step sound like a shot and sent him back to a sagebrush-covered hill in winter.

*His horse breathed heavily, steam rising from his body into the cold dawn. George leaned over the horse's black mane and let him run, pounding toward the village. The wind in his face made his eyes water, blurring his vision, but he didn't slow Abe's pace. The colors of the American flag flapped into view, and George blinked, trying to focus, and when he did he saw he wasn't mistaken. A man stood holding the flag high, his body straight and strong, his lips drawn together as he stared at the onslaught of cavalry, his look indomitable, almost tranquil. Hesitation slipped over George. He looked to the men galloping beside him, their weapons drawn, their faces contorted by wind or hatred or both. Then his horse fell and the others sped on in a volley of shots.*

The crunch of his steps shuddered through him and he saw the young Indian man facing him again. *He pulled the trigger and the Indian's eyes widened, the pupils dark and large in the still, dim light, and they wouldn't close. Why wouldn't they stay closed? Or were those Abe's eyes that wouldn't?*

George shivered in the wind that cooled the sweat dampening his clothes, bringing him out of the distorted memories. He wrapped his arms around himself and focused on getting home. When he arrived, John was sitting alone by the hearth. "George, come sit," he said.

Feeling dizzy, sick, and cold, George didn't argue, sinking into Sarah's rocker.

"It's time we talked," John said. The coals glowed as the fire died. One sparked, sending specks of light that extinguished as quickly as they appeared. "What happened?"

"Finished unloading and went to Tivoli's," George said, confessing where he had gone as if daring his father to object, to berate him for drinking, to tell him how disappointed he was, but the challenge went unmet.

"I meant with the rangers," John said.

"Nothing. We did our job and came home, that's all."

"Jack said you had a friend." John paused for a moment, and when George continued to stare at the fireplace, he continued. "You had a friend who died at Sand Creek."

"After," George corrected. In his chest, the words felt heavy, like lifting a bag of sand over his head, but they sounded thin when they hit the air.

"What happened?"

"He died."

"How?"

Silence fell on the room like frost. George could hear his heart; it sounded too slow and seemed to be keeping time with the clock on the mantel. Maybe it was the clock and not his heart he heard... Everything seemed to be mixed up.

"There was a girl, came into the masonry today. She asked to speak with you. She wanted to know about Jimmy Dobbs." Again John paused, waiting for George to speak, and again George didn't. "He was the friend?"

George nodded. The lamp cast shadows on the wall that flickered, and George watched them, letting them make him dizzy.

"Damn it, George, you've got to talk!" John stood and faced his son. John was a tall man and in the half-darkness of a room lighted by a single kerosene lamp, he was even taller, imposing, much like the brick buildings he built, much like the masonry that rose Arthurian in the gulch, something of legend. "Stop this sullenness. You went to war and came back, but it was war. Not everyone comes back. You've got to get on."

George knew his father's words were spoken from experience, but even so, he felt his father could never understand what had happened out there. "You don't know," George whispered. "It wasn't war—it was a slaughter. I could have stopped Jimmy. I didn't. I don't want to talk, to you, to Jimmy's girl, to anyone. Excuse me, sir." George stood to leave the room.

John grabbed George's shoulder, pulling him back. "No! Don't you walk out on me!" John's voice became sharp and commanding, much like it used to when George was in trouble as a boy.

George tried to shrug his father's hand off, but John's grip was firm, and the beer still thrummed in George's head. John gripped him tighter, taking both George's shoulders, and for a moment George was glad for the steadying.

"Talk to me, son, talk to me." John's fingers pinched George's skin. "I know how close soldiers become. I understand. But this has got to end!" His voice increased in volume with every word, until it seemed the whole house should be awake.

"You can't understand," George said through clenched teeth. It was then he suddenly realized that he didn't have to look up to look his father in the eye anymore; they were level, equal in height. He was a grown man; he didn't need to explain anything to his father. He jerked away, trying to free himself from his father's grip, and one of John's hands loosened its hold. "Let go of me!" George couldn't tell if he was speaking low or shouting. Every word hammered his head, and he felt a need to punch something. It came over him so quickly that he never put it into thought and didn't realize what he'd done until his knuckles cracked against John's jaw.

Both men stood stunned, the silence of the room total. George stared at his hand, the knuckles red, one cracked and dribbling blood. His mouth had gone completely dry, and his stomach tightened as if he was going to be sick. He looked up. John had his hand on his jaw. Before either could move, Sarah came through the doorway, her eyes skipping from one man to the other. George thought he saw something like fear in them and he staggered backward, turning to go to his room as she went to John.

"John, come with me and we'll put something on that jaw," she said.

George made it to his room and tried to ignore the frightened looks of his brothers as he sank onto his bed. He squeezed his eyes shut. Maybe if he squeezed tight enough it'd all go away.

With spring came the stock sale at the livery in Golden. Golden was half a day's ride downstream from Black Hawk in the foothills of the mountains. The surrounding land was hilly, and the town itself flowed up and down the hills along the bank of the stream. George and Jack, along with Jimmy, had gone to the sale for years, often buying a young horse or two that they'd ride over the summer and then sell in the fall for twice what they paid. It was such a long-standing ritual that neither George nor Jack questioned going, although George hadn't been speaking to anyone since the night he'd punched his father, and Jimmy was no longer there to go with them. The livery stable corrals were full of mangy colts pushing each other against the boards, nipping at each other's withers. George flinched as one colt kicked another in the ribs, the sound cracking into the soft, April air. He and his brother were quiet. It had been different last year. Last year, he, Jack, and Jimmy leaned side by side and assessed confirmation, color, and personality.

*"That one has good bones," Jack had said, pointing to a large sorrel.*

*"Lazy eyes though," George had answered, "not enough spirit."*

*"He'd spunk up."*

*"Not like that one." George pointed to a bay with black points and a wide, long blaze. The colt pranced in the corner, his nostrils wide, his head and tail held high. He stamped and snorted, eyeing a man's flapping jacket.*

*"Too flighty," Jack said.*

*Jimmy nodded in agreement, saying, "It'd take too many wet blankets to break that horse."*

*George smiled. "He's a good one."*

*"You're going to buy him." Jack sighed, the phrase a statement, not a question.*

*George nodded. "He's got the eyes."*

*"He's also got the moves to land ya in the dirt," Jimmy said, chuckling as the colt sprang from the others in a twisting crow-hop, spooked by a rope being tossed over the corral fence.*

*George just grinned and repeated, "He's got the eyes." Over the week that followed, he continued to repeat the phrase, every time Jack or Jimmy or his father made a comment about the colt being untrainable. It was his defense, and after two weeks the colt had made enough progress that Jack admitted, "There might be something to him."*

*"Yeah, there is, there most certainly is," George said. He patted the bay colt's neck that was now sleek with a summer coat, then swung into the saddle, urging the colt onto the road. At the edge of downtown Black Hawk, he pulled the colt to a halt, as Jimmy rode up to meet him. The colt stood with his head high, his eyes taking in every tiny movement around him. The saddle blanket was foamed and soaked with sweat, the edges dripping.*

*"That's one helluva wet blanket," Jimmy said, his grin spreading up his cheeks and into his eyes.*

*"Think I'll call him that," George said, smoothing the tangles out of the colt's mane. "Wet Blanket."*

That had been before. Now George stood away from the fence, his hands deep in his pockets. He thought about Wet Blanket. He hadn't ridden the colt since he'd returned, leaving him in the corral behind the house, letting his young siblings feed him with the rest of the stock. He couldn't face the horse, those eyes, not yet.

"George," Jack called. He motioned for his brother to come closer to the fence. Reluctantly, George moved forward. If he refused, Jack would ask him if he was okay, and he didn't want to have that conversation again. Jack pointed into the corral. "What do you think of that filly?" he asked. "The black one there in the middle."

George nodded. "Fine," he said, barely glancing where Jack pointed.

"She's well-muscled already," Jack continued, seemingly unaware of his brother's disinterest. "Could make a good delivery horse, what do you think? Seems steady, too. What are her eyes telling you?"

George swallowed, looking up and focusing on the filly. Her head was turned away, but he noted the strong curve of muscle in her neck and the wideness of her chest. She dipped her head and shook, dust rising from her coat, her movements graceful, fluid. Despite himself, George noticed this and drew closer to catch a glimpse into her eyes. Her eyes were dark, darker than most horse's, but in the left there was a fleck of gold, like a light seen from a distant home, and it almost beckoned. For a moment he saw the brown gelding of Jimmy's in them, watching as George left the horse wounded in the cold, and the empty space beside him felt wider and more open than ever, as if it would keep growing until he fell into it.

"I can't," George choked and left, ignoring Jack's calls after him.

# Chapter 8

April was a muddy affair in Black Hawk, the streets turning soupy with rain and then sticky, tar-like when the rain began soaking in. It clung to shoes, wagon wheels, horse hooves, and the hems of pants and skirts. The women swept continuously to rid their floors of the mud and never seemed to succeed. It was the kind of weather that lent well to melancholy, only the sun somehow managed to funnel some joy into the mountain valley, reminding residents that winter had passed. George didn't want to be reminded. The sun seemed to shine too brightly, even on the days it rained. The grass grew too green. He resented the hyacinths that bloomed in Sarah's window boxes, the crocuses that popped up, seemingly out of nowhere, along the foundation of the Catholic Church, the snowdrops that laced the path to the masonry. And yet, he began to find that he could shield his eyes from the colors of spring and fall into the monotonous routine of work. As long as the days followed the same ordered pattern, he could see a way forward.

The steady rhythm of the ax kept time with George's breath as he chopped logs for the kiln fire behind the masonry. This was the kind of work he liked these days, he could chop wood for hours, and when he stopped he could still feel the motion of the swing in his arms. Some days he chopped so much wood he continued the work in his dreams. He found that his father often watched him, as he split log after log, and even though George never looked to the doorway, he knew John would be standing with his arms crossed, the lines on his face shadowed valleys of worry. George knew John's expressions well. John wasn't a demonstrative man, but his face gave away his feelings to those close to him.

Since the night his fist had met John's jaw, George hadn't talked to his father beyond the necessary exchanges regarding work or niceties at mealtimes. That night had split them in a way that George wasn't sure could be repaired. He didn't know how to repair it even if he could. Once enough time had passed, wouldn't the rift heal over?

George sighed and paused in his wood splitting. He wiped his forehead with his left forearm and leaned backward, stretching; a muscle clicked in his lower back, alignment achieved again. There was a ringing in his ears like the steady chiming of a church bell. It kept going even after he'd shaken his head to rid the noise from his mind. George turned and looked down the valley toward town. Was it an actual church bell? It was the wrong time of day for a bell to be ringing, and yet as he listened he was certain that's what it was.

"Is that the church bell?" Jack asked, coming out of the masonry behind George.

George nodded, sure now that the ringing was not inside his head. He hadn't lost his mind. Relief and dread came over him equally, the dread falling like lead into his stomach, though he didn't know why. His brother came to stand shoulder to shoulder with him, and George's mind lurched back in time to them standing side by side, the reins of their horses looped on their arms, eyes fixed on Captain Tyler as he gave the company a briefing on their orders.

*"We are to scout the roads to the south for hostiles. We will be riding long hours and during those hours all must stay alert and ready to fight at a moment's notice. You never know when hostiles might choose to attack." Tyler's voice resonated through the company. "We will stop them. We will protect the innocent settlers. You will each do your duty by your family and your country."*

*George shivered involuntarily even though the August sun radiated with a relentlessness that could only come from a late summer day. He glanced at his brother.*

*Jack stood tall, a commanding rigidness to his body, his face stern, while excitement glinted in his eyes. Nervous energy coursed into George, coiled into him, and when Tyler gave the command to mount up, he and Jack sprang to their horses as one. Suddenly he felt ready, for what he wasn't sure, but ready for something, anything.*

As the memory drifted away with the smoke from the kiln fire, George glanced at his brother and saw the same commanding rigidness he had on that August day they'd ridden out of Black Hawk as rangers. Jack was listening, not just with his ears, but his whole body, preparing to move with purpose. Jack had kept his conviction through those long days of riding trails gone cold, through the short skirmishes with Sioux and Cheyenne braves, through the freezing morning at Sand Creek, the disillusioned ride home to Black Hawk. George knew he'd lost his conviction, if he'd ever had it to begin with. He wasn't as strong as Jack, he wasn't the man his brother was, and as he watched his brother listen to the tolling of the church bell with his whole being, he wondered if he could ever be as strong.

George knew the moment his brother came to a decision before Jack said a word. Jack's body softened just slightly, like a tree bending before a breeze, and George took a step forward in time to Jack's step as Jack said, "We should go find out the news." There was no doubt in either of their minds now that something had happened, and they needed to know. George matched his brother's stride, and they headed down the valley to the town below, their strides long and steady.

As they reached town, they saw a crowd had gathered in front of the post office. Aurora broke from the crowd and ran toward them, a lightness to her even as tears stained her cheeks. "They shot him," she gasped out. "President Lincoln is dead."

George stopped, turned to stone. Jack brushed Aurora's cheek and continued forward into the post office. Aurora gripped George's hand and George knew she had, but somehow couldn't feel the touch of her fingers on his palm. "George,

George, George." Her voice finally cut into his consciousness and he began to register other voices in the crowd.

"How can this be true?"

"I cannot realize it."

"Who did it? Do they know?"

"It cannot be real."

"When?"

"Did they catch him?"

"Who?"

"The actor who shot the president."

"An actor shot him?"

"This must be a ruse."

"The yellow-bellied Confederates made it up."

"John Wilkes Booth."

"Who's that?"

"He shot Lincoln."

"Lincoln can't be dead."

"How could someone shoot the president?"

"Damn rebels."

"They should all be strung up."

"Tortured, more like."

"Is it really true?"

"If I could get my hands on the man who did this..."

George made his way to the door of the post office; his hands had gone clammy, and he seemed to have lost full function of them as he took a newspaper from a wordless Jack. The headline of the column where someone had folded the newspaper into hurried creases read, "Farewell to Abraham Lincoln!" George blinked, thinking maybe he'd misread, but the words stayed the same: "Farewell to Abraham Lincoln!" Underneath the headline followed a poem by Minnie Aux. It began,

*Farewell! Farewell! Let the soft breezes echo*

*The farewell we wail to the Patriot laid low,*

*The star of our guidance, the hope of our Nation,*

*Ah! Well may we weep in the depth of our woe.*

*No more shall his strong arm be stretched forth to rescue*

*The land of our birth from the traitors' foul tread,*

*For low in the grave lies the terror of rebels,*

*But, oh! His avengers, they still, still may dread![1]*

It didn't make any sense, here was a farewell poem, but what had happened? Where was the explanation for this? George looked up in confusion, meeting Jack's eyes. He crumpled the newspaper in his hand. "This doesn't say he was shot," he said tightly. "How do we know he was shot?"

"An official letter came with the paper," Jack answered, his own voice tight as well, as if straining to keep back tears. "He was shot at a theater on the 14th. He died the next morning."

"That was days ago," George said. He knew his voice had grown louder, but he couldn't seem to control it. "Why are we just hearing about it now? If it were true, we would have heard sooner."

"It's true George, the news was just delayed," John cut into the conversation, gripping George's shoulder, and George's heart lurched at the feel of his father's hand. It took him right back to that cold, dark night when his knuckles had met John's jaw. He forced himself to not shrug his father's hand off and focused on the official letter John's other hand held in front of him. The letter read,

*The distressing duty has devolved upon the Governor of Colorado Territory to announce that at twenty-two minutes after 7 o'clock on the morning of Saturday*

---

1. Italics are direct quotes from a column in *The Rocky Mountain News* from April 19, 1865.

*the 15th day of April, 1865, Abraham Lincoln, President of the United States, died of a mortal wound inflicted upon him by an assassin.*[2]

George swallowed, but the hard lump in his throat remained. His head had inexplicably begun to throb as if he had been crying, but his eyes remained completely dry, even as he could see water glistening in the corners of his father's.

The flag in town square was lowered carefully, like a baby into a cradle, to half-mast. The gathered crowd of townspeople stood sober and silent, those who had served saluting at attention, black armbands encircling nearly everyone's arms. Black cloth draped the nearby bench and adorned the porch railings of every house on the street. All businesses had closed and the church bell tolled dolefully through the morning hours, then again through the evening hours. There was an air of uncertainty in the streets. No one seemed to know what to do or say, passing each other awkwardly, wandering listlessly. How long should they mourn? That seemed to be the question on everyone's mind.

The late April storms had given way to late April sun, and the women of Black Hawk pulled their seeds out of storerooms and laid them out in their kitchens, but no one began planting. George went into the small kitchen of the brick house on Horn Street to find Sarah fingering the brown paper packets of seeds she'd laid out on the sideboard the day before.

"You should plant them," he said.

She startled and turned, giving him a half-smile. "I don't know that it's right," she said, smoothing a crease on a packet of green winter squash seeds.

George nodded. He understood. He wanted to go back to the masonry, he wanted to feel tired from work, and not just from the grief that had accumulated

---

2. Italics adapted from the military announcement of Abraham Lincoln's death.

over the months, but it felt dishonorable somehow, as if he wouldn't truly be mourning the late president. He knew, though, that soon he'd be desperate, soon the memories would drive him back, no matter if it was dishonorable or not. Someone was going to break; he didn't want to be the one.

Sarah moved to the stove and put a log on the coals, keeping the firebox door open until the log caught. The flames snagged in George's mind and he felt them dragging him back. He turned away, his breath ragged as he tried to shove the memories down, bury them deeper than Sarah's seeds would be buried in the garden.

"Are you okay?" Sarah's voice came to him softly.

"Fine," George answered, but he couldn't look at her, and before she could ask again, he left the kitchen. The church bell began its evening mourning, and he watched as people came out onto their porches, saluting the half-mast flag hanging brightly in the alpenglow.

Days passed, and with hesitancy, the people of Black Hawk picked up their lives. One by one businesses reopened, one by one gardens were planted, one by one the rituals of life continued forward. The flag remained at half-mast, and every day as George walked to the masonry to resume his log splitting, he paused and saluted. He wasn't always sure he was saluting President Lincoln; sometimes he felt he might be saluting Jimmy, sometimes that sturdy black gelding, Abe, or even something within himself that he had lost.

# Chapter 9

Jack came into the kitchen and without a word tossed the *Rocky Mountain News* down on the bench in front of George. George was pulling on his boots, on his way to toss hay to the horses and check that Tib had filled the water trough.

"Jack, you know I don't," George began, shoving his left foot into the boot so hard the boot heel cracked on the wood floor.

"Just read it," Jack said. The lines about his mouth and eyes were tight, his eyes unblinkingly blue, showing he wasn't going to let George refuse.

George read the following:

*Our city was thrown into a feverish excitement last evening by assassination of Captain S. S. Soule, of the Colorado First. The sad affair took place about half past ten o'clock, and was evidently coolly and deliberately planned, and as systematically carried out.*

George felt as if his ribs were being stitched tighter and tighter together, and he slid the paper away. Jack pushed it back and tapped on the article, indicating for George to keep reading.

*In the evening he and his wife were visiting at the house of a friend and returned home between nine and ten o'clock. Shortly after, a number of pistol shots were fired in the upper part of the city, evidently to decoy him out, and the Captain started to ascertain the cause. Whilst passing along Lawrence Street, Near F, and directly in front of the residence of Dr. Cunningham, he seems to have been met by the assassin, and the indications are that both fired at the same instant, or so near together that the reports seemed simultaneous. Probably the Captain, expecting to be attacked, was in readiness, and when the other man presented his pistol, he did the same, but the intended assassin fired an instant soonest, with but to fatal effect. The ball entered the Captain's face at the point of the right cheek bone, pressing backward and upward, and lodging in the back part of the head. He fell back dead, appearing not to have moved a muscle after falling. The other man, from the indications, was wounded in the right hand or arm; how severely is not known. His pistol was dropped at his feet and he immediately started and ran towards the military camp in the upper part of the city, leaving a distinct trail of blood where he passed along. When the shots were fired they were standing about four feet apart, face to face.*

*Within less than a minute after the fatal shot, one of the provost guard and Mr. Ruter reached the spot. The Captain was already dead, and his murderer had disappeared. They alarmed Dr. Cunningham, and a guard was sent for. A number of persons, soldiers and civilians, soon gathered around, and after a few minutes the body was removed to the building occupied by the officers of the Headquarters of the District.*

George tried to swallow but couldn't, and despite the saliva, his mouth felt dry. He thought that he'd begun moving on from Sand Creek, that the memories were dissolving with each long day of work at the brickyard, the monotony of a rhythm he'd known before the rangers, but with the news of Soule's death they came stumbling back. He could see Soule's clear eyes consulting with Tyler as the companies rode up the ridge above the Sand Creek village. Again he remembered Soule's words, "I won't let my men attack, these Indians are peaceful," and these words mixed with the words on the paper as he kept reading, unable now to stop.

*The excitement this morning, when the facts became generally known, was intense. Hundreds of citizens visited the scene of the tragedy, and it has formed the burthen of conversation throughout the city all day. Patrols were dispatched in every direction, and it is hardly possible that he will escape more than for a day or two.*

*Probably he will be overtaken to-day. Of his identity we shall at present refrain from speaking, though there is scarce a doubt but it is clearly known. The cause is said to have grown out of an arrest made by the Captain in the discharge of his duty as Provost Marshal.*

*Captain Soule was highly respected by his brother officers, and beloved by the men in his company. He was married in this city on the 1st inst., and consequently leaves a young wife to mourn this terrible and untimely fate. It is the hope of all that his murderer and his accomplices will be speedily brought to judgement, and a punishment meted out to them such as the base crime deserves.*[1]

George glanced at Jack. "This is what I didn't want to know," he said.

"You had to know," Jack said.

"No, no, I don't want to know anymore! I can't take it!" He shook the paper, his whole body trembling. "This isn't how it's supposed to be!" He felt light-headed, as if he had stood up too fast, only magnified so that it throbbed in his temples and blurred his eyes. There on a hook by the door; he focused on John's pistol belt. Striding to it, he jerked it down. "This," he said, pulling the pistol from the holster, "this, we don't need. It only kills."

Jack eased the grip of each of George's fingers from around the pistol, taking it from him. George left the room without another word, anger burning in his heart. Or was it heartache? He wasn't sure; all he knew was he couldn't take it anymore. There had to be a way off this wagon he'd gotten on, but he knew it wouldn't happen here. Going into his room, he stuffed what he could of his belongings into a bag, then he walked straight to the corrals as if he had blinders on, past Sarah on the doorstep and Aurora coming from the barn with a pail of milk frothing over the top. He wasn't going to let them stop him; he didn't want to see their faces, too afraid that the confusion and concern he'd see there would make him hesitate, make him reconsider. Catching Wet Blanket, he tossed the saddle over the colt's back, who spooked, but it didn't faze George. He grabbed

---

1. Italics are direct quotes from *The Rocky Mountain News* article printed the morning after Soule was killed, April 24, 1865.

the cinch and pulled it tight around the colt's girth. Wet Blanket threw his head, snorting and nipping at George. George didn't even scold him; instead he tied the bag behind his saddle and put his foot in the stirrup.

"George," Jack said, grasping George's arm, "what are you doing?"

"Leaving," George said. "I've got to go, get away."

"Think about this."

"No, I don't want to think anymore. I've got to go."

"Wait a minute," Sarah said. Her voice broke through the haze that had filmed over George's brain, and things cleared for a moment. His breathing eased, as if the stitches between his ribs were being loosened like bootlaces. He knew he still had to go, needed to be away from the places and people who made him remember, but he could wait a moment for her.

Sarah went into the house and came back out with a cloth clutched in her hand. "Baked potatoes, some bread," she said, handing the parcel up to him, "to give you something to go on."

His throat tightened. "Sarah," he managed to get out. He wanted to thank her, for not questioning or reproaching, thank her for the food, but he could only say her name. He stepped into the saddle and dug Wet Blanket with his spurs. Wet Blanket sprang into a rough trot, his back rounded and ready to buck at the first snap of a stick or swirl of wind.

The land spread out like a rug being shaken and unrolled over a dirt floor. An overnight rain made the sagebrush a vibrant, silver-green and perfumed the air with a smell so fresh and fragrant it made George sneeze. Wet Blanket flinched, his skin rippling in one motion that wove into the breeze coming over the foothills of the Rocky Mountains. At one time George would have ridden toward the mountains, but this time he wanted something new, something different. Only difference could bring relief from the memories that chased him.

He thought about the young widow Soule left behind. He'd seen them together once. She was sweet-looking, with dark curls around a porcelain face, but her eyes were deep, brown and strong, as if she were ready to take on the world. Now though, George imagined those eyes were drowned in saltwater. But tears didn't seem right, and he saw them as dry, like a watering hole in a rainless summer. Maybe though, they showed nothing. Maybe they were like an empty plot of ground.

Thinking about Soule's widow led him to think about Lizzie. Did she know what had happened to Jimmy? Maybe he should have told her, talked to her. Just the thought of telling her, though, made his heart quicken, as if it were trying to come out of his chest. He remembered her eager eyes searching the ranks of rangers as they rode into Black Hawk. Those eyes wouldn't find what they were looking for; they'd never see what they sought ever again. George spurred Wet Blanket into a gallop, thinking if he rode fast enough he could get ahead of those searching eyes. The colt moved awkwardly with a stride that was at once gallop and crow-hop.

On the horizon, gray clouds dripped, and George knew that it would rain again the coming night. He began looking for a place to shelter in the storm, but all around him the land spread evenly and was unbroken by gullies or trees. It would be a miserable night, cold, wet. What was he doing?

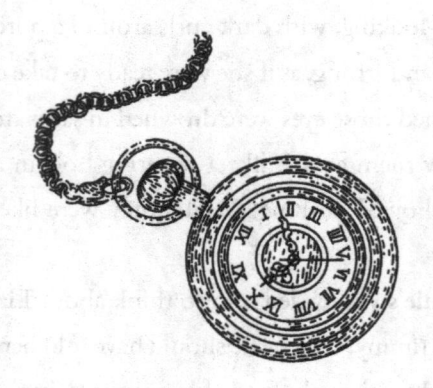

# Chapter 10

And then he was alone. It hit him suddenly with a realization that the rushing whistle in his ears of other people living, that reminded him of too many things he wanted to forget, was gone. He'd been riding for a week, and he breathed in the aloneness that stretched before him, knowing nothing would make him turn back and knowing he needed to decide where he was heading. He let Wet Blanket come to a stop and surveyed the sky. Clouds whipped across the soft blue in a wind too high to be felt on land, and he watched them pass, letting his vision blur and change them into shapes. A ship passed, followed by trailing sails, ribbons, and smoke, strands of wild oat seed-heads. It'd been a long time since he had indulged in cloud watching, and it joggled a memory of Illinois, laying in a meadow with Jack and watching white horses float by. They'd race each other to see who could find a shape first; usually Jack would be the first to shout out a shape, but George did remember one time when he'd beaten Jack.

*"A grasshopper!" he shouted, pointing so forcefully that his body bounced in the grass.*

*"No, it's an eagle," Jack said with authority, "and there is a wolf."*

*George rolled, first away from Jack and then back. The vegetation crinkled under him. "A horse, see?" He pointed into the sky again.*

*"You always see horses."*

*"Sarah says clouds is angel wings," George said, "an' angels need something to ride."*

*"Sarah thinks everything is angel wings," Jack said, and George could hear a smile in his voice.*

*Crickets began to sing along the edges of the meadow, where a small stream slipped over stones green with moss. The clouds moved, becoming wispy, trailing across the blue.*

*"Horses' tails!" George cried with youthful exuberance.*

*"That's the trail soldiers take," Jack said, correcting him again.*

*"What soldiers?" George turned toward his older brother and saw that Jack was gazing unblinkingly into the sky. Sun freckles scattered across his cheekbones and the edges of his fine dark hair were bleached almost blonde.*

*Finally, Jack blinked and then answered George's question, "The ones I'm going to join that will chase away the savages in the west. I'm going to make the frontier safe and then you and Sarah can come."*

*"Can't I come with you?"*

*"You're too little."*

*"Am not," George protested. "Someday I'll be big as you."*

*"I'll always be older," Jack returned, "so I'll always be bigger."*

*"That's no fair."*

*"Of course it is. It's how things is."*

*"I don't want to stay little," George pouted and then was distracted again by the shapes drifting by in the sky.*

Such innocence, George thought now. Clouds were just clouds, but there was something in the memory that felt prophetic. He had at one time wanted to be a soldier; he hadn't really known what that meant; did anyone really know before they actually became one? George clenched his jaw and shook the memory away, deciding he'd keep riding south, south into Arizona Territory. Maybe there in the red sand his memories would leave him alone.

George urged Wet Blanket on at a steady lope, keeping him at the pace as space widened between the sun and the horizon. By afternoon, sweat foamed on the bay's neck and chest, and George felt the need to find water. He swung down from the creaking saddle and stood looking at the land around him. Before him a wide canyon split the ground, sandy and spotted with blue winterfat and green Mormon tea. Scarlet cactus bloomed on rock outcroppings like splashes of blood, and bunches of tough browning grass grew along a gully that held the possibility of water. Holding the leather reins in his chapped hands, George headed toward that possibility.

He walked as if testing the ground for snares. Behind him, Wet Blanket snatched at bunches of grass as though nothing could disturb him. George saw the wind before he felt it. It came from up the canyon, blowing clouds of sand. Grit hit his face. The sweat on Wet Blanket dried, brown with dust, as the horse threw his head in the wind, testing the air, nostrils wide, then shied to the side. The reins went taut. George absently scratched the bay on the side of the nose until he quieted and then they walked on. The wind blew and George crunched grit. Wet Blanket danced, grass forgotten.

It was a good three miles before they came across water; a small pool, no bigger than George's hat, but water. George lay on his stomach and drank. Wet Blanket came up beside him, wiggling his lips in the water and splashing George, then, he too, drank. George stood, refreshed. He filled his canteen and said, "All right, Wet Blanket, that's it." He smacked the horse's shoulder. Wet Blanket's head went up and he snorted.

George led the horse out of the gully. He headed toward the cliffs, hoping to find some sort of shelter for the night. Lizards ran from his feet, disappearing under close-growing winterfat. Sparrows flirted around him, but there was no other sound. George turned, feeling like he was being watched, being evaluated, as if he were on trial. As he turned back to the cliffs, his eyes landed on a brick wall rising into the sky, and the tempo of his heart picked up.

George stared at the ruins before him. "Jimmy's story was true," he thought. Feeling amazement, near disbelief at the view before him, he stepped forward and pressed the palm of his hand against the stone. It was warm and soft to his rough palm, but he could feel the strength of the structure, and it felt nearly alive. Slowly he moved along the wall, letting his fingers brush along the stones as he walked. He liked the way the grains felt; it made his skin tingle and reminded him of the bricks he'd made, comforting him, as if he had come home.

As the sun moved lower in the sky, the ruins changed color. They were red like the roses in Sarah's garden, then they were pink like the breast of a mourning dove. George watched as they changed from dove pink to dove gray, to the color of slate, marveling at the change and feeling drawn to the stones even more. The ruins turned to a burnished brown like saddle leather as George followed the living wall around a corner. On the other side he saw a network of stone structures, some taller than himself, others coming just to his knees. Circular rooms, dwellings really, twice the size of any house he'd lived in, were everywhere, behind which taller structures expanded until they ran against the cliffs, stone meeting stone. And the doorways, small and arched, all faced east, slightly south, toward a large flat-topped butte with a notch in its top. George stood in front of a doorway gazing across the canyon valley, realizing the notch in the butte was in direct line with him. An urge to pray hit him and with it Jimmy's words about the doors aligned for prayer. George shifted, wondering how many had stood here before him, looked through the notch, and prayed. And who had they prayed to? Who would he pray to? Not knowing the answer, he shook off the feeling and turned to his horse.

George hobbled Wet Blanket and turned him loose to graze, then stepped through a small doorway into the ruins. He had to bend almost double to fit through the door. He straightened and looked around him. The walls rose above his head, but only just. Small windows opened the corners of the room, and he thought it was odd to place windows there. Was it for sunlight? Curiosity filling him, he reached up and felt the sandy edges of a window and rubbed the dust between his fingers until it blended into his skin. Maybe they built fires in the corners of the room and the windows were for releasing the smoke. Maybe the small high windows let the best light in. What was their true purpose? Who were the people that had lived here and built these walls? Thinking somehow the stones could give him answers, he again placed his palm against the wall. The stones were fit together precisely and had been shaped to serve the precision. His father would have been pleased with it. He always admonished George and Jack that precision mattered most, and there was never an excuse to be sloppy and lose a centuries-old trade.

"A centuries-old trade," George thought. "He was right." He stood staring at the ruins, marveling at the strength of the structures. He imagined that once these buildings had hummed with the activity of lives being lived; people coming and going up and down the canyon, tending gardens, cooking meals over open fires with the aromas wafting from one to the next calling hunters back from their travels. He could see people sharpening stones into spears or fashioning clay into bowls or utensils, weaving sticks and grasses into baskets, people shaping stones and building new walls, new houses, expanding their community as a part of the canyon.

Now though, anyone standing in this place was very much alone, and George stood soaking in that aloneness. He let the quiet comfort of the place seep into him and felt everything in him steady, and somehow he felt that he had known ever since Jimmy had told of the place that this is where he'd need to come. There was something here that he needed and at the same time he knew he couldn't stay long, as if staying would break the spell of the place, intrude on the memories, the ghosts the rocks held within. The wind whistled against the walls. Three ravens flew over silently, their wings beating steadily on their way to roost.

That night he slept deeply for the first time in months, and when he woke the sky was clear and crisp like a freshly washed cotton sheet. He felt his aloneness and smiled. There was a lightness to his body, a feeling of taking a step forward; his life was no longer a stand-still of a swirl of memories. The memories were still there, the anger, the hurt, was still there, but there had been a shift that he felt clearly, yet didn't quite understand. Wet Blanket quietly cropped the miniature broom tops of sparse bunchgrass. Sparrows gossiped and the three ravens flew out from their roost, talking loudly. In the bird calls he heard the voices of those who had stood here before him, looking across the canyon, living their lives between the circular stone walls built by their own hands. Then it seemed as if Jimmy were there beside him saying, "See, isn't it wondrous?" George lay a silver coin on the doorstep as he left.

# Chapter 11

George had seen wild country before, when his family had traveled from Illinois to Colorado Territory and when he'd ridden with Tyler's Rangers, but this country was different. There was so much space, so much emptiness, it was the definition of desert. Maybe it was because he was all alone that the wildness was more apparent, or maybe it was because he'd grown in consciousness.

Pulling Wet Blanket to a halt at the top of a bluff, buff colored sand blushed in yellow, George scanned the expanse of landscape in front of him. At first it seemed completely empty, as if he were the only one to have ever traveled here. He knew he wasn't, but there was this strange sense of aloneness, this strange sense of coming upon something untouched, like a snowfall that no one has walked upon yet, or like the roundness of vole tunnels. George shivered as a breeze caught his shirt and cooled the sweat on his skin. Wet Blanket's skin rippled in response to the wind, and his ears flicked back and forth in rapidity as if he, too, were all too aware of the emptiness. And then he whinnied, his shrill cry breaking the silence in such a way that made George startle, gripping the reins tighter.

Wet Blanket raised his head and fixated on something in the distance with his brown eyes. George followed his gaze, keenly aware of how much better his horse could see. The wind ticked through the stems of bunch grass like a clock counting the seconds by.

Then he saw it: dust was rising in the desert valley below them. A dust storm? George watched as it moved, Wet Blanket whinnied again, and George knew it had to be created by animals. The dust rose in bursts and rolls, obscuring those causing the rise. Then they came into focus: horses, nearly one hundred of them streaming across the desert floor. Slowly, George was able to make out colors—bays and blacks, sorrels and chestnuts—and the long backs and legs favored by the army. These were horses let loose or escaped on a battlefield, banded together and surviving in the brutality of the desert environment. The herd moved as one living, breathing thing, each animal responding to the one in front of it. Their movement reminded George of water spilling over stones, and he thought of the spring fed stream that ran behind the masonry in Black Hawk. The water was always cool, always clear, the kind of clarity of a newly forged looking glass.

The horses rounded a hillock and came into closer view, racing in the sand spray. A splash of white caught George's eye and he shifted his gaze to the end of the herd. Behind it rode three Indians astride pintos, flashy against the buff of the dust and the variations of brown of the army horses. The sight of them made George hold his breath, and the energy in the air suddenly made him aware of every vein in his body. Muscle memory, days of being told to watch, to chase after Indians, made him gather the reins, sit tall, his knees tightening against Wet Blanket's sides in preparation.

Shifting the gathered reins to his left hand, he reached with his right to where a rifle would have been sheathed. Hitting the empty air there tipped him off-balance. Wet Blanket shifted and danced to the side, knocking rocks down the slope. George pulled back on the reins, trying to still the dancing hooves; he didn't want more rocks knocked down, he didn't want to be given away. Stealth was what gave a person the upper hand, it's what kept a person safe. Why didn't he have a gun? What was he thinking, leaving with an empty scabbard?

Wet Blanket stilled and George focused again on the horses below. They were closer now, the Indians still behind the herd guiding them toward a gap, a gully between the hills. They hadn't seen him; George felt sure of it and let his breath out between his teeth. Wet Blanket bobbed his head, pulling at the bit, and George held him tight, as he lost sight of the horses and Indians in the gully.

And then the thundering of hooves caught his ear, making him turn as if pulled by a string. The closeness of the herd surprised him. The gully bottom seemed so far away down there in the desert valley, and yet, here were the horses appearing within an eighth of a mile of him. The horses' hair was swirled in sweat that foamed white. George had always thought that foamed sweat on a horse's chest must be what the white caps of waves in the ocean looked like. He had never seen the ocean, but he had a picture in his mind of what it looked like.

A deep brown gelding stumbled as he came onto the hilltop, and the horses behind him bumped into each other, nipping and snorting. The gelding pinned his ears and his hooves cracked on the chest of the tall sorrel mare behind him before other horses took their places. A flash of white appeared on the far side of the herd, and all three Indians on the patched Indian ponies came into view.

They were focused on the horses in front of them, driving them toward a destination they must have known clearly in their minds. The last one to come up out of the gully pulled his pony to a halt, turning to face George. The Indian sat still and straight, his hands poised six inches from the black and white mane of his mount, his dark eyes gazing directly at George. He wore leather trousers and a loose, beige cotton shirt that seemed at once strange and fitting on his strong, sinewy frame. George saw the muscles of the Indian's jaw tighten, and felt his own do the same, as if their thoughts were running the same course. The Indian's face was smooth and fresh with the desert air, darkened by the sun, but not yet weathered by it.

Both Wet Blanket and the Indian's pony stood with their heads high, their ears straining forward, their muscles tense as they waited for direction from their riders. Wet Blanket's nostrils quivered and flared, and as the wind turned in his direction, his skin shivered and he stamped his left front foot. He was ready to run, ready to race the pinto across the desert, ready to win that race, and George was almost willing to let him try. But he kept the reins tight, his and the Indian's eyes still locked, waiting for the other to make the wrong move, or the right one. George wasn't sure what the wrong move might be, what the right move might be. The Indian was an enemy, wasn't he? George didn't have a weapon, though, and was this Indian really doing anything that made him an enemy to George?

Then, suddenly, with a gesture that was so quick George would have missed it had he blinked, the Indian spun his splashy pony and galloped after the herd, disappearing toward the horizon.

# Chapter 12

George remained fixed in place, his eyes following the movement of the Indian and pony that seemed to move completely as one entity. There was no separation between the two; no light could be seen between horse and rider, as if they had been fused together like two bricks that fit exactly into place. The fluidity, the completeness between them, amazed George. He'd grown up with horses, he'd ridden them ever since he could walk, and yet there was something that this Indian had that he didn't. He wanted what that Indian had, and he let out a short laugh as he realized he was jealous, jealous of someone who was supposed to be his enemy. There was irony there, and George knew it.

The herd of horses had disappeared from sight, and, with a sigh, George turned Wet Blanket, continuing south once again. They dropped down through the gully the herd had come up. It was rocky, a trail more easily climbed than descended, and George let Wet Blanket go slowly, giving him a loose rein, so that the horse could lower his head and balance himself as he picked his way between the boulders and loose stones.

Upon reaching the bottom, George brought Wet Blanket to a halt and checked the height of the sun. Three hours of sunlight left. That gave him a couple of hours to find a place to set up camp for the night. He hoped he could find some kind of shelter, a tree, a shallow cave, but the land in front of him didn't look very promising for either. Having come down from the plateau and into the valley, the desert lay wide and flat before him, scattered with small green shrubs that looked too brilliantly colored to be part of the sand-scape. He sighed and rubbed his shoulder, suddenly feeling sore and tired and wishing for a hearty meal, but because there was no possibility of that he kicked Wet Blanket forward.

The sun had sunk to an hour before sunset, and George was just giving up finding a sheltered place and simply pitching camp where they were, when he caught movement out of the corner of his eye. He jerked Wet Blanket around to face the movement, his breath catching, his hand again reaching for the empty space where a rifle would have been at any other time. Coming toward them were two riders, riding strong-boned bays that looked like they had once been a team that had drawn delivery wagons or pulled a plow across a farm field. The horses were steadily loping, and as they got closer, the riders didn't slow their pace. George pushed aside the impulse to swing around and run in the opposite direction. He knew Wet Blanket could outrun the bays on a good day, but they had been riding all day, and he wasn't so confident that Wet Blanket wouldn't fatigue in a chase. So, he stood his ground as the two bays came rushing upon him and closed him in on either side.

The man on the right side of him had a thick brown beard and wavy, tangled hair that came to his shoulders. He wore buckskin trousers and a beaded buckskin jacket; the beads were red and brown and created a mosaic across the shoulders of the jacket, fringes ran down the sleeves, but some were ripped and missing, showing that the jacket wasn't new. He looked keenly at George from brown eyes that were deeply set, making them darker and hard to read.

"Who are you?" the man asked. He had a low voice, but instead of being gruff, it was melodic, and George had the inexplicable thought that he'd like to hear this man sing.

"George." George answered the question simply, not evading the questions, but not giving his full name, either. "And you are?"

"Bill, Wild Bill, to be exact. You may have heard of me."

George shook his head. "No, I haven't, but it's an honor, I'm sure." He let just an edge of sarcasm slip into his voice, daring to push the boundaries of meeting.

"You better believe it!" The other man, the one on George's left, exclaimed, and George's attention went to him. He was slimly built, but had square shoulders and a square jaw. He, too, was wearing buckskin, his jacket lacking the embell-ishments of beads, but was less worn than Bill's. His beard was a scruffy, dirty blonde, and his hair unkempt, although it looked like he had attempted to cut it recently. "He's a legend."

"Oh?"

"Yup, he's the fastest gun ya ever seen."

"It's probable," George acquiesced. He glanced between the two men on either side of him, wondering what they wanted from him, what they might do to him. Were they outlaws? Or merely men out wandering as he was?

"What you doing riding alone in the desert?" Bill asked. George knew he was being appraised, and he tried not to shift under the eyes of the man.

"I'm passing through."

"Heading where?"

George shrugged.

"If you don't know where you're going, then how do you know you're just passing?"

"I'm passing through," George said again, emphasizing the "passing." He wanted to make sure that this Wild Bill knew he wasn't going to tread on his territory.

Bill nodded. "Where're you camped for the night?"

George swept his hand at the land around them. "Seems to be plenty of room."

Bill chuckled. "There's plenty of room. Not much shelter."

George shrugged and heard the man on his left shift; he suddenly had a feeling Bill was more trustworthy than his companion. "It won't be bad for one night. By tomorrow we'll be somewhere else."

"Come back with us, spend the night at my cabin," Bill said, and his tone implied that George didn't have a choice. George knew that Bill wanted to keep an eye on him; strangers were to be watched. And so, he acquiesced, accepting the offer of a roof over his head for a night.

Wild Bill's cabin was tucked away to the east of where George and Wet Blanket had come down off the plateau. To get there required George to do some back-tracking over the ground he'd covered that day, and he tried not to let it bother him. It's not like he had to be somewhere at a specific time. He didn't know where he was going; he could be going anywhere, and the cabin of a gunslinger in the desert was as good a place as any. The cabin was cobbled together with strangely shaped logs and continued back from the logs into the bank behind it. Beside the cabin was a network of corrals, in which a dozen horses milled; most, like the horses being driven by the Indians, were ex-army horses, presumably found on the plains, although George wouldn't have been surprised if some had actually been stolen. He caught himself looking them over closely, searching for a certain brown gelding, and then berated himself for doing so.

George dismounted next to Bill at the hitching post and began to unsaddle Wet Blanket. Wet Blanket cocked a back hoof, settling in for a rest.

"Tom'll take care of your horse," Bill said, indicating the other man.

"I'd rather do it myself, if it's all the same," George answered. He had to make sure of Wet Blanket's care and which corral he was put into.

"Understand. Horses are family." Bill patted his own horse's shoulder and then he unsaddled his mount, calling to Tom to put his saddle away while he began to rub down the sweaty sides of the animal.

When the horses had been brushed and turned out into a paddock together with water and an armload of coarse hay, George followed Bill and Tom into the cabin. The interior was dark and smelled richly of the earth, a drier richness than the root cellar at home in Colorado, but still a smell that said you were underground where growing things began and drew their nutrients from. George breathed the smell in, finding it comforting even though the company made him wary.

The cabin was simply furnished with a table, a chair and a few crates acting as chairs near the middle of the single room, a wood stove to the right of the door, beside which was an odd assortment of cans and crates and a small pile of brush for burning. Two cots were set up against the back wall; they were covered in bedding that George knew to be army blankets. Above the cots were pegs on which clothes hung, mostly buckskin, with the exception of three cotton shirts and a woolen jacket.

Tom went to the stove and opened it, stirring the coals with a stick and then blowing them back to life. He moved a cast-iron kettle to the more direct heat, checking that it had water in it. Bill took off his gun belt and hung it deliberately on a peg by the door before turning to George. "Hungry?"

"Yes," George answered. He still wasn't sure what this man's motives were, but there was something oddly likable about him.

"So am I. Lucky for us Tom's a good cook."

"More like, ya won't cook. Someone's gotta keep us alive," Tom grumbled, as he set about cutting potatoes and onions into a pot.

"Come on, you know I'd cook if you asked." Bill rummaged in the crates by the stove and brought out a hunk of meat, tossing it onto the table and hacking it into chunks, which Tom added to the pot. As the meat hit the heat, the aroma of salt pork sizzled into the confines of the cabin.

"Tell me, George, what set you traveling?" Bill asked. He sat down in the lone chair and pulled out a pipe, lighting it and puffing tobacco smoke to mix with the aroma of cooking pork. He gestured to one of the crates. "Take a seat."

George sat down, and even though it wasn't a real chair, it felt good to be sitting on something other than the ground or a rock. "The usual," George shrugged dismissively, "an itch to see the world."

Bill looked sideways at George, and George knew his answer wasn't believed. "More like the war," Bill said, knowingly, and George acknowledged this statement with a nod.

"Get your horse in the army?" Tom asked.

"No," George answered, "got him at a sale in Colorado."

"I didn't think he seemed like an army horse," Bill said, "with that much spirit to him. Too good of a horse to be army. Not gangly enough."

This man was observant, George thought.

"Ever consider selling him? I could use a good horse like him."

George smiled and shook his head. "Nope, he's too good of a horse to consider selling."

Bill nodded and puffed at his pipe. "Understand, understand. I had a horse like that once. Now it's just old plow horses or washed up war horses. Seems like there's a lot of them out here. You see any?"

"I saw a herd earlier in the day."

"Whereabouts?" Bill sat forward.

"North. Twenty miles or so."

"Indians?"

George nodded. "How'd you know?"

"We've been exchanging that herd for the past month," Bill said, leaning back with a sigh. "It's a game, I suppose. They've won, unless we happen upon them on the way to Deadwood. Where'd you say you were going?"

"I didn't say," George said. "What takes you to Deadwood?"

Bill grinned. "I hear the gambling trade is strong there, and I always like a good gamble. You play poker?"

"I've played a few times."

"How 'bout a game while we wait for dinner?"

George nodded in agreement and moved his crate closer to the table while trying to remember the rules of the game. He'd played it a few times growing up in Black Hawk and once or twice with some of the rangers, but as with alcohol, poker wasn't sanctioned in his father's house.

Bill shuffled the cards with such deftness it was hard to believe he'd been born without a deck in his hands. He dealt the cards and they began to play, the rules coming back to George as the game went along. They played for the win instead of money or material things, and George was glad of this; he didn't want to go losing Wet Blanket in a poker game. There was a relaxed air about the game that reminded George of learning to play checkers as a boy with his father. John had been more patient then, George thought, remembering how he'd calmly corrected George's mistakes, and, he assumed now, let George win. He didn't win every time, but more often than he should have. The game became more competitive as George grew older, and then at some point they had stopped playing. He couldn't say when the exact moment they'd stopped occurred. Maybe it had trickled to a stop, like the way a cistern dribbled water for a minute after the pumping had ceased.

Bill won the poker game, and George wasn't surprised. Bill didn't seem to be, either. "All right, now, you owe me something," Bill said, and George stiffened.

"We weren't playing for anything," George said, keeping his voice carefully neutral.

"We weren't, but the winner always gets something in poker."

George swallowed. "What do you want?"

"Tell me where you're going."

George breathed in, filling his lungs with as much air as he could, and then said, "South, I'm going south, and whatever place is south is the place I'm going." It was the truth: he was just going in a direction, looking for something that was different, somewhere that would take his memories, let him start over, and he hoped that Bill would accept this answer.

"South. That's it, no territory, no town?"

George shook his head and shrugged. "I didn't stop to put that much thought into it."

"I see. Trying to disappear?"

George nodded. For a moment silence fell on the room, then he said, "Or trying to make something disappear."

"A lot of us have that problem these days," Bill acknowledged, and from where he was leaning against the wall Tom nodded his agreement. "There's a town, Globe, Arizona Territory. It's a good place to disappear. Out of the way, and you can keep your secrets 'cause everyone else is keeping secrets, too."

"Globe, you say."

"Yep. Not a bad place. Not a good place, either, but it's a place."

"Why are you telling me this?" George asked.

"Why not?"

"You seem like someone who doesn't give information unless you're going to get something out of it."

Tom grinned. "He's got ya figured, Bill." The smell of stew on the stove was beginning to permeate the room even more deeply, and Tom moved to stir the pot. He gathered bowls from a pile of odd dishes on the floor and scooped servings into each, placing them steaming on the table along with tarnished and bent spoons that had seen better days.

George took a bite and savored the taste of meat and potatoes. It was a simple stew, but it had been many days since he'd had a hot, hearty meal, and he hadn't realized how much he'd been craving it until he took that first bite. It was hard not to eat it like a starved wolf, but he did his best to remember his manners and waited for Bill to state his price for the information he'd given.

"I don't always want something in exchange," Bill said, as he began to eat the stew, his manners more refined than George had expected, making George more conscious of his own. "Every once in a while I simply want to help a fellow wanderer out. You ought to know, Tom."

Tom shrugged, and George couldn't decipher whether it was a shrug of agreement or not, but he didn't press further, turning all his attention to the food in front of him. When he'd finished his first bowl, Tom refilled it without him having to ask, and George thought that maybe Tom was a man to be trusted after all; he was definitely observant.

The filling meal made George feel drowsy, and he nearly nodded off even sitting on a crate with no back to lean against. He shook himself and stood. "I'm going to check on my horse," he said.

Bill waved his hand dismissively. "He'll be fine. Sit and have a drink." Bill pulled out a flask. "Best whiskey you can get."

George shook his head. "No thanks. Not much of one for whiskey. Besides, you've shared enough with the food and a roof for the night." He began to head out the door where dusk had fallen, making the world look soft, bleary almost, as if it, too, was tired and ready for a good night's sleep.

"Well, if you are looking to repay the kindness," Bill said, his words falling slow and deliberate, "you can help get the horses back before heading on your way."

George stopped, standing in the doorway, his hand on the doorframe. Without shifting to face Bill he said, "I thought you didn't have the time."

"I wouldn't if it was just two of us, but with three it'd be easier to gather the herd back."

"Won't they be guarded?"

"Might be, might not. I've got an extra gun you can borrow since you don't carry one. Why don't you carry one?"

# Chapter 13

In the early morning dark George slipped out of the cabin, careful to close the door without a sound, and went to the corral. Wet Blanket whuffed air out his nostrils in uncertainty, but he let George bridle him and stood still for the saddle. He shied at the gate, but the noise wasn't anything out of the ordinary for horses in a corral. Still, George's heart sped up and he looked toward the cabin, half expecting the door to open. When it didn't, he latched the gate and swung into the saddle, then turned Wet Blanket to the east, away from the cabin and past the other corrals. Once beyond the corrals, he kicked the gelding into a gallop, riding first east for a few miles, before veering back to the south. He didn't really believe anyone would follow him, but nevertheless he kept his horse running hard until long after the sun rose.

When Bill first brought up his helping them get the herd of ex-army horses back from the Indians, George had thought he'd simply talk his way out of it. But then came the question about not carrying a gun, and with it the desperate need to outrun his memories—to find a place where he wouldn't be questioned—pushed aside the comfort of the warm meal. He couldn't address the reasoning for why he had no gun; that would mean facing things he wasn't ready to face. And he couldn't be caught up in stealing horses, no matter if it was a continual back and forth exchange. He knew he'd just have to leave before morning, and so he had.

George rode deep into Arizona Territory, his memories still riding tandem, playing out like a drama on a desert stage. There needed to be another step forward, but George didn't know how to take that step and frustration had begun to creep back in, a frustration that he couldn't escape his own mind no matter how fast or far he rode. Wet Blanket was covered in a dust of dried sweat that became paste as he sweated again each day. George knew his horse needed a rest, a good long rest of a day or two or three, but something pressed him onward, as if someone was pressing a dagger in his back. He had to move forward and ease the pain; he needed somewhere to forget, and the name Globe swirled in the back of his mind. He rode deeper and deeper into the red sand. In frustration he kicked his horse into a hard run. And so, he rode into Globe.

Globe, the name that said you could see the whole world in one town. A globe, like a map of the world caught in a ball of glass; only this globe was caught between hills sloughing with silver mines and dotted with strange plants that grew stalks the thickness of a child's wrist and dropped crimson flowers to the ground. George rode the streets of the town. They were dry, dusty, and red, and when rains came they'd be slick, sticky, and red. Red clay. Wet Blanket's hooves churned up clay dust. Foam fell from the corners of his mouth and covered the ends of his bit.

Dust rose in a cloud as a horse bolted toward them, riderless, stirrups flapping. A large palomino charged after it, carrying two riders. A shot was fired, the bullet whirring between the legs of the riderless horse, who sprang into a series of crow-hops, its back rounded, its head dropped between its front hooves. Wet Blanket stiffened to a halt, his legs locked, his head so high George could barely see between the black-tipped ears. The riderless horse kept running, disappearing around a hill.

"Shoulda just shot him," one of the riders said.

"He'll kill himself one day anyway," said the other, halting the palomino at the hitching rail in front of the saloon. Neither acknowledged George. The two men pushed open the doors of the saloon, giving George a momentary glimpse of the residents of Globe, men with scruffy beards and muddy clothing playing poker and fingering their firearms, women in short skirts with brightly painted lips.

The town boasted a hotel, a bank, and a general store, all of which had an air of straggling along like stray cows. The bank's windows were boarded, the building looking as if it would topple into the jail beside it with the next storm. The hotel didn't go for much advertising, simply stating "Hotel" in big white letters on a sign that hung crookedly from the porch roof. The front steps were newly repaired, however, the red mesquite wood vibrantly in contrast with the gray of the rest of the buildings. In the window of the general store a sign advertised beans and tobacco, selling for twenty and thirty cents a pound, respectively. But the sign on the door stated, "Closed," with an air of permanence.

George slacked the reins, and Wet Blanket drank from the water trough. This was the kind of place he wanted to come to, a place where he could melt into a crowd that was always changing, never taking root. Ever since Wild Bill had mentioned Globe, it had lingered there in the back of his mind. In a small nameless town to the north he had casually asked directions from an old miner. The old man had peered at him from under his wide-brimmed hat and bushy white eyebrows and said, "Ya know that's where outlaws go. There ain't law in that town. The law's forgotten it."

George had nodded and again asked the way, and with slight reluctance the man had given directions. Now, as George actually found himself in the town, he wondered if the man had truly been reluctant or if the reluctance was in his own mind. Still, it was a forgotten town, where one could be forgotten, and he wanted to be forgotten or to forget himself.

Wet Blanket tossed his head, whinnying at the row of tethered horses. Several pulled on their ropes, straining to see who the newcomer was and whinnying in reply. George tied Wet Blanket beside them and entered the smokey saloon. As he stepped in, he wasn't sure what to do; it wasn't like the brewery back in Black Hawk or even the back rooms of main street businesses where he played the occasional poker game with young miners. Tables clustered together, their surfaces scarred, reflecting those who sat around them. George felt as though everyone had noticed him, and every eye in the room was sizing him up.

A woman slipped her hand onto his arm. "Sugar," she said, her voice husky with smoke, "buy a girl a drink?"

George nodded wordlessly and moved with her to the bar, where the bartender poured two shots of whiskey. George handed one to the woman, looking at her for the first time. Her face showed wrinkles of age that she had attempted to hide, her eyelids painted a heavy blue. Her hair fell in unnatural curls to her bare shoulders, the sleeves of her dress pulled down to show her skin, revealing a mole close to her left collarbone. The dress, a faded maroon and cut deeply in front, showed the tops of her breasts that were squeezed together by a corset pulled too tight. George was surprised that her skin there, too, showed wrinkles of age. He stared. Maybe it wasn't age, he thought, charitably. Maybe it was the tightness of the dress.

The woman held her shot up. "Cheers," she said, her voice inflecting slightly, and George reached for the other shot, knocked it over in his bluster, then felt heat rise up his neck.

"Don't do this often," the woman said, laughing. She called to the bartender to pour another, and this time she handed the shot to George. "Cheers," she said again.

George knew he should clink his glass against hers and drink the burning liquid, but he stood there, his eyes fixed on the golden substance. He hadn't known what color it was; the few times he'd had a swallow from Jimmy's flask he'd of course seen nothing, and the temperance of his father's house had kept any alcohol from passing over the doorstep. Would this make his memories as uncontrollable as those beers had? His mouth filled with the bitter taste he'd woken with the morning after that night at Tivoli's. "I don't think I can do this," he said, quietly. He set the glass on the counter and dug in his pocket for coins.

The woman downed her shot without even a small cough. "Why you here?" she asked. "You know this is where folks come to be forgotten. Sure, once it wanted to be something, but it's too out of the way." She leaned against the bar. "People don't come looking for you here." She laughed again, and George thought he heard an edge of bitterness to it.

"Why?" George asked as he glanced around the room. No one paid any mind to him or his new acquaintance, all caught up in their own drinking, gambling, or flirting, as if an unspoken pact of not intruding had sealed them all from noticing a stranger.

The woman shrugged. "Too far from anywhere worth being," she said. "There's silver in the hills 'round here, but mines rise and fall. When they fall, they fall hard. Miners drink and long for women and stay around for the next rise." She took George's shot from the bar. "If you don't want it?" she inquired, and when George shook his head she tipped it back. "Thanks, sugar."

Watching her drink the second shot without a wince, George wasn't sure he wanted to belong in this place. "Does everyone here really want to be forgotten?"

"Sure, don't we all at some point?" The woman pushed her hair off her shoulders. George thought she must have been pretty once. "I followed my husband here," she continued, "sure we'd make a fortune and have something to be proud of. We got a claim and started digging, but after months had only struck enough silver to buy a turnip. Cash ran out, and my husband got work in a mine nearby. Seemed like we'd make enough to get out of here." The woman paused, twirling the glass in her fingers, then looked at George sidelong. George motioned to the bartender and placed another coin on the counter. The bartender filled the woman's glass, shaking his head and saying, "He's young, Ellen, have a care," in a voice so low George almost didn't hear him. He didn't care, though, that this woman was duping him into buying her drinks. Even as he knew he wasn't staying, he wanted to listen to someone else's story for a moment, and maybe forget his own, at least for the time.

"But it wasn't, as they say, ordained. While my husband was working in the other mine, another man looking for a fortune started digging on our claim and hit a rich seam. 'Course my husband accused the man of stealing, which was true, but the man said it wasn't stealing if a mine had been abandoned. That logic was hard to argue with, but my husband did. Soon he was dead over it, and I was left alone with nothing to get me out of this place. So I stayed and became Ellen the barmaid, a forgotten woman in a forgotten town." She smiled, and George was surprised to see no sadness in it. She gestured at the people around them. "Everyone here has committed a crime of some kind," she said, "but we don't talk about it. Every horse at the rail is stolen from one place or another, and they'll all have new owners within the hour. We don't talk about that, either." Again she laughed, the kind of laugh a person gives when they wish what they'd said was funny. At the same time, the laugh wasn't false; it was as if she'd come to believe her life, this town, was a kind of comedy.

Her tale finished, Ellen leaned her elbows on the countertop, drawing attention to her chest, and dropped her eyelids. The gesture was so casual, it took George a moment to understand the meaning. When he did, he felt his face flush and found himself wishing for that shot of whiskey. On the heels of this thought came the definitive realization there'd be no way for him to forget who he was in this place. It wasn't reinventing that he wanted. His thoughts turned to Wet Blanket, tied at the end of the rail, and he glanced at the door. "I should go," he said. He couldn't risk his horse being stolen. That gelding was all he had and after weeks of travel, he suddenly knew that he couldn't let anything happen to the animal. Maybe he could still feel something after all. Maybe that was why he couldn't stay in a place that forgot its inhabitants.

Ellen smiled, this time soft and sad. "Good," she said. She straightened her dress and shook her curls, letting them fall once again over her shoulders, then turned, laughing, to a newcomer. "Buy a girl a drink?"

Once out the door, George immediately checked for the bald face of his bay gelding, and relief flooded him to see it still there at the end of the rail. He looked down the row of horses tied beside his own. They were of all sizes and colors, some sleek, some mangy, and on one George recognized an army brand, the US slanted and blurred, indicating with what haste it'd been burned on.

The horse was a brown gelding with a scrubby tail. His hips were pointed, and he sank onto his hocks in a way that was strangely familiar. George went to the army horse, clicking his tongue softly. He patted the bony hips, noted the spur-scars on the belly, ran his hands up the long, awkward neck until he could catch hold of the halter and turn the horse's face to his. There were the tan-brown eyes with too much white around them that George remembered as he had forced the bit between the gelding's teeth that cold morning after Sand Creek.

George stroked the nose of Jimmy's brown gelding, his fingers quivering as the horse's lips explored his hand, and his breath came ragged as he remembered that cold snowy morning, the cold of Jimmy's body as it was buried in the half-frozen ground, the cold empty space beside him where Jimmy should have been. He again felt the emptiness of the space Jimmy once occupied and in it swirled the memories of how he had left the innocent brown gelding unfed, uncared for in the frozen, midnight darkness. Shame iced through him and he leaned his forehead to the gelding's, breathing in the dusty scent, and forcing back the sob that was trying to rise up his throat. Music from a pianoforte spilled off-key out the cracks in the saloon doors, the sound of laughter rising then falling, broken and worn out, reminding him of where he was. There was too much sadness in the sound, too many broken hearts tinkling down the piano keys, and George knew with even more surety that he wasn't staying in this town and neither was the brown gelding.

In silence he left Globe behind. Wet Blanket set an eager pace, glad to have a companion following behind, and the brown gelding trotted along, his joints moving loosely, as if hardly staying together. "I'll never leave you behind again," George said softly, making a promise to the gelding. But deep down he knew it was a promise to Jimmy.

# Chapter 14

G eorge followed his own trail back into the canyons and desert mountains above Globe. The mountains weren't as dramatic as those of Colorado, but there was something wild about them in the jagged rocks and striking abundance of vegetation. He'd passed a river somewhere, and he headed toward it, thinking he'd follow it downstream, south again. When it came into sight, he brought the horses to a halt and breathed deeply. The air was tangy with sage. He searched the map of his mind and checked the placement of the sun, locating south. Wet Blanket pawed the sand, bobbing his head. George knew he wanted to graze, but he kept the reins gathered. Wet Blanket would have to wait until they camped for the night. The brown gelding nudged Wet Blanket's flank, who pinned his ears and threatened to kick.

"Come on," George said. He tapped Wet Blanket with his spurs, and they continued to the river bank. He turned south, downstream, and pushed on, wanting to put many more miles between himself and Globe. He had a feeling that no one would come after him, but he didn't want to be close enough to be caught in case someone did.

The cliffs on the opposite bank cast shadows into the river. Those shadows lengthened, the colors changing from browns and greens to bronze and slate on the stones and shrubs. Yucca grew large, as tall as his horses' chests. He'd never seen yucca like this, and it made him wonder if it really was yucca or if he'd misidentified the plant. The air cooled, and George buttoned his coat, letting the reins go slack against Wet Blanket's neck. The gelding began to nibble at the coarse grass, and George gave into the horse's hunger, dismounting and untying the brown gelding from the saddle. He looked into the horse's eyes, finding more depth there than he had at the hitching post in Globe. He rubbed the soft nose with his knuckles, almost harshly, and tried to remember the name Jimmy had called the horse. He remembered the day Jimmy had been issued the gelding. It was the same day he had been issued Abe, the black killed at Sand Creek.

*"Honest eyes," George said, rubbing his new mount's cheeks, "I'll call him Abe."*

*"Hey, boys, better write the president, he's got an ugly beast as a namesake," Jimmy said, laughing. His joviality spread down the ranks, boosting the spirits of the rangers and readying them for the long ride ahead.*

That was as far as the memory went, the laughter. George could remember the sound, but the feeling that came with it was lost. As far as any further conversation on names for the new mounts went, he couldn't remember it. He rubbed his eyes, the cheerful camaraderie of that moment still echoing in his mind, and he couldn't help wondering if they had known what was coming next, would they have been so cheerful? On the heels of the thought came frustration: why did he have to keep remembering? Forcing himself away from the memories, he turned his attention back to the two geldings.

George hobbled the horses and went to the water's edge. He dipped his fingers in the river, finding it icy cold. He leaned against a boulder, feeling the warmth still collected there seep through his clothes to his skin. As he leaned there something softened in him. His shoulders relaxed, knots that had gathered between his shoulder blades and at the base of his neck untied, leaving him with a feeling of release. The canyon was so still that he could hear the horses cropping grass. The sound was soothing, and he began to drift, his relaxed mind sending him into his own memories, all the way to his childhood.

*"We are going on a picnic,"* Sarah announced, bouncing baby Aurora on her hip. *Aurora was a month old, his first sister, and George was smitten. Even then, her red hair shone and caught people's attention, and in brotherly protectiveness George and Jack would vie to fend off the onlookers.*

*They walked to the nearby park, George, Jack, and Tib running ahead to find the best place to spread the blanket. From the grass under a young oak, George looked back to see his father and Sarah coming along the path, and boyish delight seeped into every bone of his body. It wasn't often that John took a day off to spend entirely with his family, and it made the sunshine that much brighter to George.*

*Once the picnic was eaten, George lay on his back on the red-and-white checked blanket in the warmth of the sun and the moment. Beside him, John cradled Aurora, his strong arms a gentle cocoon for his daughter. "Did you hold me?" George asked, rolling onto his side.*

*John smiled and nodded. "Used to rock you to sleep every night." He paused to tuck Aurora's blanket under her chin. "Sometimes I'd fall asleep in the rocker with you. I think it was your soft snoring that would set me adrift." John's eyes had gone soft and gray with his remembering.*

*"Really?"*

*John chuckled and chucked George under the chin gently. "You were a fussy baby and slept best when being held."*

*"You were trouble even as a baby!" Jack exclaimed, and George jumped up, tackling his brother to the ground. They tumbled off the blanket into the grass, tussling until they rolled down the hill, getting grass stains on their clothes, landing in a laughing heap at the bottom.*

As the memory faded, George wondered when those conversations had ended; when had he stopped being brave enough to ask his father questions? He should have said goodbye to his father; he should have taken the time. Pushing away from the warm boulder, George kicked at the stones on the river bank, sending them skittering and splashing into the water. Wet Blanket tossed his head, snorting and trying to run in spite of the hobbles. George leaped and grasped hold of Wet Blanket's reins. "Shhhh, shhhh," he soothed. Wet Blanket backed up, head high, blowing air out his nostrils. The brown gelding continued grazing, unbothered by the other horse's nervous ways. Putting consistent, yet gentle pressure on the lead, George stepped closer to the spooked bay until he was close enough to cover the gelding's eyes with his hands. He continued to make soft shushing sounds, focusing all his energy into calming his horse. The routine felt natural. He didn't even have to think of what he needed to do, it was all instinct, and soon Wet Blanket responded, settling and dropping his head. "Thatta boy," George whispered and leaned his forehead to the whirl of hair in the middle of Wet Blanket's white blaze. He closed his eyes and breathed in the sweet, grassy smell.

George followed the river in its canyon until the canyon split in two, then turned into the smaller one, the one heading more directly south, and followed it to where the horses could climb the bank. Above the canyon the air was sharp and woke George. His thoughts cleared. He turned the horses south again, this time angling west as well. The horses stepped lightly, as if they, too, had been cleared of anxieties. Sparrows the color of the sand sang and fidgeted in the scrub oak, and each time one flushed, Wet Blanket snorted, tossing his head up and down. The brown gelding remained calm. "As steady as an arrow," George thought. Arrows. He remembered Jimmy saying something about arrows and searched for the memory in the recesses of his mind.

*"This is the last horse I'll ride afore seeing my Lizzie again," Jimmy said. George couldn't remember where they were or what they were doing in that particular moment, but he could remember Jimmy's voice. "Yep, he will be my arrow home."*

"Arrow," George said aloud to the empty sky and sparrow-filled desert. "That's what I'll call him." He glanced at the brown gelding. "Hear that?" he said. The gelding trotted loosely, joints seemingly unhinged, tail swishing at the few flies buzzing at his flanks. His eyes were fixed on the distance in front of them, continuing onward as if nothing had happened. George smiled; having found the brown gelding was a chance for him to right a wrong, a chance to do something for Jimmy. The memories could now stop haunting him. But the question "what if they don't?" niggled in the corner of his mind.

# Chapter 15

Another week went by and then another, and George began to feel aimless. Memories continued to shift across the landscape, a landscape that rolled and tumbled, ever changing, ever the same. Being alone no longer felt desirable, and each day he hoped to come upon a camp or dwelling of some kind, any kind. Every time one came into view, though, he skirted it, fearing that encountering someone would only lead him to discover that he'd forgotten how to speak. His horses were thin, but their muscles had been toughened by the miles, and they obeyed his demands without hesitation. They were now riding through grasslands, lush and ripe for cattle grazing, punctuated by mesquite that were at once bushes and trees. Where the bark cracked, the wood showed through red, a blush of something secret, and the leaves were green with a brilliance as if trying to compete with the colorful birds that lived in the branches.

Before him a mountain range covered in low, gnarled shrubs rose, and he pushed his horses toward it. He felt a draw to them somehow, as if there was someone or something calling him there. He came upon a streambed where a small trickle of water spilled along the rocks in the bottom, overarched with silvery sycamores. George dismounted and let his horses drink, walking to a sycamore and laying his hand against its trunk. He pulled back surprised, the bark that looked smooth actually hairy beneath his touch. He ran his hand over it again, feeling the texture of each hair on his palm soft and velvet-like, the way he'd always imagined a seal would feel when he saw the drawings in an encyclopedia as a child.

Both horses' heads snapped up, their ears twitching, nostrils wide and sucking in air. George looked in the direction of their gazes. A man leading a black donkey came down the edge of the streambed, both carefully picking their way between the rocks. He wore a wide-brimmed hat pulled low to shade his face, and his clothes hung loose and dusty from his wiry frame. The donkey was heavily laden, the packs covered in white canvas, and he plodded resignedly behind his master.

For a moment George thought about mounting and riding away so he wouldn't have to exchange any words with the man, but just as he began to gather Wet Blanket's reins, he stopped, feeling the man notice his presence, and instead of mounting he untied his canteen and bent to fill it in the cool trickle of water.

"Hola," the man called, a hundred feet still between them. Despite the lowness of the hat-brim, George could see the man smile, wide, toothy, and friendly.

"Hello," George answered. He didn't know Spanish, but he did know that hola meant hello. He tied his canteen back onto the saddle as the man came up beside him. Wet Blanket reached his nose to sniff the donkey, then squealed, pawing the air with his left front hoof. The man grinned and pushed his hat back, revealing a face browned by the sun. Wrinkles creased the skin around his eyes as if he spent most of his life squinting, but he had one of those faces that could have been thirty or sixty years old.

"Ese caballo tiene fuego," he said, and then shaking his head added, "Mi burro no tiene." He laughed, a surprisingly bold laugh that made his eyes disappear in folds of leathery skin and black eyebrows.

George shook his head. "Sorry," he said. "I don't understand."

This didn't faze the man. "Me llamo Julio," he said and then pointed to George and raised his eyebrows.

George let out a quick breath of relief; he could understand this. "George," he said.

Julio nodded and silence fell. George shifted, feeling inadequate and awkward. Julio casually checked the packs on his donkey, tightening a strap here and there. The donkey pinned his ears and flared his lips, a partial bray escaping into the air. At this, Wet Blanket snorted and backed into Arrow, who nipped, but otherwise stayed planted where he'd stopped.

"Where you going?" Julio asked.

"You speak English!" George couldn't help but exclaim.

"Un poco," Julio said, a smile toying at his lips. "Going to Durasno?"

"Durasno? Is it a town nearby?"

Julio waved his hand upstream, up into the mountains. "Day's travel," he said. "Minas de cobre y plata. Copper, silver mines. Soy minero."

George nodded. A mining town. He knew about those; he'd grown up in those towns. Maybe he could find work, stop moving for a while. "Maybe," he said.

"Muchas personas han encontrado buena suerte en estas montañas. Dios nos ha sonreído," Julio said. "I make a fortune!"

"Are you leaving?" Suddenly it felt good to talk to someone, and he liked the sound of Spanish as it rolled from Julio's mouth.

"Going home to Nogales, to mi familia." Julio squinted into the sun, as if he could measure the distance to his home by the trajectory of the sun.

"Will you come back?"

"No, pero estas montañas son especiales."

"What are these mountains?"

"Son especiales." Julio grinned.

"The name," George clarified, wondering at the same time if Julio actually had understood and was joking with him. "What are they called?" George pointed to the mountains. "Ah, si, si." Julio chuckled. "Se llama las Patagonias." He, too, gestured at the mountains. "Patagonias," he said again.

"Patagonias," George repeated. George liked the name. It sounded promising, prosperous. He wondered what the name meant, where it had come from. Who had named this range of scrub covered dirt and rock? In that moment of wondering, he made the decision to try his luck in Durasno.

"Durasno," George said, "just up the stream?"

"Follow the stream. Day's travel."

"Thank you." George felt like he should offer Julio something, if not for the information then for the extended friendship. He dug into his saddlebags, but the only thing that could remotely resemble a gift was a white handkerchief with G.W. embroidered in the corner, Aurora's embroidery, slightly uneven. It'd have to do. He held it out to Julio.

"No payment," Julio said.

"For friendship, then," George said.

Julio took a small stone from his pocket, black and smooth, almost translucent in the sun, and held it out to George. "Friendship," he said, and they exchanged handkerchief and rock, both knowing that the objects held a significant meaning to the other.

"See you another day," Julio said.

George smiled. It was the kind of farewell that would be exchanged between friends, and he was grateful for it. "See you another day," he responded and parted ways with Julio, following the streambed into the mountains and feeling certain of his way.

"Que el sol brille sobre ti," Julio called after him, and even though George didn't know what the words meant, he had a feeling they were wishing him good luck.

# Interlude

Harshaw, Arizona Territory ran down a mountain gulch in a narrow line, like precise stitching on the hem of a coat. At the bottom, the town fanned out across a hillside and dissolved into a peach orchard outside of a Spanish Mission built in the early 1700s. The town was first called Durasno, named for the peach orchard, and even though it had been nearly abandoned through the late 18th and early 19th centuries, and had passed into the hands of the United States in 1853 as part of the Gadsden Purchase, it had retained its name, until David Tecumseh Harshaw arrived. A former sergeant turned cattle rancher, Harshaw came to Durasno looking for new pasture for his cattle and instead found silver. Newspapers told of his find, bolstered by Harshaw's own boasts of the richness of the vein, and as they always did, miners came looking to stake claims, make their fortunes, and return home with their riches.

David Harshaw, though, had already claimed the mines and surrounding land, so the miners that came worked for him instead of for themselves, and Durasno acquired the new name of Harshaw. In this out of the way place it was hard to envision how the mines would be successful enough to pay all of the men that came. The ore Harshaw mined took a circuitous route to San Francisco, going by mule train and boat through Mexico and up the Colorado River until it could be loaded on wagons that would make the final leg of the journey. And shipping was expensive. But the mines were rich, and miners did make their fortunes; some even left for home. Most stayed, though, the promise of continued wealth too great to send them away, and the town continued to grow, with stores, dance halls, saloons, and a hotel lining the main street. The fact remained though, that Durasno—or Harshaw, as it was now called—was a mining town, and with that comes inevitable ups and downs, with the reliance on ore in the ground.

# Chapter 16

Durasno lay tucked in the center of the Patagonia mountains, at the convergence of three draws, where a spring ran from a rock outcropping and formed the stream that George had followed. It was more of a camp than a town, made up of tents and rude wooden structures, but George could see a store, a saloon, and a livery stable just on the closest end of the town. When he entered the town, the only signs of life were three women bent over washboards, scrubbing dust and grease from shirts and trousers. The women's long black hair shone and fell in heavy braids over their shoulders, and their skirts were tied up, leaving their legs bare to their knees. Their feet were bare as well. Behind them a copse of trees spread in what looked like an orchard.

One of the women straightened at the sound of horse hooves and shaded her eyes. George swung down from the saddle and tied his horses to a nearby tree before approaching the women.

"You a miner? Looking for work?" the woman asked before he could say anything. The other two women, who George now saw were younger than the woman addressing him, continued washing, slapping the damp clothes on the washboards and scrubbing. Their sleeves were rolled up, showing their muscles, taut and strong. George watched them flex with the women's movements, the skin that covered them chapped and rough.

"Looking for work?" the older woman repeated.

George pulled his gaze from the young women's arms and faced the sharp look of the older woman. She had rugged cheekbones that angled into a near right-angle jawline and wide-set eyes that gave her an authoritative look; this was the kind of woman to be obeyed. "Yes," he said, trying to meet her gaze, only to drop his eyes in deference for her evident authority.

The woman held a pair of trousers in her worn, brown hands, wringing water from them as she tilted her head toward a wooden structure. A sign on the door said, "OFFICE." "There," she said, "they hire there."

"For mining?" George asked, not wanting to leave the presence of these women, suddenly craving feminine company, mother, sister company. He had a vision of himself sitting on an overturned wash basin, coffee in hand, listening to their conversation like he used to with Sarah and his sister. An ache bloomed in his heart, a longing.

"Yes," she said, "for mines." Her tone indicated that he should know this. After all, it was a mining community.

"Thank you," he said, snapping himself out of his reverie. Pushing the longing as deep down as he could, he moved toward the office quickly. He knew the woman watched him walk away, as if making sure he went where he was supposed to. He knocked on the office door, and after seconds had passed, a tired voice said, "Enter."

George ducked through the door into the dimness of the building. The only light filtered through the cracks in the walls, casting a strange kind of glow that took a moment to adjust to. Once he did, he saw that the owner of the voice was a stooped man who must have once been tall, taller even than George himself, with dark hair that had begun graying about his ears and a full beard.

"And who are you?" the man asked, not unpleasantly, but not pleasantly, either.

"George Atkinson. I'm looking for work."

"Ain't we all." The man went back to the papers on his desk, scratching notes on a map in cramped handwriting that in all likelihood only he could read.

George cleared his throat. "Work, sir? Is there any to be had here?"

"Of course," the man cackled, drily. "There's always work here." He wrote some more notes, crossed out a few he'd already written. "What do ya know of mining?"

"Not much," George admitted, "but I'm a hard worker and I'll do anything."

"Anything, huh?"

"Yes."

"What do ya know if ya don't know mining?"

George hesitated. Bricks. He knew brick making, but did he really travel all this way to just make bricks? "Bricks," he said finally.

"Bricks?" The man raised one eyebrow. "How to build with them or make them?"

"Both."

The man leaned back in his chair. It groaned. He scratched his beard and picked up a cigar from his desk. Striking a match on his boot, he lit the cigar and blew smoke into the confines of the building. "Might be something," he said. "I'll need to think on it. Meantime, ya know how to work a pickaxe?"

"Yes, sir," George said. "I could."

The man nodded. "Good. Go find a place to spend the night. Come back at six tomorrow morning. You can go out with the mornin' crew." He waved George away, turning once again to the maps spread on his desk. He moved his finger over them and mumbled, "Here. We could build it here." He pressed his thumb on the map.

"You are?" George asked, pausing at the door.

"David Harshaw," the man said. "Owner of the mine."

# Chapter 17

*Dear Jack,*

*I hardly know how to begin this letter, much less what to say to you. Part of me wants to say I'm sorry, for the way I left, for the way I acted. I need you to understand that I had to leave. It was too hard to stay there...*

George reread the words he'd written. He crumpled the paper and threw it into the fire. It caught quickly, and he watched as it turned orange with flame and then disappeared in gray ash. He smoothed a fresh piece of paper on the small table in the cramped, drafty room he'd rented at the back of the boarding house. The room had been built with haste, a last-minute addition to the building, leaving cracks in the walls, but it was nice to have a roof over his head and a bed to sleep in.

*Dear Jack,*

*I have arrived in a mining town in the mountains of Arizona Territory and am working, for the time being, in the mines. The place is now called Harshaw and has recently acquired a post office, making it officially a town to be put on a map. The mines are rich and there is talk of building a twenty-stamp mill. I have hopes that my brick-making skills will be needed and...*

George set his pen down and sighed. His words stared back at him, impersonal, but he couldn't afford to start over. This would have to do. He bent to writing again.

*I am making plans to build a brickyard, if not here, then elsewhere. I am in need of a brick mold to make this happen and was hoping you will do a favor for me, brother, and find one for me, sending it to me here. I've included money to cover some of the costs and will send more to cover the balance once I know just what the costs are. I will be grateful to you.* ~~I almost wrote father.~~

*How is everyone? I do miss you all and send my love.*

*Your brother,*

*George*

George blew on the ink to dry it. This letter would have to do for now.

George plucked a peach and bit into it. Juice ran down his arm, leaving a sticky trail in the dust gathered on his skin. He tasted the sweetness of the fruit and the bitterness of its unripeness, enjoying both tastes like he had as a child, eating fruit from orchard trees and daring his brother to eat ones even less ripe.

"You know those aren't ripe." Marisol stood with her hands on her hips, her eyes sharp and accusatory.

"I know," George said. Over the past weeks he'd come to know Marisol as the matriarch of the community. Not only did she wash the miners' clothes, but she fed, housed, and entertained them, running a saloon, dancehall, and boarding house. He rented his room from her and learned to abide by her rules.

"Stop eating them," she said. Her tone left no room for argument.

"Yes, ma'am." George ducked away from the peach trees that had been left to grow wild and untrimmed for years, producing their fruit high in the branches, so that children were enlisted to climb them come harvest time and pick the fruit, dropping the peaches into skirts held out to receive them, keeping them from hitting the ground and getting bruised or splitting open.

George made his way back to the center of town. It was Sunday, and he had a feeling of aimlessness, almost wishing that the mining community didn't observe the holy day. But the inhabitants were steeped in the teachings of the missionaries who had settled the area and planted the peach trees years ago. The men he worked with tried convincing him to come to mass, but George kept putting them off, saying, "Maybe next week." Sundays had become days of restlessness. He wished he would hear from Jack. If he had a brickyard, he wouldn't have to stop working, ever.

David Harshaw stood outside his office, smoking. He motioned George over and offered him tobacco, so George filled his pipe and waited for David to speak. He could tell the man was mulling something over.

"Looks like we'll get the mill," David said finally. He tapped ash from his pipe. "That empty plot to the west, it'd be a good place for a brickyard."

"It would," George responded, knowing David had something further to say.

"I'll let ya have it for a thousand bricks," David said.

George watched the smoke from their pipes rise into the clear air. Down the canyon, a woodpecker drummed on a sycamore. "Five hundred," George said. His father had taught him to always counteroffer much lower than what you were willing to pay. It gave more room to bargain. When he had been fourteen, John had made him bargain with the owner of Black Hawk's general store when the owner was building an addition. He had been terrified, stumbling over his words and ending up accidentally agreeing to a price lower than the going rate for bricks. Embarrassment had flooded his face, and both his father and the general store owner had laughed. "Better luck next time, George," the store owner had said. This time though, he didn't stumble; he knew exactly what he was doing and was confident in his negotiating skills.

"Nine hundred."

"Six hundred fifty."

David laughed, though it was more of a scoff than a laugh. "Eight fifty and I'll loan ya tools for building without charge."

"Eight hundred, the loan of tools, and you have yourself a deal," George said. His father had also taught him to never give up easily in a bargain. It earned respect.

"Deal," David said, and they shook on it, then stood in companionable silence, smoking their pipes and listening to the woodpecker drum away. George felt a sliver of guilt over having made a business deal on a Sunday.

The pickaxe clanged as it hit rock, gripped a crevice, then slipped, rock still intact. George lifted the tool and swung again, willing the rock to break and give way. He let his biceps take the brunt of the force, to spare his elbow joints, something he'd learned his first week in the mine. The other miners had good-naturedly pointed out his error, laughing with each other, until finally one said, "You're swingin' all wrong, you know. Keep that up and you'll be down the mountain, crippled, with no money."

George had stopped, mid-swing. "I'd rather stay," he said. "Show me how?"

"Certainly." The man lifted his own pickaxe and swung, keeping his elbows bent, his hands tight on the handle. The pick didn't bounce. It bit at the rock, then let go as he lifted to swing again. "Use here," he said, touching his upper arm, "not here." He pointed to his elbow.

George swung. His pickaxe bounced, but he kept his elbows bent and the impact landed in his biceps.

"Better." The man grinned and held out his hand. "Antonio," he said. Like many of the miners, Antonio had come from near Nogales, coming to the Patagonia mines in hopes of earning a living, maybe even striking it rich. He had straight black hair that just covered his ears and fell in a perfect part down the middle of his head. There was a long white scar on his collarbone that some would have tried to cover with their shirt, but Antonio always left the top three buttons of his shirt undone, the scar starkly visible. When asked about it, he always said he'd gotten it in a bar fight; though the way he said it sounded rehearsed to George, and he knew there was more to the story. He didn't push Antonio to tell him, though; Lord knew he didn't want anyone pushing into his own past.

Since the day Antonio taught him how to swing a pick, George and Antonio often worked side by side, matching rhythm. They did their work in silence, but it was a companionable silence, and at the end of the day they went to the creek, washing the dirt away and sitting on the bank, letting the water soak any stiffness from their limbs. It felt like working with Jack again, like riding alongside Jimmy, seeming to know what the other was thinking, was going to do, and falling in sync.

The rock shifted and a chunk flaked off, rolling to George's feet. He kicked it away and matched his swing to Antonio's once again. The clatter of a mine cart came down the shaft and the men stopped swinging, as if they were one man. They lifted rock into the cart, piling it as high as possible, and then with a shout it was drawn back out by a series of pulleys hitched to donkeys on the outside. The miners watched it go, heading into the light of day, then turned to position their lanterns and lift their tools once more.

George wiped his forehead and went back to work. Down the line, someone began to sing, and others joined in. The song was unfamiliar to George, but he matched his swings with the tempo, his mind becoming pleasantly numb with the simultaneous ringing of pickaxe on stone and song.

*Dear George,*

*Your father would never admit it, but he is pleased you are going into brick making, even if it is miles and miles away from us. He has sent a brick mold, as you requested. I know you asked this of Jack, but Jack is in California, so I took the liberty of opening your letter to him. I've sent it along to him, though, with a note of my own explaining that we have taken care of your request.*

*I'm glad you have found a place to settle down, though did you have to choose such a dangerous place? We hear such tales about outlaws down there that it makes me worry, so do write and tell me I am wrong.*

*Everyone is well here. The mining has slowed. We might move back to Denver. I'll send you our new address should this happen. I can't imagine we will before next month, but you know your father.*

*Be well, George.*

*Love,*

*Sarah*

"I have a business proposition," George said one evening as he and Antonio washed away the day in the cool waters of Harshaw Creek. The creek flowed clear, and along its bank the vegetation was vibrantly green, fading in color the further it went from the bank. "I'm going to start a brickyard. Harshaw offered me land for eight hundred bricks. I've got a brick mold. All I've got to do is build a kiln and we'd be set. Harshaw is building a twenty-stamp mill, you know. Interested in being a partner?"

"In the brickyard?" Antonio asked. He splashed water on his face, the dust becoming mud and then washing away with a second splash.

"Yes. I could use the help."

"Perhaps." Antonio pulled a stem of grass and chewed the white end of it. "It'd be nice to see more sun." He brushed dust from his clothes. "Is there enough need for brick?"

"As long as towns keep growing, there will be a need for brick," George said. The likeness to his father in the statement startled him. He could hear his father's voice plainly, "We will always need brick." George had heard it too many times to count, a belief ingrained in him like a trait inherited.

"I'll think on it," Antonio said.

"Not too long."

"You have others lined up?"

George shook his head. "No, I just have to get building if I want the mill contract."

"I'll sleep on it," Antonio said, but George knew it was a yes and lay awake that night drawing brickyard plans in his mind. It wouldn't be as big as the masonry in Black Hawk. For one, it would be built with logs first; it might even just start as a kiln rounding in the middle of the site like the blacksmith's forge next door, but it would eventually be a brick building with open-latching, high windows for natural light. He could already picture the way the sun would shine gold through them.

Three weeks later, the brickyard built, the kiln rarely cooling, George and Antonio sent the first five thousand bricks stacked in wagons to the site of the twenty-stamp mill. The following week they received their first payment and sent another five thousand bricks to the mill. As George watched the wagons stacked high with brick pull away, he grinned. He brushed dirt and soot from his hands on his chaps and took his pipe from his pocket. "We are well on our way," he said to Antonio, and for the first time in a long time, George felt his life moving forward.

# Chapter 18

"Here," Marisol said, thrusting a basket of laundry at George, "take this outside for me, por favor." As the years in Harshaw had worn on, Marisol had begun to treat George as a son, and he accepted this role with ease.

"Yes, ma'am," George took the basket from her and ducked out into the sunlight. He'd learned early on to duck when going through doorways; they always seemed to be just an inch or two too short for him to walk out fully upright. Walking easily down to the edge of the orchard where the town's cistern stood, he saw Marisol's girls already there filling wash basins. The water splashed and glinted like the crystals George used to find on the hillsides around Black Hawk. He would often slip one in his pocket, but then he'd forget about it, and Sarah would find it when she washed his trousers and would leave it on George's pillow. He remembered finding the crystals and smiling, sliding them into the bedside table drawer, next to the others, clinking together like coins in a jacket pocket being saved for a rainy day.

The girls' eyes shone dark brown, sparkling in their depths with the reflection of the water. It made George's heart surge with a kind of longing he'd never felt before. He wasn't sure what he was truly longing for, but he could feel it thrumming in every chord of his being.

"Set it there," one of the girls, Lucia, said. She wiped her hands on her apron, indicating the other baskets of clothes with a tilt of her head. Her thick dark hair fell over her shoulder in glossy folds, gleaming in the sun in such a way that sent George back in time. Aurora had hair like that, thick and lustrous in coils that spun to below her waist, nearly to the backs of her knees. Only her hair was red. The kind of red that took light captive, trapping it within each strand like a candle within a lantern. He could see it now: her hair swept into a ponytail low on her neck; she never confined it in a bun or a braid, letting it tangle loosely down her back. Everyone always remembered her hair, but they remembered her singing even more. Sometimes her voice would bring miners out from underground and they'd stand, blinking bleary-eyed in the sudden light, listening to the song echoing around them, their faces taking on hazy expressions as if being transported to another world. The canyon carried her voice into every mine as if the earth itself was the song she sang, and he could hear it now just as clearly, flowing into his mind with a memory.

*George looked up to see his father pause in his work and step to the door, opening it and standing there in the doorway, his ear cocked down the gulch, a soft smile teasing at the corner of his mouth and eyes.*

*"Do they miss me at home? Do they miss me?*

*'Twould be an assurance most dear to know*

*That this moment some loved one were saying I wish he were here.*

*To feel that the group at the fireside were thinking of me as I roam.*

*Oh, yes 'twould be joy beyond measure to know that they missed me at home."*

*The longing strains of the song buoyed by the wind, brushing the heads of grass beginning to go to seed, seeping into the crevices of brick, the sound magnified by the blow of the bellows.*

*"When twilight approaches the season that ever is sacred to song*

*Does someone repeat my name over and sigh that I tarry so long?*

*And is there a chord in the music that's missed when my voice is away?*

*And a chord in each heart that awaketh regret at my wearisome stray?"*

*Her voice held the last note longer than seemed possible, without a waver, strong, coming from deep within her diaphragm, a clear alto that struck every chord so that it seemed to at once shatter silence and impart it.*

*"Do they set me a chair near the table when evening home pleasures are nigh,*

*When the candles are lit in the parlor, and the stars in the calm azure sky?*

*And when the 'goodnights' are repeated and all lay them down to their sleep,*

*Do they think of the absent and waft me a whispered 'goodnight' while they weep?"*

*John's eyes glistened, yet the smile continued to dance about his lips, his mustache twitching with the emotion, the pull between tears and laughter. This was pride, George thought, intent on his father's face. This is how his father looked when brimming over with pride.*

*"Do they miss me at home—do they miss me at morning, at noon or at night?*

*And lingers one gloomy shade round me that only my presence can light?*

*Are joys less invitingly welcome, and pleasures less hale than before*

*Because one is missed from the circle, because I am with them no more?"*

George choked, feeling a sob rising in his chest and checking it with a suddenness that made him gasp and brought him back to the present.

"You well, señor?" Lucia asked. She stood looking at him askance, her hands on her hips, her dark eyes peering at him intently.

George nodded, feeling the need to blink rapidly and not wanting to for fear of giving away his emotions. "Yes," he said finally, "just remembering."

Lucia smiled like a flower blossoming. "Memories are special. They make us who we are. Without memories we would be shells."

George grunted and turned, wiping the back of his hand across his eyes. He felt almost resentful at Lucia's words. He didn't want his memories to make him who he was. There were too many things he'd rather forget, too many things that were knife wounds in his heart. He'd rather not have them—he'd rather be a shell.

Storms came across the Patagonia mountains, dark and rumbling and striking into the town or Harshaw with a swiftness that shook the very foundations. George thought they were beautiful, like a stampeding herd of mustangs intent on running from something and not seeing what was in their path, unable to be turned back. It wasn't destruction so much as a ruffling, a changing, a reshaping of the landscape, of ideas, of what was thought to have been mastered by man. And somehow it left George feeling lonely, even in the midst of miners, even as he worked side by side with Antonio mixing, pressing, and firing brick, even as he ate dinner at the long, full table of the hotel. In many ways he was still an outsider in this world. Sometimes, he wondered if he'd always be an outsider no matter where he was, and sometimes this thought bothered him, yet other times it felt as if it was meant to be, and he accepted it with calm resignation. There was part of him that felt he deserved to be an outsider. The things he'd been a part of put him there. It was his penance.

The storm came mumbling over the mountains, the sound growing until it reverberated against the hillsides and the streets of Harshaw. It became a clamor, striking the rooftops and sending the residents inside. Lightning flashed and crackled through the sky as if all the stored dynamite had detonated.

While others hurried up the streets and darted into shelter, George walked slowly through the jagged, bright streaks crisscrossing the sky. The image of each streak echoed in his eyes, flashing on the inside of his eyelids every time he blinked. He stopped in the middle of the street and gazed up at the sky. The clouds swirled heavily, darkly, and George had a sudden remembrance of black hooped silk swirling in his face as he clung to it, uncertain and scared of the world around him.

*Rich, dark earth clung to his shoes, and the smell of soil newly dug stung his nostrils. The black skirts swished, nearly suffocating him, and his grip on them slipped, his face buried in the folds. They were cool and almost damp against his cheeks, or else his cheeks were damp; he wasn't sure. And they were dark, so dark, blocking out all light, shutting out the world from where he held on desperately. The thump of dirt on the top of the coffin made him shiver, and he wished for the comfort of his mother's arms. He choked on a sob, and an arm that was not his mother's patted his shoulder, making him inexplicably more forlorn. He clutched again at the skirts, now trying to block not just the light, but sounds out as well. He wanted to disappear.*

The clouds came lower, smothering the town, and thunder sounded with a responding shake that nearly made George's knees buckle. No rain fell, just lightning, coming with a frequency that could have been rain. Sparks erupted from a nearby shed and shutters on the house behind George banged with the violence of the wind. Acrid smoke filled George's nostrils, stinging them, and as if in a dream he turned, seeing flames leap up from where lightning had struck. He stood mesmerized. Visions of all the times he'd seen fire flashed through his mind like a magic lantern show.

*A bonfire in the town square of Peoria, excitement filling his five-year-old body as someone clutched his shirt collar to keep him from getting any closer.*

*Campfires beside a wagon that he fed carefully with dung gathered on the prairie while dinner simmered and his stomach grumbled in unison.*

*A fire in the hearth of the sitting room flickering on rose wallpaper, casting a dim light to play jacks on a rug in the warmth.*

*The hot blaze of the kiln fire, his eyes burning in the heat, his arms burning from the new effort of tending the bellows.*

*Firelight dotting through sagebrush with rangers hunkered near the flames to warm their hands and the smell of burning coffee.*

*Firelight on Jimmy's skin, reflecting in his eyes.*

*Flames bursting from tepees, consuming the hides stitched and stretched around tepee poles. Faces disappearing in the flames. Flames, fire, smoke.*

Something slammed into his shoulder, knocking him off balance. George stumbled forward and snapped back to the present, turning to see what had hit him, but as he did so he noticed hurrying miners gathering buckets to fill at the cistern being furiously pumped by Marisol, and he sprang into action as if a spring had been loosed inside him.

Smoke choked the street and wind swept its way to fan the flames, sending the blazes higher and making the air drier and hotter than it already was. George could taste the salt of his sweat on his lips, mingling with the taste of smoke, a bitterness, yet also a kind of sweetness as different woods charred. Throwing his strength into a shovel, George worked alongside other men, whose faces were smudged in soot, to dig a fire break between the burning buildings and the rest of town, while others continued to attempt to subdue the fire. All sense of time had been lost to George; he could have been out there for minutes or for hours. The lightning and thunder had passed onward at some point, driven by the wind that now continued to plague the town.

Morning arrived under pale gray clouds drifting lazily across the dome of the sky as if the violence and frenzy of the night before had never happened. George sat on a stack of bricks, his arms clasped over his legs, soot clinging to his skin and clothes. He stared vacantly across the space between the brickyard and the town, watching the small plumes of smoke still rising from the charred buildings. Doors and shutters flapped on loose hinges, windows broken and open into the shells of what once was.

George rubbed his hands over his face as if to wipe away the night, but when he looked back, the desolate street remained. A solitary white pillowcase loosed from a clothesline tumbled along the street looking too bright, too clean, against the dingy backdrop of the fire's aftermath. It didn't seem right, like the sun rising on a battlefield unencumbered by clouds or storm.

Fatigue ran deep in George's bones; he couldn't remember a time he felt so weary, as if every ounce of strength and mental acuity had been leached out of him, like spring water seeping away through moss. He leaned into his hands, pressing his eyes until he saw stars. This wasn't the place, it couldn't be the place he was meant to end up. It didn't feel right anymore, but he was tired of traveling, tired of trying to find the place that would erase his memories and let him live in peace. He didn't know where to go from here, and so he stood, turning to begin the daunting task of cleaning after a fire.

In the days that followed the fire, citizens of Harshaw packed up and left, leaving the charred shells of what were once their homes behind until the town had dwindled to a quarter of its size. George watched those leaving with something akin to envy, and tried to resume normalcy, working alongside Antonio once again to fulfill orders that still came in. The whole world hadn't stopped, just a portion of Harshaw, and George tried to move along with the world that continued to spin. And on one of the spins a letter from Jack arrived.

*Dear brother,*

*I've been in California now for two months, having followed an investment opportunity here. I'm certain I will make my fortune here, many have, and I see no reason why I can't. I hear you, too, have invested in mines there in Arizona.*

*I've met a man, Colonel C. P. Sykes, who has since left for Arizona. He is bent on turning the town of Calabasas into the gateway town to the Mexican border. He boasts that people will flock there as soon as he builds his hotel. He wants it to be two-stories, made of brick, with arched windows and doorways, and a porch. I'm writing to tell you that he is looking for a man skilled in brick making to provide the bricks for this hotel. You could be that man. It is an opportunity to make yourself. Do take it. Colonel Sykes should be arriving in Calabasas at the end of the month. He'll be staying at the saloon there and will be waiting for you to contact him. Just think, brother, you could be part of a town that will be known across the country and a hotel grand enough to be in New York City.*

*Write soon.*

*Jack*

George's hands shook as he read and reread the letter; here was his chance, here was a reason, here, as Jack said, was his opportunity. As soon as he'd finished reading the letter for the third time, making sure he hadn't missed something, some caveat for building this hotel, he knew he'd soon be leaving Harshaw for Calabasas. Calabasas. He liked the sound of the name; it sounded like a promise. Could this be the place, be the town, he was meant to live in?

# Interlude

In the 1860s through the 1880s the Santa Cruz Valley of Arizona Territory was grassy, open, wild, and nearly unpopulated; it was cattle land. Spanish missions dotted the landscape from Tucson to Nogales, stucco buildings with rounded doorways and stained glass that allowed colored crystals to pattern the opposite wall, the outer walls tan and russet red, the same colors as the valley's soil. In this valley, the town of Calabasas sprouted. Calabasas, squash in Spanish, grew like a vine, winding, spreading, blossoming, and bearing fruit. It was a rough collection of buildings, but held the possibilities of so much more. The citizens of Calabasas saw the possibilities, and the town grew. It prospered.

Above the town rose the rocky ridge-line of the Santa Rita Mountains. The rock faces were slate-gray, turning rose and orange in both the dawn and the dusk. The layered rock stood sentinel to the land below, watching over the residents, both human and non-human, in stoic protection. The mountains were the rulers of the valley, whether anyone acknowledged them as such or not.

On the other side of the valley were the Tumacacori Mountains, curving down into Mexico and joining with the Pajarito Mountains. They were softer, less imposing than the Santa Rita Mountains; they rose and fell in fluid ridges and canyons, and while still steep, could be traversed with more ease. Like a curve of a mother's arm they held the valley on the western side, cradling it instead of ruling it. And it was between these two mountain ranges that Calabasas manifested itself.

The town saw many citizens come and go, as it first was a collection of missionaries, then miners, then ranchers, and was prone to be a theater for skirmishes with Apache. After the Gadsden Purchase, it became a military fort, and it was here that Cochise was lured by Lieutenant Bascom under the pretense of peaceful negotiations, only to attempt to arrest and convict Cochise of crimes he may or may not have committed. This scuffle led to the abandonment of Calabasas once again and the military withdrew from the Santa Cruz Valley. It wasn't a town to remain dormant, though, and J. Ross Browne, an Irish-American writer, brought it back to consciousness with his words, "Calabasas consists of rich bottom lands and rolling hills, extending six leagues up and down the Santa Cruz River, embracing rich arable lands on both sides."

Colonel P. Sykes heard of the place, perhaps reading Browne's words, and it captivated him. He saw it as his opportunity to raise a town to greater heights. Having made his money in mining and as the publisher of newspapers in San Francisco, Sykes planned to turn his move to Calabasas into an investment that would secure his future and the future of his family. He planned to build a hotel, The Hotel Santa Rita, and he wanted it to be made completely of brick, two stories high, including a basement, a brick barn, and a one hundred square foot brick corral. It would be the "gateway to Mexico." His name and his hotel would be known across the country, he boasted even before he had a brick-maker. If reports were right though, he would find one in G. W. Atkinson.

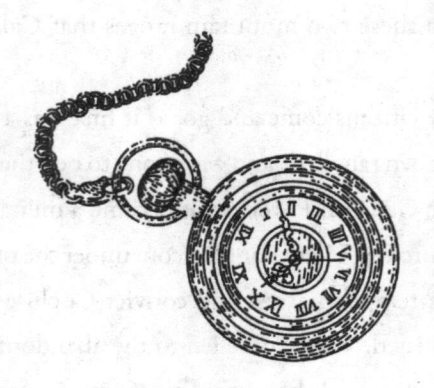

# Chapter 19

George left Harshaw for Calabasas a week after receiving Jack's letter. He rode through the Patagonia Mountains, and it was slow going; the scrub oak forest took maneuvering to get through, and he barely slept for the rumors of jaguars sighted by the miners. He kept a fire burning all night, each night of the three it took him to cross the miles between Harshaw and Calabasas, in hopes that it would keep the cats away. It either worked, or the rumors were just that, rumors, because he didn't see one or any sign of one, not even a print in the clay.

Calabasas was situated on the eastern side of the Santa Cruz river, out of the river's floodplain, and beneath the sharp rocks of the Santa Rita Mountains that rose like church spires. From a ridge on the southeast edge of the town, George pulled Wet Blanket to a halt and gazed down on the place that wanted to be the gateway to Mexico. There wasn't anything spectacular about it; it looked like any other town started by those who had found some reason to stay, and for a moment George was washed in disappointment. Yet he could tell it wasn't a mining town, which changed it, made it more promising. There weren't the hastily built shacks and rows of canvas tents that spoke of a population built of miners who fought and scraped by, hoping for their claim to pay off or for a mining company to buy them out. The buildings of this town were a mix of adobe and clapboard, blending with the mesquite grassland surrounding the town. It seemed quiet, unassuming, more of a home than a place to camp until prospects became better. George noted the permanence of the town in the way some had taken the time and care to plant trees around their houses and others lining the street; impractical trees like Norfolk pine. Cattle and horses grazed on the land surrounding the town, and as George watched, a young girl called, and a cow came to the back of the house where the girl squatted to milk. George thought he could hear the milk ringing in the pail, but the distance between them was too great for it to be so. What he heard was just the sound of a memory. The entire town fit into George's scope of sight and into his mind and settled there, pushing aside the wash of disappointment and leaving behind hope. The air felt softer somehow, as if it came from a different source than other air, as if it were birthed from the bud of hope.

George tethered Wet Blanket and Arrow to a hitching post. He went up the steps of the general store, noting the crates of squash on the porch. They were dark green, darker than the sycamore leaves along the gullies that had brought him here. It was well past noon, and George wanted something other than stale bread and jerky before he sought out Colonel Sykes. "Know where a body can get a meal?" George asked upon entering.

"Just down the street, Miss Julia serves up a mean stew and pie that'll make you wish you'd tried it days ago." The storekeeper, a rotund, balding man with a dark brown beard, looked George up and down as he talked. "You've been traveling long, haven't ya?"

George shrugged. "Few days." He glanced around the store.

"Name's Charlie Brands," the storekeeper said, extending his hand to George.

"George Atkinson," George said, gripping Charlie's hand. Charlie's grip was strong and told of days of hard work in spite of the seemingly sedentary lifestyle of a shopkeeper.

"Planning to settle here?"

"Just might," George said, "just might." He smiled then and added, "Depends on how good this food is."

Charlie laughed. "Oh, you'll stay," he said.

A rough piece of board with the word "Julia's" painted in white on it hung in front of a small house. The house was part adobe, part rough-cut boards. Flowers were planted around the foundation and in boxes at the windows, splashing red, yellow, and violet against the tan of the adobe. Beside the house were four tables covered in blue-and-white checked cloth. Two men sat at one table, their hats perched on their knees, their pistols unstrapped from their legs. One smoked a cigar, the other slurped stew from a white porcelain bowl. George took a seat at the table next to them, nodding a hello, which both returned.

"What can I get you?" a soft voice tumbled in an Irish accent asked at his shoulder.

"I..." George started, then words left his command. Wisps of blonde hair framed the face at his shoulder, gray eyes staring inquiringly at him above high, rounded cheekbones reddened and browned by sun and wind. George had never seen eyes this color of gray before, or if he had they had slipped his notice. These eyes were like the down of a dove, soft, or like rain clouds retreating leaving the freshness of rain behind. She reminded him of Sarah, only younger. He had a feeling he could tell her anything. He could love a girl like her.

"Stew," he blurted, then composed himself enough to say, "Stew, please."

The girl nodded, blonde curls, sun-bleached and fine, bobbing around her ears.

"And coffee," George called after her. Again she nodded, smiling over her shoulder. He looked away, concentrating on the hem of the tablecloth until his face cooled.

When she brought the stew, she asked, "Are you staying or drifting on?"

"I'm staying," he said decidedly. The suddenness of his certainty in this decision surprised him, and he almost added, "maybe," as if that would assuage his heart. Instead he took the hot cup of coffee from her. He had never smelled coffee that good, at least not since Sarah's kitchen. He gulped it, burning the roof of his mouth.

"Your horses look tired," the girl said. She jerked her head in the direction of Wet Blanket and Arrow, standing with their heads low, lips loose at the hitching rail.

"Rode from Harshaw," George answered.

"They'll be glad to stay." She turned, another customer calling her attention, and wiped her hands on an off-white apron that had been stained and mended more times than could be counted in a single observation. The dress that it covered, though, still had the vibrance of new cloth, following a blue-and-white pattern akin to the tablecloths. It was an unadorned dress, and every single button was precisely fastened, but the cut of the waist made the skirt flounce over her hips and fall in loose folds to the tops of her black leather boots.

"Wait," George said, "my name's George, George Atkinson."

"Julia. Welcome to Calabasas, George."

Colonel Sykes shook George's hand with enthusiasm. He was a tall man, slight in build, with a soft handshake that spoke of a life of ease, as did his clean and well-made gray suit, the collar and cuffs stiff with starch, the shirt beneath white and neatly buttoned. "You resemble your brother," he said to George.

"Thank you," George said hesitantly, not sure if this was a good thing or not.

Colonel Sykes gestured at a table along the wall of the saloon. "Shall we sit?" he asked, then, his enthusiasm getting the better of his professionalism, continued, "You're interested in building a hotel?"

"Yes." George took a seat. The Colonel didn't have any of the hardness he had expected, and he was taken aback. It was hard to think of him as sternly commanding a company of soldiers with the way he leaned forward out of his chair, but there was something in this gesture that also encouraged candor, which could have led men to follow his orders with ease. "I have a brickyard in Harshaw," George said. "I built the twenty-stamp mill there and have been shipping bricks to towns nearby."

"Harshaw. Bit of a journey to here. I'd make it worth your while if you'd move it here. Calabasas is situated to become the gateway to Mexico. People from both sides of the border will make it their destination." Colonel Sykes's voice filled with the boast and then filled the room. "My hotel will be the best in the whole territory if your work is as good as your brother says."

Jack thought his work was good, and with this knowledge, George felt confidence build inside himself. "I'll move," he said, decisively, and then wondered if he'd made the decision too quickly. What did he really know about this man? Did the Colonel even have the money for the venture?

"Good." Colonel Sykes unfolded a sheet of brown paper on the table, then called to the bartender to bring two shots of whiskey. "To celebrate our new partnership," he said. "These are my hotel plans."

George glanced over the drawings, seeing a roughly sketched two-story building with wraparound porches on both levels. He tried to decipher the markings along the edges of the sketch, finally concluding they must be an attempt at measurements. In front of the hotel, an elaborate sketch of a plaza stretched, lined with trees, a fountain rising in the center. Plans for a brick barn and corral were drawn behind the hotel, filling the paper to its edges. The plans needed work, but he thought he got the idea. "How many rooms?" He asked as the bartender brought the whiskey.

"Two hundred," Colonel Sykes stated confidently. "It needs to be able to accommodate the crowds."

"Two hundred." George repeated the number and scanned the plans again, making mental calculations of how many bricks it would take to achieve this spectacular vision of the Colonel's. It would take a lot of brick and briefly he wondered if the Colonel was aware of the cost.

"Can it be done?" the Colonel asked and then answered his own question: "Of course it can." He lifted his glass of whiskey. "To the Hotel Santa Rita!"

George lifted his own glass. "To the Hotel Santa Rita!"

The glasses clinked together and Colonel Sykes tipped his back easily. George followed suit, holding his breath while the whiskey burned down his throat so he wouldn't cough.

"Bring the bottle," Colonel Sykes called to the bartender. He filled the glasses again and lifted his high. "To the opportunity of a lifetime!"

"To opportunity!" George said, thinking he couldn't argue with that sentiment. The glasses clinked together and this time the urge to cough was less.

"To Calabasas!" Colonel Sykes let toasts roll as easily as a wagon down a hill and his ease swept George along, echoing each toast.

"To Calabasas!"

"To the Union!"

"To the Union!"

"To Mexico!"

"To Mexico!"

"To prosperity!"

"To prosperity!"

"To Hotel Santa Rita!"

"To Hotel Santa Rita!"

# Chapter 20

On the edge of town George bought five acres of land, on which he built a brickyard. The acres were fairly flat and grassy, with no trees or shrubs to cast shade. In the summer sun it'd be hot, but that didn't worry George; the heat would cure the bricks faster. His supplies had been delivered from Harshaw by mule-drawn wagon, and he'd sold his share in the business there to Antonio. He paid the driver in a bottle of whiskey and enough coins to get a room for two nights. The man spent the money on more whiskey and left town in a blurred state, his mules awkwardly jogging and nipping at each other. That had been weeks ago, and now George felt well-established, the rows of bricks for the Hotel Santa Rita stacked and curing in the sun.

From one side of the kiln, he could look across the rushing water of the Santa Cruz to rich ranch land. From the other side, he could look up the main street of Calabasas. Calabasas had grown by three saloons, a post office, and a dance hall within the few months he'd been a resident, and soon it would boast a hotel. It wouldn't be long before he'd have more orders for bricks coming in, and he thought perhaps he should put an advertisement in the newspaper. For the time being, though, it felt good to gaze across his new brickyard and know that soon a magnificent hotel would be built with his brick. This was bigger than the twenty-stamp mill, and his breath caught with excitement as he imagined people staying within walls of his brick. He imagined it as a destination, a place where ladies and gentlemen came to vacation, a place for businessmen to meet, but also a place for cattlemen to stay as they pushed their herds from Arizona to Mexico, Mexico to Arizona and beyond. Surely now, he thought, he could not be a disappointment to John.

The brickyard wasn't a place to live, though, and George became weary of camping, just as his horses became weary of being hobbled or tied. He knew if he was going to stay in Calabasas he'd need a place to call his own, a house, a barn, land. And so he'd gone to the deed office and stood in front of the claim map for near on an hour, looking at the sectors that hadn't been claimed. When he walked out, he had the deed to six hundred and forty acres.

Now, George stood and viewed the land in front of him. It expanded in an oasis of grass tufted beneath mesquite and a sky bluer than any sky he had seen. It stretched away from him to a horizon of jagged hills and mountains, just beyond the verdant, slithering river. The man at the deed office said it was good land to graze cattle, and George was inclined to agree, picturing a colorful herd scattered amongst the bushes. He saw in his mind's eye a farmhouse made of hewn stone and a barn beside it, chickens scratching, a dog keeping watch on children playing by the kitchen step. The vision surprised him, made him feel guilty in a way that he didn't quite understand.

George hadn't thought of having a family in a long time. Before the rangers, he'd always assumed that one day he would, but that assumption had dissipated upon his return. It felt wrong almost, as if because Jimmy couldn't, he shouldn't either. He felt it'd be unfair to those who didn't return from war, or maybe it was a punishment for the families whose lives were taken needlessly at Sand Creek. Here though, standing on this land, something had changed within him: a longing to come home to loved ones hooked into his heart. He took a deep breath. First things first: the hotel, then horses and the cattle, then maybe, just maybe, a family.

Wet Blanket snorted at a bird flying from a hole in a nearby saguaro. George laughed and slapped the horse's neck. "Getting ahead of myself, aren't I?" he said.

He glanced at Arrow, standing quietly. "Horses," he said. "Horses first." After all, he'd need them for running the brickyard. George had always liked horses; they were easier to read than people, and he felt he could understand them. A memory of Denver slid into his mind. It was the first year in Denver; they had arrived from Peoria in the fall and taken an apartment on a street that teemed with comings and goings. George liked to stand on the stoop of the apartment, at first to escape the cramped indoors, then later because he wanted to see the horses that went by and test his skills. At the time, his eyes were level with the horses' chests, so his focus fell on their legs.

*A set of gray legs went by, stepping high, every other step clicking together in an overreach. Heavy bones, a rounder hoof. Her strides weren't perfect, but they were steady. The feathers at her fetlocks curled and were once white, now stained yellow from days of pulling wagons through dusty streets. "There is some draft in her," he thought. Then the legs were replaced by a set of chestnut ones, smooth and lithe. Oval hooves, small and dusty, new shoes shining on the bottoms with every lifted stride; warmblood. And then a set of black legs, straight and limber, but as they passed, George noticed a catch in the left leg, arthritis, an old injury, a weakness that would send the horse to pasture if not cared for.*

*Eight brown legs, matched except for a white coronet on a right front, liquid motion, gone in a flash of wheel spokes and a confusion of pounding hooves of a group of army horses. All legs, long sinewy legs, yet muscles flexed visibly on each one, telling of a hidden strength in each shade of brown, no white, for white hooves were softer, weaker, and George understood that these horses needed to be strong, needed to be hardened.*

And it was in this way, in this observing from the apartment stoop, that George learned to assess horses, that he formed the foundation of his understanding of them, and his love of them.

A large gray colt stood at the edge of the livery stable corral, with his hindquarters tucked under, waiting for another horse to get too close. George snapped at him. The colt flickered and sprang forward. He stopped short at the fence and rolled back, slamming into a small brown mare with his chest. The mare pinned her ears, but didn't move an inch.

"I'll take that brown mare and the gray colt," George said.

Hal Connely, the livery proprietor squinted at him. He was an older man, stoop shouldered, silver-haired with a grizzled beard, fingers stained by tobacco. "Ya sure 'bout the gray?" he said.

"Yep."

Hal shrugged, his suspenders shifting with the movement, the left one slipping. He straightened it with a snap. "Be glad to be rid of him. Sorrel colt hasta go with the mare." Hal pointed at an undersized foal.

"Hers?"

"Naw, an orphan. She cares for 'im."

George inspected the colt. He had long legs; with a little time and extra feed, he might just turn out alright, maybe be a runner. George nodded. "I'll take him. Can I give you a note?"

Hal looked at his pipe. He tapped it on the corral boards, then smoked a minute. "Don't usually take notes from strangers." He tapped his pipe again, knocking the ashes from it. The little mare wandered to the fence and lipped at grass along the edge. Hal repacked and lit his pipe. "I'll take your note," he said. "Gotta place to keep 'em?"

George grinned. "Somewhat, I'll make it work."

After driving the new horses to his land, George worked away the afternoon enlarging and strengthening his corral. Wet Blanket spooked at every bang of wood against wood, shovel against sand, hammer against nail. The gray stood and watched, the little mare grazing beside him with the foal huddled against her. Arrow came and dipped his soft nose into George's hand. George scratched Arrow's ears, then shooed him; the fence had to be finished by nightfall.

Charlie said rustlers were a problem. George hadn't seen a single soul on his land, but he wasn't taking any chances with letting his horses roam loose. Cattle though, cattle were different. They'd range, and he'd take the losses. He liked the thought of seeing them ducking beneath the arms of mesquite as they grazed, rubbing the trunks smooth. Cattle would be good on this land. More horses. A dog. Julia. He'd have dinner at Julia's. He thought about her sun-lightened blonde hair, her dove-down eyes and smiled. The hammer slipped and hit his thumb, forming a red bruise under his nail. He watched it spread and wondered if love spread like this until it filled a heart. If he had been home he'd have asked Sarah or Jimmy. Jimmy would have had an answer for a question like that.

With this thought he realized how much he missed having someone to confide in, and the loss of Jimmy swept upon him with such force that he had to sit down, his hands shaking, his breath coming in quick gasps. He reached in his vest pocket and rubbed his thumb over the silver watch there. Gradually his breath evened, and he returned to his work.

By nightfall, George had the corral completed, and with an accomplished weariness he stepped inside the walls of his house. It wasn't yet finished, with no doors or windows, and the roof gaping open to the sky over the living room and bedroom. However, it was complete enough that it gave George a sense of security. In the kitchen—the one room that was furnished and had a roof, although the doorway still lacked a door to close—George lit a kerosene lamp and sat down to a meal of cornpone and cold, cured meats. As he ate, he wrote a letter to Sarah.

*Dear Sarah,*

*How did you know when you fell in love with father? Is it something that happens slowly or all at once? I think I'm in love. Only I've just met the girl, barely spoken to her. Can it happen in one meeting? What if I'm just lonely?*

He mailed the letter the next day and afterward regretted what he'd written. But it was too late to take it back: the stagecoach had left in a cloud of dust already, and all he could do was try to put his words out of mind and turn his thoughts back to putting out an advertisement.

Brick For Sale.

Geo. W. Atkinson, of Calabasas.

Will deliver brick in Nogales at $10 per

M. on cars as Nogales by the car load, or

from 100 up at $1.25 per hundred bricks.

—AND—

Will also bid on Brick put in the

wall and furnish everything.

——

Will contract to furnish Lime

in large quantities.

—-

For further information enquire at

T. D. Casanega, or address George W.

Atkinson, Calabasas, A. T.

Leave orders at Casanega's, and

will be transmitted by telegraph to me at

once.[1]

Seeing the advertisement filled George with a sense of accomplishment; he had taken the next step forward in living his life with purpose. "Everyone needs a purpose," John had always told his children growing up, "and everyone has one. Not all find it or know what it is, but if you feel you've accomplished something, then you have a purpose. Follow it." The words repeated themselves in George's mind as he ran his fingers over the typing, tracing his name there in print for all to see.

---

1. Advertisement directly quoted from original document.

# Chapter 21

George dawdled at the hitching rail in front of Julia's, tying his horse's reins to the rail slowly, looping one in and out of the other, then pulling them loose and starting over again. He ran his hand down the wide white blaze on Wet Blanket's face and over the nostrils, letting the horse lip at his fingers. The hair on Wet Blanket's muzzle was short and fine, velvety when brushed one way, prickly when brushed the other. George let his hand run back and forth, feeling the softness and the prickliness as he listened to Julia talking to a customer at a table nearby. She spoke easily, as if she knew the man well, but George heard her ask where the man was from, so he knew the man was a stranger. The man replied too low for him to hear, but Julia's voice came clearly to him.

"I hear the ocean is beautiful there," Julia said, "blue and sparkling, as if full of stars. And beaches of golden sand. They say it's prettier than the Atlantic. I can't attest to that; any ocean is pretty in my mind. We had a legend back in the old country that those who sailed the ocean without first admiring its beauty would never return to shore. The god of the ocean would sweep up and claim them for their own." She laughed to make light of the superstition, but George got the feeling she believed every ounce of it.

The man said something else and Julia responded with a careful put down. "Those clouds are calling for rain," she said, "so I don't think an evening out tonight would be in anyone's best interest."

George glanced in the direction of the table and saw Julia pat the man's arm before turning to refill another customer's coffee. A new emotion stirred in him, accompanied by the thought that he wished she wouldn't be so friendly with customers. He was so caught up in the jealousy, he didn't notice Wet Blanket nipping at him until the horse's teeth lightly grazed his fingers. George turned back to the horse, finally securing the reins on the rail and scratching the white forehead one last time.

None of the tables being empty, George walked toward the table where the man sat whom Julia had previously been talking to about oceans. George wanted to size him up. Placing a hand on the back of a chair opposite the newcomer, he said, "Mind if I sit here?"

The man shook his head. His clothes were dusty from travel and a few day's stubble ran along his jaw and chin, but he had evidently washed his face recently, and his brown hair had been combed, showing a decency that almost made George disappointed. "I'd be pleased to have the company," the man said. "Name's Albert Peck."

"Nice to meet you," George said. "I'm George Atkinson."

"Are you from around here?" Albert asked, turning a dusty, stained hat around and around on his knee.

George nodded, as he took a seat. "I've got a place across the river, and I own the brickyard here in town. You?" "Here to visit my brother, but most likely just passing through. My brother has a place up at the end of that canyon." Albert indicated a canyon to the west that wormed its way into the Tumacacori Mountains.

"Don't believe I've had the pleasure of making his acquaintance as of yet."

At this moment Julia returned to the table with a bowl of stew and a thick slice of bread for Albert. After setting the food down in front of the man, she turned to smile at George, the flash of a dimple that never fully materialized on her right cheek. "Why, Mr. Atkinson," she said, "I didn't expect you to be by today. Weren't you here just yesterday?" Her eyes brightened as she teased.

George's face warmed and he fumbled with the edge of the tablecloth. Yet even as he wondered how it was possible that someone could make him feel confident and self-conscious all at once, he kept his voice even and dismissive of his being there. "Yes, but I had work at the brickyard that took longer than expected."

"I see," Julia said, arching a single eyebrow that indicated she didn't fully believe him. "Stew and coffee?"

"Please."

"Now I understand," Albert said once she had left.

"Understand what?" George asked. He leaned against the back of the chair, resting his back.

"Why she refused my offer. She already has a steady suitor."

George shook his head. "Oh no!" he almost exclaimed. "She's not my girl." He coughed, as if the idea was just too much, but then said in a lower tone and more to himself than to Albert, "At least not yet."

Albert laughed. "I get it," he said. "I've been there. Just ask her. She likes you. She won't say no, trust me."

"A self-proclaimed expert." George took his hat off and set it over his knee. He ran his fingers through his fine brown hair, a gesture habitual to most, but in his case awkward, aware that it was to make himself presentable. "Where are you from?" George asked to move the conversation away from him.

"San Antonio by way of Nogales," Albert answered.

"Nogales isn't really in direct line from San Antonio to here," George commented.

Albert shrugged. "I like to take a wandering route."

"Why'd you leave San Antonio?"

"I got an itch in my boots. You ever get that feeling where you just know it's time to go somewhere? It starts one day as a simple thought and then pretty soon it's an itch so far under your skin that you can no longer ignore it, so you pack up your things and hit the trail."

George nodded. "I know what you mean," he said, thinking of how he left Black Hawk. The decision had been sudden, but he'd felt a certainty that he had to leave so distinctly that nothing would have stopped him. Maybe it had begun as an itch to see the ruins of a brick city planted there by Jimmy; maybe it had begun as a desire to do something that was completely his decision, that wasn't dictated by his brother or his father; maybe it had begun as a wish to prove himself, to find who he truly was as a man. Whatever the beginning, his memories had built upon the foundation until he couldn't refuse the need. When he'd left he'd thought he didn't have a place or direction in mind, but perhaps there had been direction to it. It was possible that, deep down, he had followed a specific path carved in the furthest reaches of his mind.

As he watched Julia come toward the table with a bowl of stew and a cup of coffee balanced in her brown, sturdy hands, he knew he was meant to arrive in this place as if he really had followed clear and specific directions to the exact spot. Julia focused into his sight as decidedly his north, making his palms sweat and his heart thrum in an unfamiliar way. Could he get used to this new rhythm? He didn't know, but he couldn't wait to find out.

# Chapter 22

"Ten children," Julia said. She laughed as if to lighten the statement. The sound of her laughter always surprised George, just as much as her blunt honesty did. For the past three weeks she'd been surprising him this way, ever since Julia had said, "That'd be nice," when he asked her to go walking. That first walk turned into a second, then a third, then a fourth, until every evening found George riding into town.

"Or twelve," she said.

George fiddled with a dry cassock of grass, then met her eyes. They were jovial, almost taunting, sparkling as if they held a universe of stars within them. She coughed. The cough was tight, shallow, and when she inhaled, a squeak rattled in her throat. Her face flushed. George brushed her cheek with his fingertips, finding her skin warm, but not feverish. "I worry about that cough," he said.

She stood, moving away from him and shaking her skirts out. "Twelve children," she said. "I'd like to have twelve children." She looked up at the sky. "Let's watch the sunset from up there." She pointed to a nearby hill and without waiting for George's response, set off quickly, knotting her skirts up so that they weren't dragging in the dust. She navigated between fuzzy, reaching arms of cholla, without getting so much as a single spine caught on her clothes, and the speed with which she climbed the hill surprised George.

"I always thought I'd have liked to have siblings. You could never be lonely with siblings," she said when they'd reached the top. Her breath came short and she put her hands on her back as if supporting her own frame.

George ignored the want to fuss over her, telling himself that there wasn't anything to fuss over. Instead he said, "It's still lonely with siblings."

"It couldn't be. You must have always had someone to talk to, tell your secrets to."

"Not always."

"Why not?"

"You don't always get along."

"Didn't you tell secrets to your brother?"

"Sometimes." George shrugged. "I guess when we were young. There was this meadow, by our house in Illinois. We'd lay in the grass and watch clouds. I guess we told secrets."

"Tell me more." Julia caught hold of his left hand in both of hers.

Her hands were warm, and George could feel the calluses on the palms. "You can tell a lot by a person's hands," Sarah said to him once. She hadn't gone any further, as if that was really all that needed to be said. He understood what she meant now. He wanted to draw Julia's hands to his chest, he wanted to kiss her knuckles, her calluses, to ease any soreness in them. He began walking again. "There's not much to tell," he said.

"Of course there is," Julia said, following him. "There's always something to tell. I am the only child my father ever had, I've never had many friends—you couldn't when you were constantly following gold mines. Still, there is something to tell."

"I'd say your life is more of a story."

"We all have stories. Some of us just don't know it yet." Her statement sounded like something his father would say; in fact George felt like he'd heard him say it before. They'd get along, Julia and his father, probably better than George got along with him. Julia stopped walking and when George looked back at her, her hands were on her hips, her gaze direct, unyielding.

"My mother died when I was young," he began, walking back to her.

She nodded. "Mine too."

"Jack is my only full sibling, all the others, well, they're half siblings. It's funny though, I never think of them that way. They're my siblings." He shrugged and watched the rays of sun slide behind the Tumacacori Mountains. "I'm closest with Jack. We did near about everything together, up until I left." He smiled softly, remembering, and was about to share stories of their boyhood antics, when Julia asked, "Why did you leave?"

The question sucked the air from him and he glanced at her, before focusing back on the mountains. The sun dipped lower, spreading pink and purple gauze on the horizon. A quail called from somewhere in the brush and a gray hawk circled once before dropping down into the branches of a mesquite. Finally, George turned and met her gaze. Julia's eyes seemed to reflect the sunset back at him, an unrelenting and beautiful phenomenon that lasted forever and only a second, and he knew that she would soon know every possible inch of his story.

George stood on his doorstep, and for the first time in a long time something like contentment filled him as he watched the horses shifting in the corral. Behind them the barn stood, still windowless and doorless. Charlie said the hinges would be in on the next stage. George took a sip of his coffee. It would be nice to have doors on the house, too. The roof was done now, and he had built a bed frame last week, finally able to sleep off the ground. The makings of a rocking chair and table waited for his hands to finish them in the yard. George gave a contented sigh; it was coming together, it would be a home, his home. The thought sent a shiver across his skin, the good kind of shiver that was like an inward smile.

A cow bawled and he glanced in its direction. He watched a red calf run to the bawling cow, ducking its head under its mother's side. It suckled, and the cow switched its tail, chewing her cud. George counted the red backs of the cattle standing in the mesquite, coming up with twenty. All were there, his first herd of cows. He'd bought them from Hal, making a good deal and saving Hal the trip of driving them to the stockyards in Nogales. They were on the thin side, but George was confident that a few months grazing along the river would put meat back on their bones. It gave him a feeling of contentment to look out across his land and see them, even if their ribs did stick out. He sipped his coffee and his thoughts drifted to the letter he had received from Sarah the week before.

*Dear Georgie,*

*Love is tricky. It grows both slowly and quickly, and you never know how it will grow. You once asked if I loved your father, and I answered that I loved him as much as I was able. This was a way of satisfying a young boy's real question of whether or not I was going to stay in his life, without admitting that I wasn't sure if what I felt for his father at the time was love. It was, but it was the beginnings of it, because with your father love grew slowly. It started as a spark, or a bud on a branch as spring comes. Now I can't imagine ever not loving him. No matter how it starts, love can deepen into something that cannot be described.*

It was in this letter that George felt Sarah's full forgiveness for the night he'd hit John, her full forgiveness for leaving the way he did. The letter told him that she was once again his confidante and that she'd be honest with him, that she'd always be there for him, and that she'd always be his mother.

The sun finished breaking over the horizon, coloring the clouds gold. It made him think of Julia's hair, gold and wispy around her smile. With her, he felt like he could remember how to smile, how to laugh, how to be happy. Maybe happiness was what would finally chase away the memories that haunted him. He wondered if this was the way Jimmy had felt about Lizzie. Was it Lizzie who kept Jimmy's nightmares away?

"Lizzie is sunshine," Jimmy said once.

George had smiled, thinking a girl couldn't really be sunshine, but now he knew what Jimmy meant. Julia was sunshine; she was the entire solar system. George's face flushed as this thought passed through his mind, and he cleared his throat. In the corral, Wet Blanket's head snapped up, and he turned toward the house, whinnying. The sound washed through George's body, warming him more than the morning sun, warming him more than all the thoughts stumbling about in his mind.

# Chapter 23

The horses in the paddock whinnied across the expanse of grassland, excited by the dust the cattle churned. Wet Blanket neighed shrilly back as George whistled at the herd of Herefords. He'd gone to Sonoita three weeks ago and bought an additional dozen heifers and half a dozen cows with calves. Now it was time to brand the young ones and any heifers small enough to hold down. The cows, well, he'd just have to hope no one tried to claim them as their own. He wiped sweat and dirt from his forehead as Wet Blanket instinctively blocked the path of a cow trying to turn back. A few of the calves had slowed down, and their mothers were becoming nervous, wanting to bolt back to them.

"Andy, Harold," he called, "catch those stragglers."

The two boys pulled their horses back, their hands low and heavy on the reins; even a stranger could have said they were brothers. Their father owned a claim on the other side of the river, and on Charlie's suggestion, George had hired them for the day to help with branding. The weight of homesteading showed in the browned skin of their faces, but they were still young, thirteen and fifteen, and they still had a chance to live beyond hardness. Even as he flinched along with their horses, George was glad he had given them a chance. Maybe he could teach them, if only just a little, that a horse is a partner, not an opponent to wrestle into place.

The cows filled the air with their bawling as they pushed through the gate of the small barnyard corral. Two red heifers locked foreheads. Dust billowed around them, their legs twisting as they fought. The rest of the herd pouring into the corral interrupted the scuffle. The heifers broke apart. One hopped away, her tail high and switching.

"Close the gate there, Harold," George said.

The boy jumped from his saddle, grabbing the gate in the same movement. He banged it shut, tying it. He had let go of his horse's reins and the horse pranced away. George cut it off and held it in place until Harold grabbed the reins again.

"Careful, letting go of your horse like that."

Harold nodded.

"Andy, kick that fire up." George dismounted and tied Wet Blanket to the fence. Andy followed his lead, tying his own horse, a scruffy Spanish pony, to the fence beside Wet Blanket, before going to the fire and setting a dry log in the coals. It caught fire. George pushed the branding irons into the flames. For a moment, looking at the two slim boys, George worried that they weren't going to be the help he'd hoped they'd be.

Harold loosened his lasso, twirling it over his head, and then, snapping his wrist, he let go of the loop. It landed over the top of a post and Harold pulled tight. "Nice," George said, "let's try that on a cow."

"Yes, sir," Harold said.

George heard the excitement in Harold's voice and smiled, glad again that he had given these boys a chance. He remembered when he and Jack were Harold's and Andy's ages. Their family had just moved to Boulder from Denver, following business opportunities that would last the year and send them on to Black Hawk, and George remembered feeling out of place and small, even though he'd had a growth spurt and was momentarily half an inch taller than Jack. A rancher from the outskirts of town offered them a couple days of work mustering cattle. The memory slipped into place.

*George rode at the left flank of the herd, having been charged with keeping any cattle from breaking away and running through the pungent sage that rose to the horses' withers. He glanced across to the other side of the herd to where Jack rode, and noted how Jack's attention was solely fixed on the cows in front of him. His horse broke sagebrush branches with its wide chest, the broken branches scratched George's legs, the leaves getting caught between the saddle and saddle pad, and George returned his focus to the backs of the cattle in front of him. The cattle were a mix of skinny longhorns and Herefords, browns, reds, blacks, mottled in white and brindled. They bawled, and some balked at having to push through the sage. Then a baldfaced steer broke from the herd and ran, head high, leaping with sudden agility. George kicked his horse into a gallop after it, and as he closed in and turned the errant steer he felt something settle in him. Living in Colorado would be okay. He knew he'd get used to the mountains rising on the horizon, blue and chiseled above the treeline; he knew he could love this new home.*

George let out a breath as the memory faded, thinking how he did miss those Colorado mountains, but here in Arizona there were the Santa Ritas to the northeast puncturing the sky, and to the southwest the Pajaritos broke the horizon, north of them the Atascosa and Tumacacori ranges. It wasn't as if he were mountainless here; they were just different. He couldn't describe the difference, not really. In a way they were austere, separate from the land below them, but it wasn't hostility that created this illusion. It was more like ownership, as if these mountains had an unwavering claim to everything. Maybe that was why men insisted on mining into the sides of them, trying in some way to reverse the role, bend the mountains to being owned.

"Let's get this done," George said, pulling himself away from his thoughts. He'd been getting too caught in them lately and needed to have all his attention on the task at hand if they were to finish it.

The two boys swung into their saddles, dallying their ropes on their saddle horns. George knew they were going to try their hardest. Movement along the river caught George's eye, and he paused, one foot in the stirrup. A horse and rider appeared, trotting easily toward them. As they grew closer, George recognized his nearest neighbor, Pete Kitchen, a stout, easy-mannered man who raised pigs. George raised his hand in greeting.

"Heard you were brandin'," Pete said. "Need a hand?"

"We might," George said. "Know anything about branding?"

"Know enough."

George nodded; at the very least, Pete could hold the calves down. He swung into his saddle. "Andy," he called, "you'll be in charge of the irons. Harold, let's see how good you are at catching a cow. Pete, you can hold them down?"

"S'pose I can," Pete said good-naturedly, his long mustache twitching as he smiled. He tied his horse and moved toward the fire with Andy. "Push 'em in there good," he instructed Andy. "A hot iron is best. Makes brandin' quicker. Don't have to hold a cow down as long. Since that's my job, I want these irons hot."

George chuckled. He swung his rope until he had a wide, loose loop. Wet Blanket danced, ready to go after a cow. He knew the drill, and the prospect of running down a cow excited him, as it should with any good cow horse. George held him still, assessing which cow to cut from the herd first. A young heifer lingered on the outside of the herd, and George settled to rope her first. All it took was a nudge of his knee for Wet Blanket to leap forward, bearing down on the heifer. The heifer startled, bolting toward the herd, but Wet Blanket moved quicker, turning the heifer around and moving her down the fence. George stood in the stirrups, swinging the looped rope over his head, and then with an easy flick of his wrist the rope swooshed through the air, catching the heifer's legs.

The minute she hit the ground, Pete knelt on her neck and shoulder, pressing her head down with his left hand and gripping her top front leg with his right. "Be quick an' steady," Pete said to Andy.

Andy hesitantly came toward the heifer, the brand held out in front of him.

"Quick, boy, quick," Pete said through clenched teeth as the cow tried to rise.

Andy lifted the brand, then stopped there with it poised as if he'd suddenly become a statue. The heifer thrashed again, and George dallied the rope tighter, asking Wet Blanket to take a step backward. Wet Blanket arched his neck as he pulled against the rope. "Harold!" George shouted, "help your brother!"

Harold leaped from his horse and grabbed the iron from his brother. He pressed it down hard on the heifer's hip. The hair sizzled, and the burning smell of it filled the air. Harold pulled the brand away, leaving the mark 61 red and raw on the heifer. Andy snapped into movement, jerking the rope from around the heifer's hooves, and at the same moment Pete released his weight. The heifer jumped to her feet bawling and ran to her herd. George coiled his rope. Harold stuck the iron back in the fire, then patted his brother's shoulder. Pete wiped his forehead, grinned and said, "That's how it's done."

George walked to his house in the silence that came with the cows moving back out across the landscape, grazing as they went, all sporting 61 burned onto their hips. The mark claimed the cattle as his, something that could help him track them down should a rustler make off with one. It gave George a sense of security, and even though he knew brands didn't always keep cattle from being stolen, the 61 would at least give a rustler pause. His feet left strong depressions in the sand, weighing into the heels more than the toes and leaving the sand to slowly spill back into the boot marks like that of an hourglass. He paused at the door, glancing over his shoulder, then pushed the door in, latching it behind him.

George piled some pieces of mesquite kindling in the kitchen stove, and after a couple strikes of the flint against steel the fire was crackling. He rubbed his neck, staring at the fire and thinking about dinner. Finally he cut a thick piece of bread from a loaf Julia had given him and spread butter across it half an inch thick. He put the kettle on the stove and leaned against the cooler side, biting into the chewy sourdough. Closing his eyes, he thought about Julia's gray eyes and smiled. It'd been a week since he'd seen her. He'd never known he could miss someone this much in such a short time. No wonder Jimmy used to talk about Lizzie all the time. All those months he must have been miserable, yet George couldn't remember ever thinking of Jimmy as being miserable. Except for that night...

The door burst open, the latch snapping, to reveal six men, looking darker skinned than they really were against the light of the setting sun. George jumped, automatically reaching to his side only to find empty air. His bread fell to the floor, butter side down, and he grabbed the back of the closest chair, all the while taking in the unshaven men. A wiry man, George presumed to be the leader, said something to the others in Spanish, and in response they relaxed the aim of their pistols. "Food," the man said.

George nodded, loosening his white-knuckled grip on the chair. "Bread?" he said, gasping the word out as he tried to stay calm, his heart thundering in his chest. He hoped these men only wanted food, that they would eat and leave, and he repeated over and over in his mind to act unbothered by their intrusion, to keep his nerves from blundering into provoking them. Keeping his eyes on the men, George sliced the remainder of Julia's loaf. Then he set the uneven pieces and the butter on the table. He motioned to them, and their leader jerked his head to the others, who holstered their guns before reaching for bread and slathering the pieces in butter with their fingers. How long had they been without food to eat like this? George wished he had more to offer, but he'd been too busy with building and branding to do any hunting. The bread was the best he had. He almost laughed at the ridiculous nature of this wish. What did he owe these men?

George found the few mugs he had and placed them on the table, before turning and pulling the coffee pot off the stove. He knew the coffee would be lukewarm at best and bitter from sitting all day, but he offered it to the men anyway; at least it was something. "Coffee?" he asked.

"Si," the leader said, and the others nodded.

"You'll have to share," he said. His voice cracked, but he kept his hands steady as he poured the coffee. He noticed the buttons on their shirts shone silver even though the fabric was wrinkled and dusty. Caked dirt fell from their boots, and George knew they had come by the river because there hadn't been any weather for weeks.

The leader gulped bread and chunks of butter, then took a drink of the coffee. He spat. "Este cafe es terrible," he said. His companions laughed, and George offered them water, but in the end they all drank the coffee. Please, George thought, just finish the food and coffee and leave. But once the bread, butter, and coffee was gone, the leader leaned back in his chair. "Dinero. Now." And George felt his heart become leaden, his mouth dry and unable to swallow.

George knew he had some money in his pocket, change from a purchase at the store that he hadn't bothered to put back in the kitchen drawer, and he took out the worn and crumpled bill, putting it into the hand held out to him, hoping against hope that it would satisfy. "All I have," he said. George watched the leader's face as the man looked at the money, wondering if the man knew he was lying. The man had a small scar above his left eye and his face was creased in lines, giving him the appearance of being older, but George found himself thinking that this man couldn't possibly be older than thirty.

"No puede ser que nada más tengas esto," the man said, still looking at the money in his hand. "Where is more?"

"No more," George said. It was hard to get the words out through the dryness of his mouth, but he managed it and supposed that was one good thing that had come out of his time with the rangers: he could keep himself calm under pressure.

The man leaped forward and clutched the front of George's vest. His eyes were dark and burning, but there was something else in them, deeper, hidden by the emotion of the moment. Desperation, maybe? He felt something like recognition as he stared into them. Then, for a moment George found himself back on a snowy slope, staring into the brown eyes of a young Indian, again with that flicker of recognition... Then the hand tightening its grip on his vest brought him back to the present.

George's ribs tightened, that familiar feeling that warned he was on the edge of exploding. He told himself to stay calm and take charge, but if his ribs got any tighter he wouldn't be able to take it. His breathing came in sharp bursts as he focused on the moment. These men had intruded into his home, they were in the wrong, and he couldn't let them walk over him. He couldn't let his memories derail him; no matter what he had done in the past, he didn't deserve this now. With this thought, the tightness relaxed just enough, and George took a firm hold on the man's wrist with his strong hands and clamped down on the bones, stopping short of breaking them. "No more," George repeated. "No more dinero. None."

The man laughed, a laugh that wasn't humorous, but was half unbelieving, half scared, and fell back against the wall when George let him go. George kept eye contact with the man. The man stared back as if assessing just how far George would go. Then, with the suddenness of a twig snapping underfoot, he turned to his companions, Spanish commands rolling off his tongue. All six men pulled their pistols with movement that was as fluid as rainwater. George looked down the barrels, surprised to find he felt calm, strangely calm, just waiting for what would happen next. His hands didn't even twitch. He wondered if a person was happier dying on an empty stomach than on a full one.

The leader waved his gun at the still open door. "Come." He pressed his gun into George's back, and George began walking as if in a trance, the rest of the men circling him. The men's footprints were shallow, the sand sliding back to almost erase the boot tracks. The barn looked dark and bleary in the dimming light. George blinked and moved his eyes up to the sky. A nightjar flew along the crest of the only white cloud there.

The gun jabbed George, and he bit the inside of his bottom lip to keep from swinging at the man behind him, focusing his eyes on the barn again. Stepping through the creaking barn doors, the honey-colored beams became clear. He remembered the feel of the ax and the cross-saw when he cut the timbers. Charlie had helped him, and in return George had re-shingled the general store; the willing give and take of neighbors in a town that was getting to its feet. Although it had only been a few months ago, it suddenly felt like a lifetime had passed.

The tallest of the men threw a loop of rope around George's neck. George ducked at the feel of the coil, but he kept still, a tumble of thoughts spilling through his mind, trying to come up with a scenario where he would get out of this alive, but they were the ones who held the guns. Guns were faster than fists, faster than running feet; he knew this, he'd seen this, and there was still a chance if he remained calm that they wouldn't kill him. Wasn't there? The tall man chucked the end of the rope over a beam. It slithered across the top and down the other side and dangled in front of George's face.

The leader pushed the knot tight. "Dinero, where is it?"

"There is no more," George repeated. He looked into the leader's round, black eyes and thought about Jimmy. How did he feel when the rope touched his neck? Was he thinking of anything besides what he was doing? George swallowed hard, but he didn't take his gaze away from the black eyes in front of him, focusing on that spark of emotion he recognized, that he could feel deep within his own chest. For a moment the leader hesitated as if he, too, had seen it, had recognized that feeling of desperate longing for a past to be forgotten. His fingers loosened the noose a small part of an inch.

Then the tall man came in with a glossy, taffy-colored horse, and the moment was broken. The leader pushed the knot back against George's throat, and with much shouting among themselves, the men managed to get George into the cracked leather saddle. Another man tied the rope off on the beam. Then, as if in slow motion, the horse was led forward. The rope scratched and tightened and George began to gasp for breath. Were they really going to hang him? He shifted, turning in the saddle, and hands were on him, pushing him back in place. Then the man halted the horse just before it was out from under George.

The leader looked up at him. "Dinero?"

"Kitchen...drawer." George gasped, telling the truth now and hoping they would let him down. They had to, didn't they?

"Si." The leader turned, leaving a round dent in the hay with his heel. The other five holstered their pistols and followed out the barn door, one catching the horse's reins and leading it away. Reaching the end of the rope, George was pulled back, over the cantle of the saddle, over the sleek rump of the horse, fine horse hairs pricking their way through his pants to his skin. The rope scratched George's neck and hooked on his chin, pushing his head up and back, and then it jerked, closing around his lungs, as his body hit air, swinging there in his own barn. George fought for a breath of air, just one, just so he could know what his last breath was and managed to get in a gulp of the dry, dusty, air. The last air Jimmy breathed would have been cold and wet with snow. George wondered which was better, a cold resignation creeping over him, like spider-webbing frost. This was it. This is where it all ended, where he paid his penance for the wrongs he'd done, paid his penance for not being the friend Jimmy needed.

The gold and scarlet sky showed through the open door, and an evening breeze whisked dirt and bits of grass into George's eyes. His breathing rasped after a long interval, and he closed his eyes, counting his last breath again. He heard the house door slam and then shouts of Spanish crashed through the barn walls along with the spinning and pounding of many horse hooves; it all seemed too loud.

George's thoughts jumbled in his head. Faces flashed through his mind: Julia, Jimmy, Sarah, Jack, Aurora, his father, Evan, Tib, Lizzie, Captain Tyler, a Sioux brave leaning back on his pony, faces of rangers whose names were erased from memory. He wanted to cover his face with his hands, as if by doing so he could hide from the faces in his memories, and as he reached up, his hands caught on the coarse rope around his neck. That's when it hit him that his hands weren't tied; they hadn't tied his hands. How had he missed that? And he held the sudden realization in his mind so tightly that it became almost his only consciousness, pushing away the merry-go-round of faces.

The rope stuck into his hands as he grasped it above his head. His arms flexed, strained, as he pulled. The rope loosened around his neck and he gulped air. This wasn't his last breath, it felt more like a first. With the strength of that breath he tried to work his left hand up higher, but his hands slipped. The rope tightened, burning his palms and chin, a shock of pain running up and down his spine. But that had been a first breath, not a last, and he had to make sure of that. He reached and pulled up again, fighting for another breath of air and sucking it into his lungs.

The air, cooler now, passed through his sweaty shirt to his skin, making goosebumps rise, but he didn't notice. All he knew was he had grasped the rope and, if he was strong enough, he had a chance to live. From outside came the sharp crack of a horse kicking the paddock fence and then the harsh squeal of displeasure from another. The low bawl of a mother cow floated in on another brush of wind. A window shutter slammed from the same breeze. George felt the nighttime groans of the barn through his hands. He knew this barn—he'd built it with these two hands—and it knew him; it wasn't going to let him die. He eased his hands higher on the rope, biting the inside of his cheek so hard in concentration that it began to bleed. The rope loosened again around his neck, and he took another breath.

If he could just get one hand on top of the beam. He held himself with his left hand, reaching above with his right until he felt the coarse beam. He smoothed his right hand against the side to the flat top and clung to it, then lifted himself. The rope went slack, slapping against his sweat soaked back. He clasped his left hand over the beam. A spasm of shivers ran over him. Desperation burned through his veins. What kind of desperation had Jimmy felt? Did he flinch? Was there a moment where he wanted to live? George wanted to, he had to, he had to make things right. He didn't have to pay penance, he had to make things right. Dying wouldn't make things right, only living could, but his arms ached. What if he wasn't strong enough?

The muscles in his arms stretched and tingled with the strain. His right hand scraped back, losing its grip on the beam. George closed his eyes again, his breath coming sharp and fast, beating out against the wind gusting through the door. Julia's beautiful, laughing face turned dizzily in his mind, and he knew he had to get down. He couldn't leave her; she needed him, and there were so many memories he wanted to make with her. Tears ran down his cheeks, and he wasn't sure if they were from the strain or from the realization that for the first time in a long time he wanted to create new memories.

In a sudden burst of will he held himself with his left arm, and with his right hand worked the noose until he could pull the loop over his head. The rope dropped, swinging below him. He grasped the top of the rope and let himself down hand over hand, dropping onto the barn floor. He lay on his back watching the ceiling spin. Specks of dust settled after being puffed up by the impact of his landing, and George blinked them out of his eyes. He was alive; he'd done it. He expected to feel more relief, but the sensation of the rope was still around his neck, and he put his hand against where the rope had pulled. The sweat on his palm stung the welt there and came away flecked with blood. The rope continued to swing, and George covered his eyes with his hands. He noticed he was shaking.

Early the next morning, George saddled Wet Blanket, the saddle seeming unusually heavy, and rode into Calabasas. The sun clasped the mesquite and turned the sand copper, playing with pieces of dust stirred by Wet Blanket's hooves. There were only a few people out when George rode into town. He touched the brim of his hat to them, trying to make it seem like any morning, but he felt jumpy as a new calf, and his whole body ached. Wet Blanket pranced and spooked at the noise of a housewife throwing dishwater out of a street side window. George spooked too, almost dropping one of his reins.

Tethering Wet Blanket in front of the general store, George went steadily in through the door that was propped open with a cow skull. He readjusted the bandana around his neck to cover the angry welt and rope burned skin there.

"Good morning, George," Charlie said, cheerfully. He continued measuring coffee beans into burlap sacks, the smell of them permeating the air. On any other day it would have made George go to the potbellied stove in the corner and pour himself a cup of coffee from the pot that lived there. Today he went straight to the counter.

"I need a pistol, Charlie." The words came harshly from George's lips.

Charlie looked closely at him, narrowing his eyes and drawing his thick eyebrows together. "Rustlers getting to your cattle?"

"No." George didn't offer any explanation. What would he say, I was hanged in my own barn? How did one go about telling that kind of story? He leaned against the counter, forcing himself to appear relaxed, even nonchalant, and said, "Do you have one?"

Charlie nodded, concern now mixing with the curiosity in his eyes, and reaching below the counter, pulled out a Frontier Six-Shooter. George took it and carefully turned it over in his hands.

"I'll take it," George said, even as his heart thudded at the weight, the smooth steel barrel of the pistol cold in his hand.

George saw the surprise in Charlie's face. "Alright," Charlie said after a space of silence that almost tipped into awkwardness. He wrote the purchase on a scrap of brown wrapping paper. Then said slowly, "I've never seen you with a gun. Why now?"

George ignored the question and jerked his head toward a dark leather gun belt that hung on the wall. "I'll take that, too," he said.

Charlie let out a huff of air, still watching George closely, and added the price of the belt to the price of the gun on the scrap of paper. "Is that all?" he asked.

"Can you put it on my account?" George asked. "I'm clean out of money at the moment."

Charlie nodded and clicked his tongue, as if he wanted to say something more, but he didn't.

George took the gun belt off the wall. He slid the six-shooter into the holster and slung the belt over his shoulder. Had pistols always been this heavy? He remembered the one he carried as a ranger as being lighter, almost weightless. Had pistols changed since then? "Thanks, Charlie," he forced himself to say and headed toward the door before any more uncertainty could catch up with him.

"You might want these." Charlie tossed a box of bullets to George.

George caught them and quickly stuffed them into his vest pocket as if they had burned his fingers. The rough-cut floorboards creaked as he crossed them to the door. He tipped his hat down to shade his eyes, to hide his face, and as he stepped out, Charlie called after him, "George, be careful, won't you?"

George didn't respond or turn back, but went out, letting the door swing shut on its own. He untied Wet Blanket and stepped into the saddle, loping out of town to the crossroads where he pulled up, letting the horse dance in place. He studied the tracks made by the men that he had followed from his ranch to the fork. George then looked down the trail that led home, a right angle to the men's retreat south. A bird whistled from a nearby cholla and in the distance dust rose from a cattle herd. What was he doing? He needed to think this through, come up with a plan for going after the men. And so, he loosened the reins and let Wet Blanket lope out toward home.

When he arrived, he tied the gelding and went into the house, through the kitchen door hanging crooked on its hinges from being opened with such force the night before. Sitting down in the chair with the crooked back, he took his hat off, slapping it onto the table. He pulled the gun from its holster and held it in his right hand, feeling its weight, trading the gun to his left hand, then back to his right. He fingered the trigger and stood up. If he pulled it a bullet would fly, and where would it go? Could a trigger really be pulled without any harm coming from it?

Looking out of the east-facing window, George could see the range of his ranch stretching out in a seemingly immeasurable distance. Memories came swimming into his mind, memories of pulling his pistol and taking aim, the smooth skin of the Indian no older than himself with eyes as brown and deep as a horse's. Had he pulled the trigger?

*He ran up the bank alongside the other rangers told to turn back and his foot slipped. He stumbled forward a few steps, but continued on. The sounds of the cavalry's small arms fire chased up the hill after him. Breathless at the top of the ridge, the rangers all turned as one and stared down into the trees along the creek. Flames shot up, burning down one teepee after another in bonfires the color of red and orange, yellow and black.*

George blinked until the memory became a dull throb in his ears. He leaned heavily against the sill and pressed his head against the frame, trying to clear his mind of the violence.

George straightened and looked at the gun resting across his palm. He put it back in its holster and stepped across the kitchen to the opposite wall. The flat end of a nail stuck out there and he hooked the belt on it. He turned and picked up his hat, knowing he just couldn't do it. Revenge wasn't what he wanted;

there was no point to it. He just wanted to know why. How could someone wish death? Why hadn't he said something to Jimmy? He should have shown Jimmy he understood. Without a second glance at the pistol, he stepped out into the sunshine. It softened his memories, but they didn't leave. They refused to.

# Chapter 24

George let Wet Blanket walk slowly and thought about how he would propose to Julia. He had always expected that when he asked her he would have a ring, but the ring was long gone, jingling in an outlaw's saddlebag, or perhaps being worn by the wiry leader of the band. It was time he asked, though. He needed to ask her, he felt it as staunchly as he'd felt the need to leave Colorado, so ring or no he was going to.

Should he use her full name or just her first name? Did it really matter?

Wet Blanket's head bobbed as he walked. Birds darted between mesquite branches, busy with their own lives. Lizards basked in the sun and disappeared in a flash when they heard the horse's hooves.

Should he tell her that her ring was stolen or just that it hadn't arrived yet? George took a deep breath. "Well," he said out loud, "let's just get there, huh?" Wet Blanket flicked his ear at the sound of George's voice. George tapped him in the ribs. Wet Blanket shot to attention with a snort and broke into a trot. George urged him into a lope, and soon they were riding down main street, a trail of red dust behind them.

"George!" Charlie hollered at him from the door of the store, and George slowed Wet Blanket. He supposed Charlie deserved an explanation, and so he pulled the gelding all the way to a halt.

"Charlie," he said, keeping his voice casual, as if nothing unusual had transpired between them.

Charlie came down the steps to stand by Wet Blanket's shoulder. "You okay, George?"

"Yes," George answered and meant it. He was okay now and felt ready to answer any questions.

Charlie rubbed the gelding's neck. "Good, good," he said, and cleared his throat. "A couple days ago I wasn't so sure. Something was wrong, wasn't it?"

George nodded and then found himself telling the whole story. As he spoke, Charlie didn't say a word, letting George get it all out. "I didn't go after them," George finished. "I couldn't."

Charlie shook his head. "How many men can say they've survived a hanging?" he said, then added in a more serious tone, "You should have told me before. I am your friend, you know. You were right not to go after them. One gun against six isn't great odds."

"Perhaps I should have said something," George agreed, and in saying so he knew that he would tell Julia the truth about her ring. She deserved to know the truth, even if it made her fuss.

"You're sure you're well?"

"Yes, more than well." George grinned at his friend—it felt good to acknowledge Charlie as a friend—and said, "I'm on my way to propose to Julia."

Charlie beamed. "That's great news! I knew you'd get around to it sometime, but was starting to wonder what was taking you so long. You'd better get going before you lose courage."

George chuckled and felt his face warm. "Thanks, Charlie."

Charlie stepped back and George clicked to Wet Blanket, moving on down the street. He felt lighter having told Charlie and now he knew how to tell the story.

It was simple really: he just had to speak, let the words come out. He hoped the words, "will you marry me," came out as easily.

George tied his horse to the hitching rail in front of Julia's along with a dozen other horses that ranged from groomed gambler's mounts to scruffy miner's ponies. He walked past them, pausing to cast a judging glance over a sturdy black with a white muzzle. He scratched the horse's forehead and moved on.

Julia was rushing to refill her customers' coffee cups. George skirted around the tables to the stove, on which a pot of stew simmered, and hunks of cornbread wrapped in flour sacks were on the doors of the warming ovens. The smell of the food was rich and inviting, and took him back to Sarah's kitchen when he, Jack, and his father, later Evan and Tib, would return from the masonry to the fragrance of venison roast that had been slow cooking on the stove all afternoon.

"George!" Julia set the coffee pot down with a clatter, before throwing her arms around his neck and giving him a kiss. "What brings you to town?" she asked.

He felt his face flush. He still wasn't used to her outright show of affection. He'd never met anyone before who wasn't embarrassed by showing how they felt even when other people were around. The unreservedness of her unnerved him and for a moment he couldn't remember what had brought him into town. "You," he said, answering her question just at the moment where it almost became too late to respond.

"Mind giving me a hand with that table for a minute?" Julia said, giving him a soft smile that he knew was his smile alone, "and then I'm all yours for a few."

"Not at all," he said, smiling back. He couldn't help but smile when he was around Julia, and he could almost forget the events of the past few days, could almost forget the persistent ghost of memories past. He took two bowls of soup from her hands, letting his fingers brush hers, setting his skin tingling in a way he'd never admit to anyone...well, maybe only to her.

"Well, you ain't as pretty as the gal that took our orders," a cowboy said when George set the stew down.

"No, but the stew's mighty good."

The cowboy laughed, and he and his companion fell to the stew with a quickness that spoke of many days on the trail, seeming to forget that anyone had brought it to them. A man at a neighboring table tipped his chair back, chewing on a toothpick. He wore a brown felt hat and an ivory-handled pistol strapped to his thigh. "Heard there's been some trouble with thieves 'round here," he said.

"I'm certain as much as any place," George said, feeling his spine involuntarily stiffen. "Do you need more coffee?"

"Yeah," the man said. "I heard talk in the next town over of gettin' up a posse. Seems there's a band that's takin' more than cattle."

"That so?" Before the man could respond, George turned away to get the coffee pot from the stove, remembering the even teeth of the leader of the men, and the scratch of rope on his neck. He could talk about it with a friend, but he wasn't going to talk about it with a stranger—not yet anyway. Julia needed to know before anyone else did. He heard Julia's laugh and the stiffness brought on by the man's words softened. Watching as she joked with a miner, her manner all ease, all cheerful, all trust, George knew it was her, he wouldn't be here, but for her. And she ought to be told.

George winced as Julia applied salve to the welt on his neck. "You could have been killed," she said, her voice cracked with emotion as if she were holding back tears or anger. George didn't look to see which, but he waved her hands away; he hadn't wanted to cause her this distress, and he didn't want to cause her any more. Even though he knew this was impossible, he felt an overwhelming impulse to shield her from everything, and it made him restless.

"It's fine, I'm fine," George said. He got up and went to the door, worrying his hat between his hands and noticing that those same hands still ached from the strain of pulling himself out of the noose. The town had quieted, and Wet Blanket stood alone at the hitching rail. His head was up, his ears forward, watching the world around him. He had one back hoof cocked, and his tail swished lazily at flies.

"I'm glad you didn't go after them." Julia touched George's shoulder, her voice quieter now, more leveled. "A ring isn't that important. I know you love me without it." Her breath warmed his ear as she leaned in closer.

She was right. Just because the ring had been stolen didn't mean they couldn't get married. He pivoted and caught her hands, struck by how well they fit into his. "I do, Julia, I do love you." His voice was deep with the emotion sweeping over him. He felt as if he were racing a summer thunderstorm across desert, unsure if he would beat the lightning to safety, and undeniably exhilarated by the race. "And even though I no longer have a ring to give you, will you, Julia? Will you marry me?"

Julia's eyes sparkled as if they'd been laced in crystals. "Of course," she said and let him pull her close. She stopped him just ahead of his lips brushing against hers. "I did think, though, that just telling me about the ring being stolen was your way of proposing," she teased. Before he could respond she closed the space between their lips, and George's ability to form coherent thought drifted away.

Three months later a column in the paper was headlined, "Santa Cruz Valley's first cattle rancher marries."

*Last Saturday, George Atkinson and Julia Jordon exchanged vows. It was a simple ceremony held at the Hotel Santa Rita and performed by the circuit preacher Thomas Lusk. The now Mrs. Atkinson wore a white cotton dress trimmed with lace her mother had made and had white lace in her hair. She carried a bouquet of mariposa lilies. Mr. Atkinson wore his best gray suit and took his hat off. Most of the town attended, as well as settlers of the surrounding area. A luncheon was served afterward consisting of roast beef, mashed potatoes, and an abundance of squash, as well as biscuits and four kinds of jam. A sugar pound cake was also served with sweet cream. It is said the recipe for the cake came from Mr. Atkinson's mother in Denver, Colorado. Mr. and Mrs. Atkinson are now living comfortably at Mr. Atkinson's ranch stead after a weekend honeymoon to Tucson, and Julia's Cafe is for sale. Rumor has it that the Dugan family are looking into its purchase.*

George folded the paper; he'd cut the column out later and send it to Sarah. He'd written to her and to Jack of his engagement, and both had sent back their congratulations. *Wish I could make it there to see you walk down the aisle,* Jack had written back. *Can't believe my little brother is soon to be a married man. Must feel good to beat me in that respect. As soon as I'm able, I'll come for a visit and meet this woman who has you gushing poetic phrases in your letters to me.* The letter had made George grin, and had also made him miss the camaraderie he and his brother had shared for so many years. Maybe it was still there, just in a different form than it had been growing up.

Sarah's letter had been full of congratulatory exclamations and motherly advice, as well as a note addressed to Julia, which had prompted Julia to write back and ask for Sarah's favorite cake recipe that she could use to make the wedding cake.

"Nice article," Charlie said, leaning across the counter.

"It covered most everything," George said, and with a grin added, "especially the food. Julia will be pleased, and that's what matters most." As he said the words he realized just how true they were. From now on that would be what mattered most, even though the thought left him feeling shaky. A sense of purpose, someone to cherish, to come home to, made him feel like he was finally living again.

"Take a look," George said, handing the paper to Julia. A smile crinkled her eyes as she read the article about their wedding.

"It was perfect," she said.

"Yes," George said, remembering how beautiful Julia was walking toward him across the lawn. The white lace tied in her hair, twirled around her bright cheeks with the flyaway curls that always framed her face. It was her eyes that were especially beautiful, full of sparkling light as though they had caught the entire Milky Way inside them. To come home every day to those eyes, this was what life was supposed to be. He drew Julia into his arms, the paper crumpling between them, and kissed her.

# Chapter 25

George patted the little bay mare on her withers, then rubbed his hands over her sides to where her stomach sunk between her hips and her ribs, indicating that the foal had dropped. She'd foal within the week, and George could already smell the sweet milky breath of the newborn foal. "It's one of the best smells in the world," he'd told Julia once, and Julia had smiled, saying, "You'll be a good father." He'd blushed and wondered when that time would come. Julia must have seen something of his thoughts cross his face, because she said, "We will have children, it just isn't the right time yet."

But they'd passed their first anniversary and still no baby cried or laughed, and George began to feel as if maybe they weren't meant to have children. Julia hadn't given up, though, and so he didn't voice his doubts. He wasn't going to be the one to smother her dreams. Now, as he rubbed the mare's sides, though, he couldn't help but wonder if there wasn't some truth to what Julia said. Maybe this would be the year that would bring the breath of their own child into the world. The mare let a whoosh of breath out her nostrils and cocked her left hind leg, her head lowering and ears relaxed back, so that she took on a donkey-like appearance.

George gave the mare one last pat and whistled for Wet Blanket. The gelding came trotting, ears perked forward, eyes bright and ready. George slipped the bit between the yellowing teeth and led the horse to the barn, where he saddled him. Then, at an easy lope, he rode the horse to the brickyard. He needed a load of 10,000 bricks made and ready to ship by the end of the week, and he was feeling the crunch of time. The kiln fire was burning hot when he arrived; Manuel, his apprentice, was already hard at work. Manuel was young, not much older than twenty, his round face holding an unmistakable youthful quality. He walked with an assurance, a confidence, though, that made him older, his strides long and deep, his back straight, shoulders squared, chin leveled; a man who was ready to take on whatever the world threw at him.

"Four thousand to go," Manuel said by way of greeting him.

"We might just get her done," George said, feeling relieved that they actually were making headway. The bricks were to be sent to Bigbee, a budding mining town to the east, and were to build a hotel which would be called The Copper Queen. The proprietor of this new hotel had stayed at the Hotel Santa Rita a month ago, and, complimenting the make of the bricks, had been sent down to George's brickyard by Colonel Sykes. George had taken the commission eagerly. Work had been trickling in at a slow speed; an order for five hundred bricks from Nogales, an order for a thousand bricks from the Peck ranch, another order from Nogales for eight hundred; all these orders coming in over the span of four months. When The Copper Queen order had come in, he'd tacked an advertisement in the store for an apprentice and bought a ham from Pete Kitchen to take home as a celebratory dinner.

George went to the office and checked the tallies Manuel had made. Four thousand bricks to go and then they could turn their attention to the growing stack of orders on the desk. The Copper Queen order had opened the tap, and they had enough work to keep them busy through the rest of the year. "Let's get two thousand pressed today," George said, feeling a sudden fire to work hard and long, "and if we do, come for dinner."

"It's a deal, boss," Manuel said.

Side by side the two men fell to work. They worked with an ease and quiet. Manuel had proved to be a quick learner, and George rarely had to provide correction, making their work go fast and smooth, like the way the Santa Cruz River ran just yards away. A silver cross on a strip of leather around Manuel's neck indicated an influence from the nearby missionary at Tumacacori, and once he mentioned a sister, but otherwise his life and past remained unknown to George. Still, George had grown to trust the young man and found him a good companion.

The day wore on and with the heat of the sun and the kiln fire, both men grew hot, sweat soaking their shirts, their faces red with the heat and exertion. George pushed bricks into the oven, then turned to Manuel. "Go cool off," he said, gesturing toward the river.

Manuel wiped his forehead and then the back of his neck with an already dirty handkerchief and nodded. "I won't take long," Manuel said.

"Take as long as you need." George rubbed his shoulder. "I'll be down in a moment to cool off myself." Just thinking about stepping into the river, he could feel a coolness sweep over him. A vermillion flycatcher dove after an insect and then landed on a stack of bricks on the edge of the yard, looking as if he owned the world, the wings of his prize sticking out of the sides of his beak.

The days moved on like this, in a rhythm that George found soothing, and every evening he returned to a dinner that always seemed like a celebratory meal because it was made by Julia's hands.

One such evening Julia said, "I was in town today," as she set the stew pot on the table. George could tell she was leading to something and waited for her to continue. He buttered his bread, watching her out of the corner of his eye. She was flushed and had undone the top buttons of her blouse. She sat down. He heard her breathe in sharply.

"I was in town today," she said again, making George smile, "and saw Kathy Dugan. She looked tired. I thought, maybe, we could take the boys for a week, give her a break."

George nodded. The boys, Thomas and Samuel, were seven and three years old. Their half-sister Kathy had been thrust into the role of mother a year ago when their own mother died. Kathy was seventeen, running a cafe, caring for two young boys with a barely present father, and all of this took its toll. George thought about the last time he had seen the boys. Samuel played in the dirt track in front of the cafe, his clothes, hands, and face coffee-brown with grime and sun, his black hair overdue for a trim. Thomas hovered at the hitching post, and George thought he saw him pull a leather string from a saddle, but couldn't be sure, so he hadn't brought it up to anyone. The boy's face was hard, like someone much older, and reminded George of someone, but he couldn't put his finger on who.

"I don't know, Julia," George said. "They're rough, they're..."

"They're motherless," Julia said, her Irish stubbornness edging its way into her voice.

"They speak Spanish."

"They also speak English. They do, after all, talk to their sister."

George felt a little ashamed for using their Spanish as a point to not take them in, but it was the first thing that came to mind. Julia would get her way, they'd take the boys in, but he had to let her know that he didn't feel right about this. "I don't trust Thomas."

"George, he's a seven-year-old boy!"

"He steals."

"He needs guidance, that's all."

"Are you sure you could manage them?"

"All they need is some love." Julia caught his eyes. Hers were deep, gray, earnest, and they looked right into him. He couldn't say no, and he knew better than to try.

"Alright, yes, we can take them for a week. Just a week."

Julia smiled. "Good. I'd kiss you, but you need a wash first."

George laughed. Once he had wondered if he'd ever laugh again; Julia had sent that worry into the past, and although the pangs of memories still haunted him at times, coming to him in often unexpected moments, he felt he'd turned the corner to happiness. And maybe there was enough happiness, enough love to share with two young boys.

Kathy handed a squirming Samuel up into the wagon. Julia pulled him into her lap, cuddling him in spite of the dirt, until he calmed and sat playing with a small piece of fabric he clutched in his hand.

"Thomas," Kathy called, "come, Mr. and Mrs. Atkinson are waiting."

"No," Thomas said, not looking up from where he was drawing in the dirt with his bare toes. His smooth black hair fell across his forehead, hiding his eyes, but not the tautness of his mouth or the sharp set of his jaw.

Kathy sighed and brushed at her hair, which was curly and brown and could have been pretty if stress hadn't stolen its luster. Her shoulders sank and George could tell she was resigned. She was tired of trying to get Thomas to behave, and why shouldn't she be? She hadn't asked for two young boys to be left in her care, boys of a Mexican mother whom she never understood. Or was he presuming too much? He didn't really know that she didn't speak Spanish, and she could have loved her stepmother. He loved his stepmother. If he admitted it, he loved her more than his real mother, but he tried not to think about that. When he did, he ended up feeling guilty, desperately trying to bring the few memories he had of his mother to the forefront. He wished he could see them fully, but they always remained like clouds readily blown away.

"Come," Julia said, "we have horses, a new foal, and I'm making a pudding tonight." Julia's voice was coaxing, as if she were trying to convince a stray dog to take a tidbit from her hand.

Thomas moved toward the wagon. Relief spread across Kathy's face, and Julia kept talking until Thomas got in. "There, we go," she said. "We will have fun, I promise."

"Thank you," Kathy said. "Thomas, Samuel, be good." Lines creased her forehead and her eyes were red. She could have had pretty eyes, deep emeralds, if they weren't so tired. She stood with her hand on the side of the wagon as though she didn't really want them to leave.

"They'll be okay," George said, suddenly feeling that he and Julia were doing the right thing. "It's just for a week. Let you catch your breath."

Kathy nodded. "I know, I know." She swallowed, and George hoped she wasn't going to cry. He never knew what to do when people cried.

Julia smiled at her and said, "I'll take good care of them."

Kathy composed herself. "Yes," she said. She stepped back from the wagon and waved at the boys. Thomas slung his legs over the back of the wagon and gazed at the ground below his swinging feet. "Hold on," Julia told him and then in a lower voice to George, "Let's go."

"Alright then," George said. He clicked to the team, who startled from their doze and moved out at a slow trot. Their hooves clopped on the packed dirt of the road, and the wagon creaked. Julia held onto Samuel tightly and kept one eye on Thomas the entire drive back to the ranch. She had taken on the care of these boys and she had taken it on fully.

"Thomas, finish your porridge," Julia said, "then go out and help George." The sun was already coming in the kitchen window, making the room even warmer along with the heat from the stove, the fire in it built up to cook breakfast. Breakfast took longer with the two young boys, between getting them to the table, making sure they ate and put their dishes in the sink, and washed their faces before going about the day's activities.

Thomas picked up his spoon and let the porridge drip from it in clumps. "No." Thomas pushed his bowl away from him. "No lo quiero." His face was stoic, his lips pinched together in a straight line.

"English, please," said Julia, pushing his bowl back to him. She spoke softly, with a patience that George marveled at; he could never be that patient.

"No, no lo quiero," Thomas said, louder this time.

"Don't raise your voice," George intercepted. He and Julia had agreed that she was in charge when the boys were in the house, after a couple days of crossed signals, but he couldn't let Thomas speak in that manner. Julia coughed. George wasn't sure if it was a cough to remind him of their agreement or not, but he turned to her. Their eyes met and George still wasn't sure of the meaning of the cough, but he mouthed, "Sorry," in case he had over-stepped what they had agreed.

Thomas hit the table with his fist, catching the edge of his bowl and spraying the contents. For a moment the only sound was the bowl spinning on the table. Samuel's dark, luminous eyes widened and began to fill. His mouth was full and oats clung to the corners and his lips began to tremble.

George stood, overstepping or not, he couldn't let this outburst go unchecked. "Come with me, Thomas." He reached for Thomas's hand. Thomas pulled it away, shouting, "No! Dejame ir, no me toques! Tu no eres mi padre! Estupido! Estupido!"

Samuel began to cry and Julia scooped him up, trying to shush him. She looked at George over the top of Samuel's head, her eyebrows drawn together, her lips tight, and George knew she was worried that they weren't going to last the week. George gripped Thomas's hand and they left the kitchen.

Thomas dug in his heels, twisting and trying to pull away, until George was practically dragging him, but George didn't stop walking until he got to the barn. Once there he let go of Thomas's hand and said, "I'm not going to whip you."

Thomas straightened and for the first time looked directly at George with dark eyes that hid emotion well. "Why not?" he asked, speaking the first English words George had heard from him.

George picked up a pitchfork and handed it to Thomas. "You can start with these stalls," he said, motioning to the four stalls within the barn, "and then the chicken coop. I don't want you to stop, until all are clean, do you understand?"

Thomas nodded.

"Good." He opened the first stall and stood leaning on the gate until Thomas began to stab at the manure, lifting and pitching it into a wheelbarrow. "I'll be in the corral when you are done," George said. He left Thomas alone in the barn, hoping that the boy would do the job and not run off. He was nervous, wondering if he had done the right thing. Thomas had spoken though, in English, directly to him. That had to mean something. Still, as he haltered the new filly he was breaking, he couldn't help but glance back at the barn, expecting to see Thomas running from it.

"I'm done," Thomas said. He climbed the corral fence where George was still working with the new filly. It had been nearly two hours since George had left Thomas in the barn, and in that time George had resisted the urge to check on the boy. He had worked the filly slower though, so that he could stay alert to the world outside the round pen. A sense of relief passed over him when he saw Thomas come to the fence, but he kept his focus on the filly, not wanting to show that he was watching and waiting for the boy.

George pulled the cinch tight on the filly. He could feel the filly's stomach expand against it and he pulled tighter. Once the air was out of the filly's stomach, he didn't want the saddle to slip. The filly responded by nipping at George's pants. George ignored it and let her loose, shooing her away. The filly jumped away, all four feet leaving the ground at the same time. When she landed, she stood shaking by the fence, her head high, her eyes glued on George. George turned away and walked over to where Thomas was sitting on the fence. He climbed up and sat beside the boy.

"See that filly?" George asked. "She wants to be close to me, but I can't let her yet. She has to accept the saddle first."

"Why?"

"It's about understanding, understanding that you don't have to be afraid of new things."

"She looks scared."

"She's still learning. Soon she won't notice it at all."

They sat there in silence. The filly settled, lowering her head and lipping at some grass. George glanced at the boy beside him. Thomas stared soberly ahead, no creases on his face to suggest any sort of smile. The expression was too old to be on the face of a boy that young. George wondered how he could make this dark, hard little boy smile. He reached out and patted Thomas's knee. Thomas didn't move, staring intently at the filly.

"How would you like a horse of your own?" George said, surprising himself by asking such an impractical question. The boys were only here for a week, yet somehow he seemed to forget that for a moment.

Thomas shrugged. "Si, supongo," he said, slipping back into Spanish, but George understood it as an affirmative that he would like a horse. The filly took a few steps. "She's ready," George said. He jumped from the fence and clicked to the filly, who turned toward him, stepping gingerly across the space between them. She bobbed her head and George scratched her wide white face.

"Her," Thomas said.

"What?"

"Her."

"Full sentence, please," George said. He tied a rope to the filly's halter and led her over to Thomas. He knew that Thomas meant that he wanted the filly to be his, but he needed to hear Thomas ask.

"Can she?" Thomas shifted, his eyes darting, refusing to focus on any one thing. "Can she be, ser mio?"

George smiled. "Yes," he said, "yes. Come down and meet her."

Thomas jumped off the fence. The filly snorted and backed up. "Move slowly," George said. "Horses startle easily, especially young ones."

Thomas nodded and took a step away. The filly lowered her head, her ears twitching.

"Go ahead. You can pet her," George said.

"Name?" Thomas asked as he stroked the filly's nose.

"You can name her."

"Magdalena," Thomas said with certainty. The filly lowered her head, nibbling at Thomas's shirt. George waited for the boy to smile or laugh, but Thomas didn't. Instead he scratched the filly's cheek, his fingers becoming gray with dust.

"Magdalena it is," George said.

"Magdalena, ella es una buena chica. Ella es una buena potra. Ella crecera grande y fuerte y correra libre y salvaje. Ella es una bonita potra, una bonita potra." Thomas's voice was quiet, calming, and the filly closed her eyes, leaning her forehead into his hand, her ears flickering back.

George felt something well in his chest. He wasn't sure at first what the feeling was, but then he recognized it as pride. And along with it came the beginnings of a new understanding for his father.

"I gave Thomas the new filly," George told Julia, as she cleaned the kitchen after dinner. The boys had been put to bed, so they had the evening to themselves. George looked forward to this part of the day and poured himself a cup of coffee. It steamed and he breathed in the fragrance. The smell of coffee always soothed and steadied him.

"You did?"

George couldn't tell if she approved or not from her tone, and her back was turned so he couldn't see her face. "I thought it'd help."

"I think you did right," Julia said. She turned and smiled at him. "I knew this would be good, for him, for us."

George sighed with relief. He wasn't sure he had done the right thing, but now he was. It was good. Having something to care for would be good for Thomas, and he voiced this aloud.

Julia nodded. "It will be. It'll occupy him, maybe make him a boy again."

"He is a boy."

"Not really. He's forgotten that he is a child and can be happy." Julia wiped down the kitchen table, then straightened, breathing in shakily. "Pour me a cuppa, won't you?"

George poured her coffee, handing the cup carefully to her and listening to her breathing. She sipped the coffee and after a moment her breathing became less audible.

"He named her Magdalena," George said.

"Pretty, very pretty. It fits her."

"It does." George topped off their cups.

"I wish I knew what their mother called them," Julia said, her voice wistful, her eyes watching the steam float up from her cup.

"Thomas and Samuel?"

"She had to have had her own names for them. I think it'd make them feel more at home if I knew."

"We can ask Kathy," George said "She'll know."

Julia sighed and rubbed her neck, seeming to be thinking of some memory of her own. George wondered what it was, but he didn't ask, knowing she needed him to reassure her at the moment, not ask her to share her memories.

"They've only been here three days. You'll figure it out," he said gently, then remembered that they only had four more days left and worried that she wouldn't figure it out by then. A week was too short, it really was.

"I think," Julia began and then she stopped, focusing on her coffee cup. George waited. He didn't like rushing people into what they were saying. There didn't seem to be a point to doing that. It just made people flustered and forget what they were saying, creating unnecessary confusion and discomfort.

"I think," Julia began again. "I think we should adopt them."

George gulped his coffee, then set it down. He went to the window, looked out at the darkness, and shoved his hands deep into his pockets. Somehow he had expected this, but in another way he hadn't wanted her to bring it up. The sky outside the window had darkened with clouds. It would rain in the night, but with any luck the sun would be shining in the morning and maybe there would be something that would make Thomas smile. George was determined to see the boy happy, and deep down he felt that they could do some good for these boys. But to adopt them?

"George?"

"What about Kathy?"

"She's not ready to be a mother."

"But to let her brothers go?"

"I think she would. Besides, she could visit."

George nodded, although he wasn't fully convinced. He could feel Julia's eyes on him, but he refused to meet them. If he did, they would break him too easily, and he'd agree to talk to Kathy.

Small footsteps sounded in the doorway. "Ju'ya, you sing?" Samuel asked. His raven-black hair had a slight curl to it that gave his features a rounder, even younger appearance, and it was tousled, belying his restless attempts to fall asleep.

Julia went and gathered him up. "What are you doing up?" she said and disappeared with him down the hall. George smiled. Julia would be a good mother. But their discussion wasn't over. He didn't need to look in her eyes to know that.

# Chapter 26

"They can stay another week," George said. He stood in the doorway, watching Thomas and Samuel as they ran to gather eggs. Thomas swung the basket high above his head and whooped. "Oye, oye!" he shouted, and the chickens squawked, running and flapping their wings. Samuel flapped his arms in imitation, his bare feet kicking up dust.

"Another week is good," Julia answered. She came to stand at his elbow, brushing her cheek on his shoulder, as if she had an itch. There was something about the way she did this that made George feel warm through.

"I'll ride in and talk to Kathy," he said.

"There's no need. She said it'd be okay."

George turned so he could look squarely at Julia. "When?"

Julia folded a dish towel and placed it over the back of a chair, smoothing the wrinkles in the cloth carefully. "Kathy," Julia began and then she stopped. She rolled the corner of the towel between her thumb and forefinger. "When I first talked to her about taking the boys," Julia began again, "there was no end time."

"No end time?"

Julia nodded. "They're here as long as…"

"Forever," George interrupted her. "They're here forever."

"If we want them to be."

"Is that what you want?"

Julia took a deep breath and met his gaze, her eyes clear and determined. "Yes."

George held her gaze for a moment, reading her emotions, feeling them tip him into agreeing. But it was a big step; it wasn't just changing their lives for a few weeks, it was changing their lives forever, and forever was a long time. His pulse quickened with the thought, the responsibility, also something close to excitement, and he turned to watch the boys in the yard. Samuel carried an egg cupped in both of his hands and tiptoed to Thomas. He placed it in the basket as though it were something about to break. Thomas swung around in a circle, the basket getting higher as he picked up speed. George remembered doing the same as a boy, feeling the pull of the basket, and spinning until he fell, laughing, to the ground. He waited for Thomas to do the same, but Thomas stopped spinning and stood looking beyond the barnyard at the desert spotted in mesquite and cholla and tough grasses creating a mosaic of browns and reds and greens.

George wondered what Thomas was seeing, what he was thinking, and thought, laugh, just laugh. And then he knew that he wanted these boys to stay; he wanted to be there when Thomas laughed.

"Okay," he said. "They can stay."

Julia smiled. "Good," she said. She went to the stove and flipped the flapjacks browning in the cast-iron. "Call the boys in?"

Work at the brickyard had piled up in his week-long absence. George read through the orders stacked on his desk and arranged them in order of importance, then took out a clean sheet of paper and carefully printed, "HELP WANTED: Looking for an able-bodied man for work at a brickyard. Direct interest to George Atkinson."

"Manuel," he called as he stepped out of the office, "take this to the general store and have Charlie post it."

Manuel took the paper and scanned the words on it. "Yes, boss," he said. "It'd be good to have help."

"Sorry I haven't been around much lately."

"Understand you've had your hands full."

George nodded. He picked up a brick and rubbed its edges, which were simultaneously rough and smooth. The feel of it took him back to the ruins of the brick city he'd come through. Was that already years ago? A wish that he had stayed longer, that he had wandered through what was left of each home, that he had taken more time to sit and understand the place lingered in his mind. And at the edge of that wish he could feel the ghost of Jimmy. It made him catch his breath and reach out to the empty space Jimmy had left behind him, finding that it wasn't as gaping as it once had been, which in turn made him feel uneasy, as if he were letting the space fill too quickly.

"Kids change things," Manuel commented, his tone indicating he knew that kind of change. George glanced at him. "You think your life is all in place, that you have everything you want and then the kid comes along. Nothing in place no longer, but now, now you have everything."

"You have kids?" George asked.

Manuel grinned and nodded. "One. She just turned a year. Walking now." He scratched his jaw and resettled his hat. "Now that's something." The deepness of his voice told of the love he had for his daughter without him even having to say the words. George wondered if he would ever speak with such love about Thomas and Samuel; could it be possible that one day he would feel that way about them, that he could love these boys as if they were truly his flesh and blood? What if he couldn't? That worry joined the worry of forgetting Jimmy too quickly, rubbing together in his mind, until it seemed they might catch fire.

The friction of his worries still smoldered in his mind as George rode out to check the cattle that evening. At the top of a rise the cattle came into view, and he pulled Wet Blanket to a halt. The cattle grazed calmly, switching their tails at flies and every so often raising their heads. One large cow with a full udder noticed George and Wet Blanket. She lifted her nose, testing the air in their direction, and then bawled long and low, calling her new calf. The calf unfolded itself from where it slept under a scrubby manzanita. The white of its face and legs were stunningly bright in the sun, and its sides weren't filled out yet. It ran to the cow's side and nosed along her belly until it finally found a teat and settled to suckling.

George leaned forward on the saddle horn, watching the cows and counting them slowly, making a mental note of three new calves. Wet Blanket shifted his weight, and George lost count as a small, yellow-faced songbird flitted by. He started counting again, but then started composing a letter to Sarah.

*Dear Sarah,*

*How long did it take you to love Jack and me? I remember you as fitting right in, an instant part of our family, but did you? Was it hard to bond with me, with Jack?*

George sat straight and gathered the reins, clicking to Wet Blanket. Wet Blanket jumped to attention and started down the hill. He sank heavily on his haunches to keep his hooves under himself. The cows moved together, each momma finding her calf, nuzzling them and lowing softly.

*Julia and I have taken in two young boys. At first it was temporary, but now they are here indefinitely. Julia has taken them in completely as if they are her own children. I'm unable to, though. I can't seem to find a way in, especially with Thomas, the oldest. He pushes me away, hiding behind his Spanish, refusing to speak English, when I have explicitly told him to.*

"Maybe," George muttered, "maybe we should send them to school." In school they would be forced to speak English. It could be good for them, but the school was so far away. It would take too much of the day to get them there and back. Julia might be willing to take them. Could he persuade her it would be best for the boys?

George guided Wet Blanket around the edge of the herd, starting to count them again. He came to the full count of seventy-nine, then added the three new calves. Eighty-two. He broke a twig from a manzanita and scratched the number on his wrist. He'd write it in his log book when he got back to the house. He turned the red twig in his fingers, thinking about the name of the shrub. Manzanita. It was Spanish, he knew, and as he turned the word over in his mind, he wondered what it meant. To him it meant a shrub with red wood and bark that the cattle used to scratch on and calves slept under, but the word must have some other meaning. "I wish I knew what their mother called them," Julia had said. At the time, he hadn't understood, but now he did, at least a little. The boys, like the tree, had other names, other meanings, and if he could find those meanings, well... He turned Wet Blanket around. "Home, boy," he said.

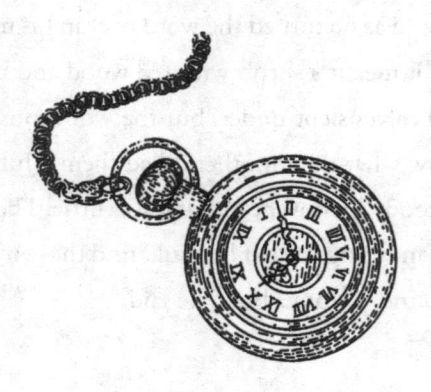

# Chapter 27

E vening fell in long shadows, like ribbons cut from a dark sky with no clouds. It came with quietness that reached through the walls of the house and into George's mind. He closed his eyes and leaned back in his chair, listening to the click-click, click-click of Julia's rocker, the only sound of the evening. His memory wandered to times playing checkers with Jack in the cool autumn evenings. John had taught them both to play. He remembered how the checker pieces scratched across the board. It had been a long time since he'd played checkers. Maybe he'd teach Thomas to play, but first he'd have to make a board and pieces, maybe out of manzanita wood. He began to doze, his thoughts soft like a wet newspaper, its type washing together.

George woke to Julia gently shaking his shoulder. "Come to bed, dear," she said.

He stretched and smiled, touching her warm cheek with the back of his hand. She kissed his forehead. "You were dreaming," she said. "Want to tell me about it?"

George took her hands in both of his, thinking about his dream. Jimmy was there. It had been a long time since he had dreamt about Jimmy, and Jimmy's face was blurry. He kept trying to get closer to bring Jimmy's face into focus, but he never could get close enough, he couldn't even get close enough to hear Jimmy's voice. What if he forgot the sound of Jimmy's voice? What if he forgot what Jimmy looked like? What if he forgot everything about him? The thought made him shiver, left him feeling clammy like after a fever has passed. He couldn't forget. Jimmy deserved more than that. "I don't remember," he told Julia.

"Alright," Julia said, but her tone told him that she didn't believe him.

"It wasn't much of a dream," he said, standing. "Come, it's late." Once in bed though, George couldn't sleep. He lay staring at the ceiling and listening to Julia's breath fall into the evenness of deep sleep. His life was coming together and somehow that made him restless, almost as though he didn't fully deserve it. He slid out of bed and went to the bureau, opening the top drawer and taking out Jimmy's silver watch. At first he'd kept the watch in his pocket, the weight of it somehow comforting. Then it became too heavy, and he put it away in the bureau drawer. When it was there he didn't have to think about Jimmy, didn't have to think about Sand Creek, didn't have to think about Lizzie, or how he'd avoided her and kept the watch when she was the one who really should have it. He opened it and tried to read the inscription, but the moon wasn't casting enough light into the room. He didn't need to read the words though. He knew what they were by heart. *My sunshine forever.*

With the morning sun, George shook off the dream of the night before, refocusing himself on the boys and Julia. He brought in an armload of dry, round wood for the kitchen stove, dropping it in the wood box just as Julia came in tying her apron, the same stained and mended apron she'd been wearing the first time he saw her. She smiled. "Thank you, George," she said and then continued, "You were restless last night."

"I thought I'd ride over to the school," George said, avoiding the unsaid question hanging in the air. "Check the distance. It might be good for the boys to go."

Julia bit her lip. "It might be better for them to stay put."

"School would help their English."

"Maybe. It just..." Julia broke off and picked up the water bucket, heading for the door. George followed her. He wanted to ask her "just what?" but waited, hoping she'd voluntarily continue. The morning was still, the kind of silence that preceded a burst of noise and energy. The birds that had sung to announce the new day had become quiet in reverence and worship of the rising sun, but they'd soon brighten the air again with their music, just as soon as light fully hit the land.

"They need to know English," George said.

"Maybe we should know Spanish," Julia answered, pumping water. The water splashed cold and glittering into the bucket. It reminded George of a waterfall he and Jack had found once, shortly after they moved to Colorado.

*Early one morning, Jack and George caught the wagon horses and rode bareback into the mountains, ducking under pine branches, and whooping wildly. Coming around the edge of a jagged rock that stood like a watchtower, they entered a gully, the bottom of which ran with a clear stream. They rode upstream and came upon the source, a spring pouring from the rocks in a glimmering waterfall. They drank from it, and it was the best water George had ever tasted.*

As he remembered, he could almost taste that water again: it had been so pure and fresh and clean, as if everything in the world were perfect, or would be if the whole world could drink that water. They had sworn to never tell anyone else about it, a secret between brothers, and it made the spring that much more special. A desire for Thomas and Samuel to have the chance to make such memories washed over him, but if he couldn't get Thomas to speak with him, he didn't see how this could happen.

"English is more important," he said, finally.

"Do you think?" Julia straightened, her hands on her hips, gazing towards the river. "Go to the school and see what it's like," she said, "but don't force the boys. We might have to meet them halfway." She picked up her full water bucket and walked back to the house. George watched her; she stepped so lightly even with the weight of a water bucket. Then he went to the barn and saddled Wet

Blanket. If he was going to get to the school in time for the beginning of classes, he needed to leave right away. Wet Blanket danced. Cool mornings always made him younger, and George couldn't help admiring the gelding's movements, even when Wet Blanket came close to stepping on George's feet. George pressed his palm on the gelding's shoulder, feeling the warmth and energy there. This is what it meant to be alive. He wished he could give this feeling to Thomas, but they needed a common language to do that. English must be that language. Spanish couldn't be...could it?

The school was a squat adobe house. George imagined that it had once held a family, picturing dark-haired children with round bellies and mangy dogs keeping watch around herds of gray and white sheep. Now though, the house was converted into a school with windows knocked into the walls and a bell hanging by the door. George tied his horse beside the group of animals already tied to the hitching rail, watching a tall Mexican boy hobble his donkey with a strap of what looked like flour sacking. Children ran around the building, shouting and laughing, their black and brown and blonde hair tousled, their bare feet and legs dusty. These were the children of homesteaders, of squatters, miners, and migrant workers. Children born and raised in the dust or on the move, toughened by circumstance, but still children, children who knew how to play, laugh, and just be in the world. George made his way to the door, knocking gently as he opened it. "Hello?"

The schoolmistress, a small woman with tight facial features, turned. "Hello," she said. "What can I do for you?"

George strode forward, holding out his hand. "My name's George Atkinson," he said. "I was wondering if I could observe."

The schoolmistress shook his hand, her own hard and bony. "Miss Ellen Oberly. Are you with the school board?"

"No. I have two young boys who speak mostly Spanish. I'd like them to go to school, but wanted to observe the teaching first, if that's okay?"

"Yes. Most of my students are Spanish speaking. Of course, the goal is to get them speaking English." Miss Oberly's manner was brusque. "Please, take a seat in the back," she ordered, making a shooing motion with her hand.

George nodded and sat on the bench along the back wall. He leaned against the cool adobe wall as Miss Oberly rang the bell. Children came pushing and stumbling over the threshold and took their seats at the makeshift desks in a slightly orderly, slightly chaotic manner.

"Silence." Miss Oberly's sharp voice commanded silence more firmly than the strictest general. A little girl in front with long black pigtails whispered something to her seatmate in Spanish. Miss Oberly cracked the girl's desk with her ruler. "English," she snapped. The girl winced away.

"Class, open your readers," Miss Oberly said, "to page ten." She stood firmly at the front of the room. "Miguel, read the first line aloud."

The Mexican boy who'd hobbled the donkey stood and read in a clear, even voice, "A fat hen. A big rat."

Miss Oberly nodded. "Antonio, the next line."

In a similarly clear manner, Antonio read, "The fat hen is on the box." Again Miss Oberly nodded. "Good, good," she said.

These boys read English well. George was impressed. Thomas and Samuel could learn so much coming to school; just see how these children were reading without any hesitation. Even the smallest children were reading correctly, George thought as the little girl in front stood and read with only a slight lisp, "The rat ran from the box."

Miss Oberly wrote, "Can the hen run?" on the blackboard. "Class, copy this question onto your slates," she told the children. Every child in the room bent over their slates and the only sound was their chalk scritching and Miss Oberly's shoes tapping slowly between the desks as she checked their work. George stood to look over the shoulder of the boy closest to him and saw even letters, carefully copying the question on the board. He sat back, satisfied and pleased by what he saw.

At recess, George stood stroking Wet Blanket's nose, listening to the children's chatter. He was disappointed to hear most of it was in Spanish, even though the last words Miss Oberly had said before letting them loose were, "Remember, only English during recess." Why weren't they speaking English? The boy called Antonio ran to the hitching rail after a ball that had gotten away. "Hello, Antonio, isn't it?" George said.

The boy looked at him with widened eyes that reminded George of Thomas's, the ball at his feet.

"Do you like school?" George asked.

Antonio continued to stare at him.

"School." George gestured to the schoolhouse. "Do you like school?"

Antonio picked up the ball and ran back to his friends, speaking to them in Spanish. One of the other boys ran just beyond the schoolhouse, then turned and held his hands up. Antonio threw the ball to him, shouting, "Coger!"

Something wasn't translating to these children. They could read and write in the classroom, but outside Spanish prevailed. Miss Oberly seemed to command such obedience, and yet English was scarce, making George wonder if they were learning anything. They could parrot the lessons, but did they actually understand?

Miss Oberly approached him. "Mr. Atkinson, will I see your boys?" she asked.

"Do you know any Spanish?" George asked in return.

Miss Oberly laughed, a short, bitter laugh. "No. The children need to learn English. I don't need to learn Spanish."

"How do you know they can understand you?"

"They will learn to. If they want to live here, they will learn to."

These had been his own arguments to Julia, but hearing them come from someone else, he heard how false they were. Maybe Julia was right. Maybe he did need to learn Spanish. How could they expect the children to learn English if they didn't try to learn Spanish as well? They needed to meet on some common ground, didn't they? Wouldn't that make things easier for everyone?

# Chapter 28

"Charlie, do you know any Spanish?" George asked, setting a bag of sugar on the counter. It had been a few days since he'd observed Miss Oberly's school, and he'd continued to mull over the merits of making the boys learn English or learning to speak Spanish himself. He worried that he wouldn't be able to learn a different language, but what if the boys couldn't either?

"Un poco," Charlie said, laughing a bit sheepishly as if he were a child caught telling a white lie.

"Do you think it helps?"

"With what?"

"Your communication," George said. "I've been thinking it might help me with the boys, Thomas and Samuel."

"You thought about sending them to school?"

"Yes, but the school..." George trailed off, trying to find words that would be less judgmental. "I don't think it is teaching English. The children repeat what the teacher says in class, but outside they still speak Spanish. They aren't learning the meanings of English words."

"That's a strong opinion," a man coming up beside George said. "Herbert Brown. I'm the owner of *The Arizona Weekly Citizen*. Would you mind elaborating on your thoughts about the school system?"

"You want to print my opinion?" George asked, stepping back and looking Herbert Brown up and down. The man was stocky, broad-shouldered and bushy-bearded. He had the keen expression of an observer, one who was always looking for a story, or for someone to state an opinion he was interested in.

"Yes. People want to hear the opinions of residents. It's important." Herbert Brown took a small notebook from his pocket, along with a stub of lead pencil, quickly ready to take notes as only a reporter could be.

"To who? You?"

"To everyone," Herbert Brown said. "What's your name?"

"George, George Atkinson," George responded automatically, and Herbert Brown wrote down his name.

"Think about it, George. Like I said, people are interested in citizens' opinions. I'm staying at the hotel. Come find me when you want to talk."

Charlie grinned at George as Herbert Brown left the store. "You know how to catch attention," he said, shaking his head.

George tried to make light of things by laughing. "Not something I always enjoy," he said, then asked, "Do you think it helps?" bringing the conversation back to the original discussion.

"It helps. Less misunderstanding."

George nodded. "Some common ground."

"Yes."

"It's important," George said, more to himself than to Charlie, as he thought things through. "Think I'll go talk to that reporter."

"I knew you would," Charlie said. "You know you'd make a good politician."

"Now that's where I draw the line." George left the store and crossed the street to the hotel. He was surprised by how quickly he'd come to the decision to share his opinion, but then he'd changed a lot in the last few weeks, and anything was worth it to help get closer to understanding the two little boys living under his roof.

In the *Arizona Weekly Citizen* the next week his words appeared in the local news column:

*Of the use of Spanish in the public schools, George Atkinson from Calabasas, tells of an experience of his own. He visited the closest school recently. Most of the children were Mexican and he wanted to see how the law of the territory, that all children be taught in English, was working. He was astonished and pleased at their progress. They could take up a reader and go through their exercises with the utmost correctness. And spell—they could spell the words with precision and correctness. His pleasure changed though, when he found they were no better at practical English than before. Their acquirement was only parrot English. They would say the words, or spell them, but had little or no idea of their significance. "There is one thing sure," says Mr. Atkinson, "They ought to learn English but they haven't got the right way yet. In Calabasas district $8000 has been expended on the school, and yet there is only one Mexican boy there who speaks English."[1]*

Julia folded the paper and handed it back to George, her expression pleased, a glitter of "I told you so" in her eyes. But instead of saying so she pointed to an ad next to the column. "Next time you're in town see if you can't get some of that breakfast cocoa?" she asked. "I want to make a treat for the boys." The ad stated: *Unlike the Dutch Process No Alkalies or Other Chemicals are used in the preparation of W. Baker & Co's Breakfast Cocoa, which is absolutely pure and soluble. It has more than three times the strength of Cocoa mixed with Starch, Arrowroot or Sugar, and is far more economical, costing less than one cent a cup.*

1. Italics directly quoted and paraphrased from article in *The Arizona Weekly Citizen* 1894.

*It is delicious, nourishing, and EASILY DIGESTED. Sold by Grocers everywhere. W. Baker & Co., Dorchester. Mass.*[2]

"I'll see if Charlie carries it," George said, wondering what she thought of his words printed there adjacent to the cocoa ad. He was about to ask when she reached over and squeezed his hand. He knew before she said it, that she was proud of him.

"Brick," Manuel said, "el ladrillo." He and George were sitting on a bench in front of the brickyard office where a swath of shade was cast by the building. From the bench they could look up Main Street and watch the activity of the town, visitors and locals weaving around each other in a way that made George think of an anthill. He used to study them as a boy, lying on his stomach and poking them with stems of grass.

"El ladrillo," George repeated, attempting and failing to roll the "r."

Manuel smiled, something that had become more frequent as the two men got to know each other more through the Spanish lessons each day when they broke from work to have lunch. "Now say it together," Manuel prompted, and took a bite of the flaky empanada that made up his lunch.

"Hago un ladrillo," George said slowly, pronouncing each word with care.

"Good, bueno," Manuel said, and George felt relieved that he had gotten it right.

"Gracias...por...ayudar."

"Ayudarme," Manuel corrected, "y eres bienvenido."

The men fell silent, both finishing their lunches and drifting into their own thoughts. Noise from the main street of the town came drifting down to where they sat. Wagon wheels and horse hooves and the shouts of teamsters signaled the

---

2. Ad quoted directly from *The Arizona Weekly Citizen*, January 6, 1894.

arrival of a stagecoach, and both men turned to see who might get off. The dust settled as it came to a halt in front of the hotel, and after a moment a well-dressed man and woman got out. The man tipped his hat with a flourish to the stagecoach driver, and a worker from the hotel rushed to grab the carpet bags set on the side of the street.

"Colonel Sykes esta de vuelta," Manuel commented, then translated, "Colonel Sykes is back."

"Si," George answered, "and brought su esposa."

"Si!" Manuel stood and wiped his hands on his pants. "Estás listo para volver a trabajar?"

George nodded, standing and stretching the kinks out of his spine. The creak of shafts and jangle of harnesses signaled the stagecoach had begun to move again. Soon it passed by, the horses jogging at a lengthy trot.

Standing to the side of the round corral, George watched Thomas lead Magdalena through the gate. Thomas held so tightly to the lead rope that his knuckles were white. Instead of having him turn the filly around and close the gate, George closed it behind them. It swung shut silently, and he was careful to not let it bang when he latched it. "Alright," George said, "let her loose."

Thomas reached up and untied the lead rope from Magdalena's halter. He waved her away. Magdalena tossed her head, her mane snapping, her forelock blowing back to reveal the small crescent moon on her dark brown forehead. She trotted to the far side of the corral.

"Keep her moving," George said. "Don't let her think of anything except you moving her forward."

Thomas jiggled the rope in his hand and took a step toward Magdalena. He stopped and glanced at George. George nodded. "Swing the rope, guide her with your arms and your eyes." The instructions flowed out easily, as if he had given them before. He hadn't, though, and then he realized they were the words his own father had used when George had trained his first colt. With the thought of his father came the now familiar pang of regret that he hadn't repaired the rift before he'd left. He'd tried writing, had even sent one of the letters, but the words on the page just seemed hollow. He hadn't heard back from John.

Thomas moved toward Magdalena again and swung the rope. She snorted and started around the corral at a trot, her hooves cutting crescents in the packed dirt around the corral's edge. Thomas moved with her, continuing to swing the rope, but not as confidently as his first swing.

"Swing higher," George said. He climbed the corral fence to watch from the top of it. "Let her know you mean it."

The rope fell slack. Thomas straightened his shoulder and took a big gulp of air, then snapped the rope into the air, swinging it as high as he could. The rope swooped through the air, knocking his hat off. The hat hitting the ground spooked Magdalena. She leapt forward, her back rounded, her head went to the ground, and she kicked her back hooves so that the bottoms of them saw the sun. It was the highest buck George had ever seen a horse throw. He cringed. Not even Wet Blanket had thrown a buck that high. What had he done giving Thomas a horse that could buck like that? Maybe he hadn't thought this through, giving Thomas an untrained filly. Training was dangerous. Thomas could get hurt, seriously hurt.

George jumped off the fence and went to Thomas. "Stop, that's enough," he said, his throat choking with a strange sense of panic.

Thomas turned, his brown eyes full of confusion. "No?" he said. Magdalena circled the corral at a stiff lope, the small size of the pen keeping her strides from becoming long and fluid. She whinnied, and the sound was piercing, echoing between George and Thomas as they stood facing each other, George fighting for words to explain why he was telling Thomas to stop.

"We don't want to do too much," he said finally, as his heartbeat slowed again. He watched Thomas's shoulders sink, knowing he had taken steps backward with the progress they had just made. "That's enough." He tried to think of other words to say, but none came. So he just repeated, "That's enough, that's enough," until he wasn't even sure what it meant himself.

Magdalena stopped running. She lifted her head until her chin rested atop the fence and squealed. She reared, her hooves hitting the boards, sending a shiver through the wood all the way around. George thought he felt it hit him as he watched the vibrating movement, but then he realized it was Thomas shoving him away with his small fists balled.

"No, no he terminado," he said, "not done, not done."

George held the boy by his shoulders. Thomas swung his fists, but George kept out of the way and let him punch. Thomas stopped and George saw the streaks the tears had left on the boy's face. He wanted to wipe them away, but he couldn't bring himself to do it. Instead, he let the boy go, finally able to voice why he had stopped the breaking of the filly. "I don't want you to get hurt." He wasn't sure Thomas heard him or understood, so he said it again: "I don't want you to get hurt." Then he desperately tried to think of what it might be in Spanish. All that mattered was that he got through to the boy that George was trying to protect him, that breaking a filly was no joke. "No querer," he started, then stopped, searching his mind. "No querer you daño."

A flicker of a smile went across Thomas's face, although it didn't quite make it to his lips. "Tu espanol es malo," he said.

George smiled. "We'll take it lento, bueno?"

Thomas gazed at Magdalena, where she stood quiet now on the far side of the pen. She dipped her head and then pawed, sending another shrill whinny into the air. From the paddock, Wet Blanket answered her with an equally loud cry and came running to the fence, pressing his chest against it in an attempt to come as close as he could. Thomas picked up the lead rope and coiled it into a perfect circle. "Bueno," he said.

After turning Magdalena loose in the paddock with the other horses, George pumped water into a bucket and splashed his face, letting it run down his neck and dampen his shirt. The day wasn't hot, but between the worrying and the arguing he felt as though he had a fever. The water soothed his skin.

"I heard you," Julia said, coming up beside him and wrapping her arms around his waist. "You spoke Spanish."

"Not really," he said, leaning into her embrace and then pivoting to face her.

"Yes, bad Spanish, but still." Her eyes were bright with love and pride.

He indulged her with half a smile and then said, "I don't know that it'll be enough."

"It will be, trust me," she said, tightening her hold on him. He desperately wanted it to be true, but would it really be enough?

# Chapter 29

George tethered Wet Blanket and Arrow to the hitching rail in front of the barn. He saddled Wet Blanket first, tossing the heavy roping saddle onto the horse's back as if it were nothing more than a dishtowel, saddling being second-nature, without the need to look at his hands. He stared over the horses' heads to where blue sky met the riverbanks in a clash of color. A large black bird circled slowly in the distance, tilting first one way and then another. George wondered what it saw to keep it in such a circle, or if it saw anything at all. Maybe it was just passing the time, waiting for a rodent, a snake, a small bird to appear, unaware of the presence above.

The cinch tight and tied, George moved to Arrow, swinging another saddle up easily. This saddle was less worn, the straps still stiff, the seat still shiny and unscratched. George ran his hand over the smooth, unblemished leather, remembering when his father had given him a new saddle. He was fourteen, fifteen maybe, and the saddle he'd been using had become too small, as if made for a doll and not a young man.

*"Time you had a man's saddle," John said, watching as his son carried the lightweight saddle to the barn. George set the saddle over a rail in the barn amidst*

*the others, carefully, as he'd been taught, so as not to break the bone tree that held the saddle together.*

*John fingered the worn leather peeling from the horn. "It's time," he said again, but there was something in his voice that made George feel as though his father wasn't quite ready to let George give up this old one for a new one.*

*"This saddle's fine," George said.*

*John smiled. "No, you need one that can be your own, that you will take with you, that will become part of you."*

To this day George didn't know what secret memory that old saddle held. He could never ask his father questions like that, questions that would open a window into his father's emotions. He remembered how the new leather felt, shiny, almost slippery under his fingers, like this saddle was now. He pulled the cinch tight and buckled the bucking strap as Thomas came around the corner of the barn.

"Julia told me to come out here," Thomas said, his words clear and precise.

"You can check the herd with me," George said. "Got you a saddle. You can ride Arrow here."

Thomas nodded and stepped carefully to Arrow's shoulder. The horse turned his head, blowing into Thomas's hand. Thomas's lips twitched as if a smile was trying to make an appearance. "Alright," Thomas said.

"Bueno." George untied the horses, handing Thomas Arrow's reins, before mounting Wet Blanket. "Mount up."

Thomas hesitated, twirling the ends of the reins. He stepped to the gelding's side and raised his left foot toward the stirrup. Arrow moved away, making Thomas hop on one foot a moment. George held Wet Blanket steady and Arrow took the cue, settling and standing still for Thomas to slip his foot into the stirrup. Thomas grasped the red mane and pulled himself up somewhat awkwardly, but he settled into the seat naturally, sitting tall, heels down, eyes forward.

"Ven," George said. He started Wet Blanket off at an easy trot, leaving Thomas and Arrow still at the hitching rail. He wanted to glance back, make sure that

Thomas could get the gelding turned around and moving, but restrained himself. Soon he heard Arrow's hooves and the horses fell in step.

"Arrow was my friend's horse once," George said, surprising himself with this admission. It felt good to say it aloud though, and he continued. "Jimmy. He and I were in the army. Arrow was his horse then. I had this black that I called Abe, you know, after the president, Abraham Lincoln."

Thomas nodded, but George wasn't sure he really knew about Abraham Lincoln and maybe was just nodding to acknowledge he was listening to the story. Either way, George took it as a sign to continue. "Jimmy never fussed much about his horses, but sometimes at night he'd sneak Arrow bits of corn cake. I teased him about it once. He denied that he'd ever done such a thing, saying that if anyone was sneaking their horse corn cake, it was me. He was right about that. Sometimes Abe had more of my meal than I did. Deserved it though. That horse would have walked through fire." George fell silent, picturing Abe's large black head with his eyes that were placed almost too far apart.

"Why don't you have Abe?" Thomas asked.

George swallowed, gripping the reins tighter and fighting the urge to hide his hands away. "He was shot. Dead in an instant." He felt the bluntness of his own words. Momentarily worrying that they were too blunt, he blundered past them with, "He had the softest muzzle of any horse I've ever had. Just like that fabric, what's it called? You know, that soft, silky stuff, that changes colors in different light. And he was all lip. I never once felt his teeth. Heck, he might not have had any." George forced a short laugh and glanced at his companion. Thomas was looking steadily between his horse's ears, but his round black eyes were alight with attention. The horses' hooves thudded dully on the ground, muffled by grass and loose soil. Their short shadows fell to their right as they rode south along the curve of the land, unintentionally following the way the river turned.

"Why do you have Arrow?" Thomas asked.

George cleared his throat, uncertain how to tell the story. "Jimmy," he began. "Jimmy, didn't make it back." He knew his words were careful, too careful, but he didn't know how else to tell a boy who had just turned eight what really happened.

"He killed?"

"Si." George spoke Spanish, hoping somehow it would make up for not telling the whole story. "Yo tome, Arrow, un recuerdo, a remembrance of Jimmy." George scanned the land ahead of them and tried to ignore the dampness that had pooled in the corners of his eyes.

"Mira, mira," Thomas said, his voice splintering the silence they had fallen into. "Look, alli, there." He waved in the direction of the river.

George saw what looked to be a cow lying on the bank, but something didn't seem right. A rock settled in his stomach. He didn't want to go toward it, even as he turned Wet Blanket. Arrow followed before Thomas asked him to. They came up on the cow quickly, too quickly for George to prepare Thomas in any way.

The cow lay sunk in the sand, covered halfway up her round rib cage and bloating stomach. Her neck was stretched out, her head turned to the side, eyes open and rolling. She had to have been stuck there for hours, perhaps even days. Why hadn't he ridden out to check the herd sooner? George dismounted and went to her head, lifting it and listening for her breath. He didn't hear anything, but still they had to try and pull her out. George took his lariat from his saddle and pushed it over her head and down to the bottom of her brisket. Tying the rope off on his saddle horn, he backed Wet Blanket until the rope became taut.

Thomas sat quiet and white-faced on Arrow, staring at the cow as if he could never look away. George pulled the cow's head out of the sand, checking again for breath and still not feeling or hearing any. But when he passed his hand over her eye she blinked, giving him just a sliver of hope she'd be okay. Yet deep down he knew though that there was no hope she'd live. He mounted Wet Blanket, clicking to him and guiding him backward. Wet Blanket sank on his haunches against the pull of the rope. The cow moved only slightly, sinking back when George let Wet Blanket rest.

"Come on, come on," George said in quiet encouragement, asking Wet Blanket to back again. Wet Blanket strained, his hooves cutting into the ground. He snorted, throwing his head. The cow began to come out of the sand, the suction letting loose in pops and squelches. Wet Blanket halted, his sides heaving. George dismounted again, checking the rope around the cow's neck. He wished he could get the rope around a leg, but he couldn't get a grip on a leg; she was still too deep in the quicksand. There was no reaction when he tapped her eye, and he knew there was really nothing else he could do. He brought Wet Blanket forward, letting the rope slacken and slid it off. His chest tightened as he turned away, coiling the lariat and tying it back on his saddle.

"Let's go find the rest of the herd," George said, unable to look at the young boy.

"The cow?" Thomas said in confusion.

"Nothing we can do. She's dead." He swallowed around the tightness in his throat, in his chest. "Sometimes things like this happen," he said to Thomas and to himself. "Death is part of it all," he added, although he wasn't fully convinced himself. Thomas gave a nod, as if he understood, and it made George's heart ache.

They found the rest of the herd a mile downriver. George counted them, looking for a motherless calf and not finding one. Two losses. "We'll push them back up river," George said, skirting around to the south of the herd. He whistled at them and called out, "Hup, hup." The herd fell together, bawling to their calves, and began to move. Arrow fell into step beside Wet Blanket and George glanced at Thomas. Thomas seemed to have disappeared inside himself, his large eyes blank of emotion, and George felt a near overwhelming guilt that he had somehow broken the boy's heart.

Samuel climbed into George's lap as he sat on the step of the house, looking out at the barnyard, listening to Julia make supper in the kitchen. It had been a long day, and George's shoulders ached. He wished he could have done more for the cow mired in quicksand along the river, but even as they approached her he had known she was gone.

"Sometimes it happens," he'd told Thomas, trying to sound matter-of-fact, trying to be the practical adult. Was that the hardest thing about having children? Having to be the one that didn't break down, the one with answers, not questions? Thomas kept silent on the ride back. Any bonding seemed stripped away, and George didn't know how to get it back, so he stayed silent too. Maybe the mutual silence would tie things back together, but when had that ever solved things in his past?

He sighed, and Samuel looked up at him with the easy smile of a child too young to be fully aware of loss. George smiled back and ruffled the boy's hair. It was soft and clean, curling just a little at the ends. His cheeks were beginning to fill out again, as a baby's should, and even though dirt couldn't be kept entirely off, it wasn't caked on from days of not being washed.

"I help mama in jardín," Samuel said proudly. He held up his hands, as if to show George the dirt under his nails as proof.

"Look at that," George said, while thinking, did Samuel just call Julia mama? It wasn't that surprising, really. Samuel was young and adaptable. Why shouldn't he call Julia mama? Still, it surprised George, suddenly making it all seem very real. These boys were his and Julia's. He was a father. The thought made his hands shake.

"You cold?" Samuel asked.

George couldn't help laughing. "No, no," he said.

Samuel grinned and bounced on George's knee. He sank back, rolling his head on George's shoulder, then he sat straight. "Where Tomi?"

"Grooming the horses," George answered. Sitting there with Samuel filled him with contentment. It made everything else fade away, become less important. Family was what really mattered in the world. The realization made his heartbeat quicken.

"Me go see," Samuel said, squirming off George's lap and running toward the barn, his bare feet kicking up small puffs of dust.

"Stay away from their hooves," George called after him, and as he did so he realized Samuel had called Thomas by a nickname, Tomi.

Julia came to the door, wiping her hands on her apron. "This came today," she said, taking a letter from her pocket and handing it to him. George recognized Sarah's handwriting and ripped open the envelope.

"You were in town?" he asked as he unfolded the letter to the soft waves Sarah's pen made on the page.

"Yes," she said. "Samuel was restless and I needed seeds." Her voice was tight, tired, and George looked quickly at her. Her hair lay damp on her forehead and her cheeks were pale except for bright red spots on each cheekbone.

"I would have gone tomorrow for the seeds," he said, stepping around the question he wanted to ask.

"I know." She smiled, thinly, then turned back into the kitchen. George reached and caught her arm, pulling her back and down onto the step beside him. He pressed the back of his hand against her face, her skin damp and hot.

"Are you okay?" he asked, unable to keep the question in any longer.

"Of course," she answered, letting out a lilt of a laugh. "I'm fine. Just tired." She squeezed his hand and kissed it. "Come, supper. Call the boys."

He kept hold of her hand. "Samuel called Thomas, Tomi. Maybe that's what their birth-mother called him."

"Tomi." Julia smiled. "Tomi." She rubbed the back of his hand with her thumb, thoughtfully. "That must be it."

# Chapter 30

*D*ear George,

It didn't take me long to think of you as my own son, but you received me as such. With Jack it was a little harder. It took both of us longer to accept the other. That doesn't mean I didn't love him, though. It was just different and harder, and some days I wanted to give up trying to reach him. Eventually though, he accepted my presence and I accepted him as my son. There were many times when we moved forward and then something would set us back. I could never predict what would slide us backward. Sometimes it was like standing in quicksand and almost being able to step out, then sinking again, never quite able to get anywhere, although feeling like you were at times. Frustrating, yes, but in the end finding what we both wanted and needed. I have every confidence that you and Thomas will find this as well. Don't expect it to happen overnight. Just keep reaching out to him and one day you will find that he is no longer shutting you out, no longer pushing you away and every setback will be a distant memory that hardly feels real.

The weather has turned colder here. Snow will fall before long. I'm almost looking forward to it. It gives one a chance to slow down and take stock of things. I guess you don't get snow there, do you? What is winter like? I think I'd miss snow, but Arizona must have its own ways of charming people.

Yes, Arizona had charmed him, or the people here had. He knew for sure Julia had, but there was something more. It was a feeling that started deep in his stomach and spread through his veins as if it were blood giving him life. He couldn't say exactly what the feeling was, only that it pulsed when the sun hit the river banks just right, giving them a vibrancy of amber that seemed to belong to another world, or when Julia let her hair fall, waving down her back and shoulders.

*How I wish I could meet your Julia and your two boys,* Sarah's letter continued. *Arizona has been good to you and it makes me glad you left, although I still miss you around here. Your father misses you too. He won't admit it, but I can tell. That's the thing about being with someone every day for so many years. You know how they feel without them even saying a word.*

Sarah was right. He knew Julia wasn't well, even though she'd never said anything. It was time he did something about it.

George entered the small waiting room of the doctor's office and glanced around. There were benches along the walls, and above them landscape sketches hung. George took off his hat and leaned to get a better look at one. The scene was very familiar: a curve of river, with a steep cutbank on the far side, a one armed saguaro on the right with an oblong hole in its center. Hadn't he seen that cactus before? The sketch was deftly done. Whoever the artist was, they were good.

"Can I help you?" the doctor said, coming out of the back room.

George started, being so absorbed in the picture that he hadn't heard the man's footsteps. "Yes," George said, recovering himself. "Name's George Atkinson."

"Nice to meet you, George. Albert Carmichael." They shook hands, and George subconsciously sized the man up. Albert Carmichael was a tall, thin man with untamed red hair and an easy smile that dipped slightly to the left. He was younger than George had expected, but his manner encouraged trust.

"Come on back," Albert said.

George followed him into the back room, grateful to be the only one in the office. He didn't want people to see him there. Somehow it felt like going to a doctor's office invited rumors to get started and showed a kind of weakness that he didn't want to exhibit, even though he wasn't there for himself. The office, like the waiting room, was bright and clean, even inviting, despite the long wooden table in the middle of it, the metal instruments laid out on the side counter, and the amber colored bottles lined up and labeled on open shelves on the back wall.

"So, what seems to be troubling you?" Albert asked.

"My wife, I think she is ill," George answered, "but she won't admit it. If I describe her symptoms, could you prescribe something?"

"I can try." Albert motioned for George to take a seat. "Is the illness sudden?"

George shook his head. "No, I've been worried for a while now, only it seems to have gotten worse. She's had this cough, and her breathing becomes strained, especially after she's been working or when she gets anxious or excited. Sometimes when she laughs it turns into a cough and then she can't seem to get a deep breath." George stopped, noticing that his hands were shaking. He pressed them to his legs to steady them and hoped the doctor hadn't noticed.

"And it's happening more often now?"

"Yes. Now there seems to be times she's feverish. Her face goes white except for a spot on either cheek. Sometimes there is a rattle in her chest, and when she coughs it doesn't seem to do anything." As he spoke, he could picture Julia's face as clearly as if she were standing there with them, her skin draining of color until it resembled the ivory white of a porcelain doll, her countenance becoming just as fragile. George felt the fear and urgency that always came with seeing her that way crawl into his mind, just from the visualization.

Albert stood and went to the back shelf, running his fingers across the labels. "It sounds to me," he began, shifting the bottles, picking up one and setting it back, finally selecting a large one and crossing the room back to the counter. "It sounds to me like asthma. Your wife has never had it diagnosed?"

"No, not that I know of."

"Does it get better when she drinks hot coffee?"

"Yes, I think. She drinks a lot of coffee."

Albert nodded. He took a small, empty bottle from the counter and poured some of the liquid from the bottle he'd taken from the shelf into it. "Does she grow mint or lavender?"

"I think so."

"Good. Pouring boiling water over mint and lavender leaves and breathing the steam often helps relax the lungs and makes breathing easier. Have her try that next time she seems to be having trouble. If that doesn't work, have her take a drop of this. Just a drop. Arsenic is strong and it doesn't take much. It has proven to be successful with many, though." Albert handed George the small amber-colored bottle.

"Thank you." George put the bottle in his pocket. "How much do I owe you?"

Albert waved him away. "I don't charge for first visits," he said.

That couldn't have been true, but George didn't argue. He'd learned that many found it disrespectful to argue a generous gesture, and he respected this young doctor. "Thank you," he said.

"Don't mention it. Tell your wife to take care of herself."

George smiled. "I will."

As he passed the sketch in the waiting room, he remembered where he'd seen the saguaro. It was north, almost to Tucson, a mile or so from the stage road. Julia had shown it to him on their journey back to Calabasas after the honeymoon trip they had taken. *"I call it sinsear," she said. "I think it is the oldest cactus around. Seeing it is what made me believe I belonged here."*

*It rose above them, over twice George's height. They had to stand several feet back to see the cavity some bird had made in its trunk. "What does sinsear mean?" George asked.*

*"Ancestor." She smiled at him. "Our ancestors are everywhere. This cactus is one of mine." And it was in that moment he felt how truly lucky he was to have her as his wife, as his family.* Now, though, as he stepped from the doctor's office with the small bottle of medicine in his pocket, fear plagued him.

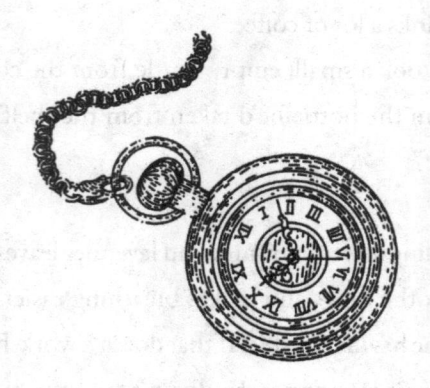

# Chapter 31

"You had no right," Julia said, her jaw tight, her cheeks and forehead flushing red. She pushed the bottle of arsenic across the kitchen table to George. It scraped gratingly, leaving a long scratch on the wood. "I don't need some doctor's medicine," she said, "and you certainly had no right talking to him about me."

"You're my wife," George said, glancing at the bottle, but not picking it up.

"That makes it okay?" Julia stared at him, her eyes seeming to catch fire. "Privacy, George."

"You can't keep ignoring it. Your breathing. Just admit it." George succeeded in keeping his voice even, but he couldn't meet her gaze.

"Don't you ever get out of breath?" she snapped.

"This is different." George paced the room in frustration, then turned to face her again. "You are ill. It's called asthma."

"I'm fine, just fine." Julia gripped the back of a chair, the chair with the crooked back, her breath coming short and fast.

"No, you're not. Why can't you just admit it? You say I have no right to talk to a doctor, but what gives you the right to keep things from me?" George was on the verge of yelling. He had never yelled at Julia and he didn't want to start now, but he wasn't going to walk away, not this time.

"I'm fine. I'm not keeping a bloody thing from you." Her eyes flamed and George had never felt heat like that before, not even during his time with Tyler's Rangers.

"Damn it, Julia!" George shouted. He slammed his fist onto the table and felt the sting of the impact all the way to his shoulder. Julia flinched, sucking in her breath, the wheeze of it hanging in the ringing silence that follows noise. An unexpected lump rose in George's throat, and he fought to swallow. Neither one moved, time moving so slowly George could feel it. For a moment he wondered if he could grab it and turn it back. "I don't want to lose you," he said, finally admitting his fear to her, to himself. His voice was strained.

Julia's breath wheezed in and out. She loosened her grip on the chair and stepped back, her knuckles white like her face.

"Please," George said, his voice coming back to its usual volume, "at least try the steam and the mint and lavender." When she didn't answer he added, "It can't hurt, right?"

Julia looked away. She smoothed her apron with her hands, the color returning to them as she did so. Her cheeks remained pale. "Don't you ever do this again," she said. George wasn't sure if she meant the doctor or shouting or hitting the table or all three combined, and he didn't ask. He felt suddenly tired like he did when he'd sit down after a long day's ride. Julia turned and moved the kettle onto the heat, as if resuming her work. George watched her, preparing to leave, when she said, "Pick some mint for me, won't you?"

As it had in Black Hawk, work at the brickyard created a routine and a rhythm that kept his mind busy enough that he didn't have to think of the things that worried him: the memories and the present stresses that kept him awake at night.

Every day, George threw himself into the work, working until noon when he went home to take one or both of the boys off Julia's hands.

"Did you hear the news?" Manuel asked George as they began preparations for the work of the day, interrupting the rhythm George had started to fall into as he always did in the morning.

George stopped with a bag of sand lifted halfway to his shoulder. "What news?"

"Thieves were caught just miles from here. There was a big shootout. Two deputies died and several of the thieves. They had lots of loot in possession."

"When did this happen?" George asked, wondering how he could have missed such an event. He lifted the bag to his shoulder and moved to the trough where they mixed the elements of the bricks together before pressing.

Manuel shrugged. "Yesterday morning," he said, inflecting his voice upward, as if he wasn't positive when the event had occurred. "It's in the paper."

George cut open the bag of sand and emptied it into the trough. "I might walk to the store and get a paper," George said, shading his eyes to look up the street.

"Si," Manuel said, as he sliced open another bag of sand and began pouring it into the trough, as well. The grains sent dust motes into the rays of sun shining down from the clear, open sky.

"The Peterson brothers can wake the kiln fire when they arrive," George said. Now that he had three employees, he was able to spend more time on his ranch, and he felt confidence in Manuel's ability to be the boss in his absence. It had become natural for George to pass this role to Manuel, and Manuel took it on without question, as though made for the role of supervisor.

"Si, I'll put them to work." Manuel grinned.

George laughed. "Good," he said and headed up the street to the general store, where he picked up the paper and read the account of the apprehension of the thieves.

*A band of Mexican thieves were apprehended six miles east of Calabasas. In their possession were ten stolen horses, six head of cattle, three cow hides, a pearl-handled pistol, three military rifles, a saddlebag of coins, a gold necklace chain, and a diamond ring. Three of the banditos were shot and killed in the shoot-out that ensued before the capture, two more sustained superficial wounds. Deputy Fred Martin and Deputy Peter Danby were fatally wounded, Deputy Martin dying at the scene, Deputy Danby passing on after arriving at Doctor Carmichael's office. Sheriff Anderson is working to find the owners of the horses, firearms, and jewelry. The money is believed to be mostly from the robbery of a stage carrying a payroll that occurred three weeks ago.*

George folded the *Arizona Weekly Citizen* carefully in the original creases. A diamond ring. What if it was Julia's ring? It was unlikely; he didn't even know why the idea came into his head, but once it was there he couldn't shake it. He had to talk to the sheriff and stepped to the counter hoping Charlie would know where to find the man. "Where can I find this Sheriff Anderson?" George asked.

"Sheriff Anderson." Charlie tapped his fingers on the countertop as he thought. "Anderson. He works out of Tucson, I believe." He stepped aside to help a woman with a bolt of cloth. George stayed at the counter and waited for Charlie to come back.

"Was he the one that caught those banditos?" Charlie asked, coming back.

George nodded, feeling an edge of impatience.

"Check over at the hotel. He might still be around." Charlie laughed a little. "Lawmen like to hang around their victories."

Again George nodded, folding the paper with the account of the apprehension on the outside.

"Did the banditos have something of yours?"

"They might have." George put his hat on and set a coin down for the paper. "Thanks, Charlie."

George let three wagons and a pair of cowboys pass on the street before crossing to the hotel. The lobby had been recently repainted, and it shone clean and bright in a way that imbued a kind of newness to it, encouraging people to stay, to feel as though they had arrived in the best hotel between Santa Fe and San Francisco. To George it spoke of Colonel Sykes's personality and firm belief that he would make Calabasas the gateway to Mexico, yet. He went to the clean, polished front desk and rang the silver bell sitting there. The sound was tinny and echoed in the emptiness of the lobby.

The clerk came whistling around the corner. George didn't recognize the man. "Hello, sir," the clerk said, "and what can I do for you?"

"Is Sheriff Anderson still staying here?" George asked.

The clerk opened the ledger on the desk and skimmed his finger down the columns of names. "Yes, he hasn't checked out yet," the clerk said. "Room 11, up the stairs and to the left."

"Thank you." George went up the stairs, running his hand along the polished railing. When he found Room 11 his knock was answered by a large man with skin like leather and a star pinned to his jacket.

"Sheriff Anderson?" George asked, knowing that he was, but inquiring anyway.

"Yes," Sheriff Anderson said. "I s'pose those banditos took something of yours, too?" His tone inflected enthusiasm and he smiled, pride in his apprehending of the thieves spreading across his face.

George looked the man up and down. The pistol strapped at his side stood out against the faded pants he wore, the handle shined from use. George felt the strange tightening in his chest, that feeling of being stitched closed, and couldn't seem to pull his eyes from the pistol. How could a man wear such a weapon and use it with the ease that authority gave license to?

"Nevermind," George said, watching the way Sheriff Anderson kept his hand hovering close to his holster. Was this a habit of all lawmen or just this one in particular? "I'm sorry to bother you," he said as though he'd leave, but he stood, his eyes fixed on the pistol and the sheriff's hovering hand.

"You're George Atkinson, ain't ya?" Sheriff Anderson said.

George glanced up, wondering which stories about him this sheriff had heard.

"People respect you. They say ya never wear a gun and ya don't need one. That true?" A smirk on Sheriff Anderson's face told George he was skeptical, but also curious, as if wondering how a person could really survive like George did.

"I don't wear a gun," George agreed, though he couldn't help feeling pleased upon hearing that people respected him.

Sheriff Anderson regarded him. "Heard you fought in Indian wars. Takes a certain kind of man to live through that."

"It takes a certain kind of man to live at all," George answered.

Sheriff Anderson gave a short guffaw, but he nodded with a kind of approval. "We could use a man like you as a lawman. You'd make a good one."

"Lawmen use guns," George said. "I won't."

"That's what'd make ya a good lawman. Ya already command respect without one. Just think what you'd accomplish with one."

George shook his head. "I don't think you heard me," he said, trying to keep the edge out of his voice, though he wasn't sure he succeeded. "I won't wear a gun. It's not that I don't. I won't."

Sheriff Anderson didn't seem to hear him. "Think 'bout it. We could use a man like you. I'll be here a couple more days, then I head back to Tucson."

"Thank you for the offer, but I have to decline."

"Just think 'bout it."

George had to give it to him, Sheriff Anderson was persistent. He hardly remembered why he had come in the first place. It came back to him. Was it completely impossible that the ring was his? "The ring," he said, abruptly, before he could talk himself back out of asking about it. "I had a ring stolen, my wife's engagement ring—" he changed his mind mid-sentence. "Nevermind, it was too long ago."

"Wait," Sheriff Anderson said. "I still have the ring. When was it stolen?"

George hesitated before admitting the length of time it had been. "Two years ago."

"That's a long time, but come in." Sheriff Anderson stepped out of the doorway to let George enter. "Can ya describe the ring for me?"

"It was silver, with three diamond flecks flat in the band." George paused, trying to remember the details of the ring. "There was a blue tint to the fleck in the middle. And it was a small ring, barely fitting on my pinky."

Sheriff Anderson opened a box, poking through it for the ring. He held it up. The light from the window glinted on it as he turned it back and forth, inspecting it, matching it to George's description. He passed it to George. "It looks very like what ya described," he said, sounding surprised.

George set the ring in his palm, knowing instantly that it was his. He took his time though, checking the ring over and then finally sliding it onto the tip of his pinky. It barely went to the bottom of his nail. "This is the ring," he said.

Sheriff Anderson smiled. "I'd agree." He shook his head in disbelief. "Two years. Your wife is one lucky woman."

"She deserves this ring, that's for sure," George said quietly.

George found Julia in the garden when he arrived home; on her knees beside the new squash plants, she carefully plucked the weeds away. Samuel lay stretched in the sun, asleep within an arm's reach of her. His cheeks showed red even through the tan, his lips just parted. George glanced around for Thomas and saw him sitting on the corral fence, watching the horses. George needed to keep his promise, he knew, and let Thomas work Magdalena again. Maybe tomorrow or next week.

"Julia?" George said.

She sat on her heels and looked up at him, wiping the dirt from her hands on her apron. It had been three days since he'd given her the doctor's remedies, but there had still been this sliver of frost between them, keeping George away from the house longer and Julia quiet in the evenings. Now though, as her eyes caught his, he knew they had moved beyond it. He reached down for her hand and pulled her to her feet. Taking the ring from his pocket, he slipped it onto her finger. It went on easily. The diamonds sparkled, and Julia gasped.

"George," she said, "where? How?"

"It's the ring," he said, laying emphasis on "the" and hoping she'd understand what he meant.

"You mean, the stolen ring? After all this time?"

"Yes. I guess it wasn't as easy to get rid of as they'd hoped," George said.

"I can't believe it." She held her hand up and smiled. "It's beautiful."

"Not as beautiful as you." George pulled her close. "I'm sorry," he whispered into her hair.

# Chapter 32

Magdalena lowered her head, curving it inward toward George. She was quiet, moving easily even in the half-light of early morning with the cool air of night still shifting across the landscape. George relaxed, turning away from the filly, dropping his hand to his side and listening for her footsteps to come behind him. The first rays of the sun appeared on the horizon as he felt Magdalena's soft breath on his elbow. He breathed deeply, letting her rest, then gave her a rubdown, gently sacking her out with the rope. She cocked a back hoof, her skin not even quivering as the rope slid down her sides and over her rump.

In the afternoon, George brought Magdalena into the corral again, and this time Thomas was with him. "Pull the cinch tight," George told Thomas, showing him how to slide his fingers between the cinch and Magdalena's belly. "Pull it tight."

Thomas did as instructed. George checked the tightness and nodded. "Good, good," he said. "Now pull it one more notch. Young horses blow their stomachs up, then once you're riding they let out the air and the saddle slips."

"Now can I ride her?" Thomas asked. George could hear the excitement in the boy's voice and smiled, remembering his first ride on the first colt he broke.

*Excitement thrummed through him like strings on a guitar tuned too tightly, and when he went to put his foot in the stirrup, it slipped. The colt skittered away and then leaped into a crow-hop as the empty stirrups swung and smacked his sides.*

*From the corral fence his father chuckled, then called, "You need to stay steady. You're too nervous. Settle yourself."*

*George breathed in and brought the colt back in, retightening the cinch and trying again with the stirrup. This time he succeeded in pulling himself into the saddle and glanced at his father. John gave a nod of approval, and George sat taller with pride, until the colt shuddered and leaped forward, and he was forced to gather the reins and focus on settling the colt. He stayed on, but only just, and got to the ground trying to hide the fact that his knees were shaking by grinning up at John.*

As George remembered, he checked the saddle on Magdalena and then nodded to Thomas. Thomas put his left foot into the stirrup, and George held Magdalena steady as Thomas swung his other leg over the filly's back, working his right foot into the other stirrup. Magdalena bobbed her head and shifted her weight.

"Dismount, then mount again," George said. Thomas did, and Magdalena remained quiet. George took a deep breath, then led Magdalena forward. She stepped out confidently and George let go of the reins, allowing Thomas to take control and direction. "Hold the reins a little shorter," George said, stepping backward to the center of the corral. "Helps keep you in control of a young horse."

Thomas shortened the reins and Magdalena tucked her head in response; George relaxed. The early mornings of working her had paid off. She had settled, and George didn't worry so much that she would do something unexpected and put Thomas in danger. He watched with pleasure as Thomas guided the filly, the filly soft and responsive. Thomas clicked his tongue, tapping his heels against Magdalena's ribs. Magdalena tossed her head, but moved into a trot, her gait smooth. Thomas sat tall, his eyes gazing straight between her ears. He turned her and brought her to a halt in front of George. A smile broke wide across his face. George felt warmed by the smile more than he did from the sun rising toward the middle of the sky.

The cattle bawled and shoved against each other, knocking into the corral boards of Hal's livery paddocks. Hal Connely leaned on the fence, chewing on a piece of straw and assessing the cattle. "A couple are a bit thin," he said, shifting the straw from one side of his mouth to the other.

"They're lean," George said, "not thin. It's been dry."

"That's for sure," Hal said, glancing at the sky. The sky was powder blue without a single shred of cloud. Rain wasn't on the way. "Been a good melon harvest, though. Did ya see those mounds at Charlie's store?"

George nodded. "Julia's been picking them every day in her garden. Squash, too."

"Good for gourds, bad for cattle."

"My cattle aren't thin," George said again, as if challenging Hal.

Hal chuckled and scratched the gray stubble of his beard. "Yeah, yeah. They look good. Better'n some others I've seen. Give you twenty a head for the cows, ten for steers, and two for calves."

"Twenty-five, twelve, and three," George counter-offered, falling easily into bartering, knowing Hal enjoyed it just as much as he did himself.

"Twenty-two, ten fifty, and two twenty-five."

"Twenty-three fifty, eleven, two seventy-five."

Hal surveyed the cattle again. He took his pipe from his pocket and packed tobacco in the bowl, putting the stem in his mouth and chewing on it. The cattle had settled and stood stamping at flies, their tails twitching, the calves pushing at their mother's udders. Hal lit his pipe and then held out his hand to George. "Deal."

"Deal," George responded and shook Hal's proffered hand.

"Come on in my office, and we'll settle up," Hal said.

In his office, a small single room with a worn desk, piles of papers hiding the top of it, flyers and newspaper clippings about stock sales and cattle prices tacked to the wall, Hal tallied the prices on a scrap of brown paper. "Six cows at twenty-three fifty, seven steers at eleven, four calves at two seventy-five," Hal muttered as he added. "Total of two hundred and twenty-nine." He counted the bills out. "That's a nice little sum," he said, grinning, showing the gap in his teeth where one of the front ones had been knocked out "by an over enthusiastic colt," as he put it.

"You'll make a nice little sum off of them, too," George answered, good-humoredly. He slipped the bills into his pocket. "Good doing business with you, Hal, as always."

"Always good doing business with you, George." Hal puffed on his pipe and followed George to the door. "I hear there's a space openin' up on the county supervisor board. Was talkin' to Charlie, and we think you should run for election. We'd recommend you."

George paused on the step. A cow bawled and a wagon passed on the street, going slow and creaking over the ruts. George rubbed the back of his neck.

"After what ya said 'bout the schools, well, that shuffled things up. New school board, new teachers, new teaching. Fact is ya made a change. Just think what ya could do as county supervisor. Ya care. We could use someone who cares."

"Politics," George said. "I don't know, Hal." There was a part of him that balked at being too involved in the politics of the place, but he wasn't sure why, as if doing so would mean permanence. But it seemed that almost everywhere he went something drew him in. He tried not to think how his father was the same way, but he remembered how in every town they arrived in, John would somehow become caught up in the politics of the place, becoming a church elder, a councilman, sitting on town committees, and Sarah would end up hosting dinners for politicians, baking for days before and serving the men with her cheeks still bright from the exertion and kitchen heat. George wouldn't put Julia through that. Was that what kept him balking at the idea? He listened to another wagon go by, laboring in the ruts, the driver cursing. "We could get these roads cleaned up though," George said, laughing a little to keep the conversation light. "The stage might actually get here on time. It'd be good for the town."

"And water," Hal said. "Ranchers are sayin' we're takin' too much here in town."

"It's a dry year," George said, trying to brush off the conflict Hal brought up, but he knew if something wasn't done, it'd turn into more than complaints. And what about the rumors of the thousands of acres along the Santa Cruz actually belonging to a New Mexico sheepherder? If it turned out to be true, they'd all be in trouble. Wouldn't it be better if he knew more about these proceedings?

"True, but we need someone who understands," Hal said.

George gave a short nod. "I'll think about it. Let me talk to Julia."

"Good." Hal took a long draw on his pipe, then said, "When ya bring yer colts in, I'll be over to take a few off yer hands, before ya take 'em down to Nogales."

"Are you sure you have that kind of money?" George asked, relieved that the conversation had swung back to livestock.

Hal laughed. George untethered Wet Blanket and swung into the saddle. "I'll send Thomas in to tell you when they're in. It'll be next week."

Hal nodded and as George moved Wet Blanket out, Hal called, "Think 'bout it, George."

That evening George stayed in the kitchen after dinner, offering to help with washing up and bringing up his conversation with Hal.

"That's the second person to ask you something of the kind," Julia said. "Some would call it a sign." She handed him a plate, giving him a pointed look, her soft blonde eyebrows raised and drawn together.

"A sign, huh?" George wiped the plate dry and stacked it.

"Yes, but only if you want it to be." Julia smiled softly. "That's the thing with signs. They only are such if you believe in signs or need a sign to make a decision.

My momma used to tell me that. I think she was right. So, do you want it to be a sign?"

"I don't know. Perhaps," George said.

"If it helps, I think you'd be a good county supervisor."

"You do?"

"Of course. You'd be able to bring the ranchers and the townsfolk together. You're liked by both. People like you, George. They'd be happy with you as a supervisor, as someone to represent them and look out for their interests, for the community's interests. You care, George. That's what it comes down to, and that's what would make you good at it." Julia looked directly at him, her eyes now earnest, and put her hand on his arm.

George met her eyes and for a moment they stood like that, caught in their own world. George leaned in and kissed her forehead. "I guess it's settled then," he said finally. "I'll run." Even as he said it, he felt a sliver of unease and the worry that he was becoming too much like his father articulated itself in his mind.

*George Atkinson is a wheel horse in the Republican party and will make a good supervisor. He will poll not only the vote of his own party but will also draw largely from the democrats, who recognize the weakness and unfitness of their own nominees and his fitness for the office he aspires to. Everything he has is in Pima county and her interests are as dear to him as his own. He can be trusted and will be trusted. He has the confidence of the people and will proudly keep it.*[1]

"I'm not sure I'm a wheel horse," George said, laying the paper out on the kitchen table, "but they got one thing right: what is dearest to me is right here."

"Everything they said about you is true," Julia said. She lifted the paper and read it again. "You should send this to Sarah. She'd be proud."

George nodded. Julia was right, Sarah would like to see the column. Behind that statement and thought hovered the thought, would John be proud too? Was this finally something that would show John the kind of man he was, the kind of

---

1. Italics directly quoted from *The Arizona Weekly Citizen*, October 27, 1888.

man he'd become? Julia must have caught a sense of his thoughts, for she rose on tiptoe and kissed him. "You're a good man," Julia said. "He knows that."

# Chapter 33

George woke when his hand slid onto Julia's pillow and found it cool and absent of her soft hair. He sat and blinked into the dark bedroom. "Julia," he whispered. There was no answer. He pushed the covers back, and his feet hit the braided rug on the floor. He made his way to the kitchen where he could hear the fire popping in the range and the carefully quiet movements of Julia. Another sound came to him, a wheezing and gasping, and fear gathered coldly into his bones. "Julia?" He called in a half-whisper as he entered the kitchen.

Julia looked up, startled. "I—" she began, forced to stop as she gasped for a breath. She leaned against the table, gulping air into her lungs.

"Julia?" His voice was now much louder, as if she were further from him than she had been a moment ago, even though he was beside her. George took hold of her shoulders. "Here, sit down." His instinct to protect her, to care for her righted itself through the fear, and he helped her into a chair. Julia fluttered her hand at the stove. George's eyes followed her movement and saw the kettle on. In movements that seemed somehow distant and too slow, he put more wood on the fire. Not knowing what else to do, he rubbed the heel of his hand between her shoulder blades, hoping to ease the tension building there.

Julia pushed against the table, gasping for any shred of air. Her body shook. "Where's the arsenic? Did you try the arsenic?" George asked, even as he saw the bottle on the table.

Julia nodded. "I tried." Her voice choked as if she were close to tears. George brushed her hair off her forehead. Her skin was hot and damp, feverish. How had he not noticed her condition the night before? Why hadn't she woken him? Why, why did she have to be so stubborn?

"You need a doctor," he said. "I'll get Thomas and send him for Albert."

Julia shook her head. "He...can't...do...a...thing..." She managed to force the words out in a thin wheezing voice, a voice that had lost strength and will, so unlike the Julia George knew that it frightened him even more.

"He could try," George insisted, never having felt so helpless in all his life. Could she take another drop of arsenic? Albert said to be careful with it, but just one more drop, wouldn't it help? He'd said it had helped many. George tightened his jaw in an effort to suppress tears. The kettle began to boil, and George poured the water into a bowl and placed it in front of Julia. She leaned over it. The steam rose and condensed on her cheeks. George held his breath, listening to her breathing, the scent of mint wafting in the air. He heard the clock in the hall counting the seconds too loudly. Julia's shoulders heaved as a gulp of air made it into her lungs. George stroked her hair, trying to keep his hands from shaking; she couldn't know how terrified he was, he needed to be the strong one, the one that protected and made things right. The doctor, he needed to get the doctor. "Just try and relax," he whispered. He left her and went down the hall to the boys' room.

"Thomas." He shook Thomas's shoulder hard. "I need you to go for the doctor."

Thomas sat, blinking in confusion. He wavered as he stood and George steadied him. "I need you to go now, fast," George said.

"Why?" Thomas managed to say, his voice still muddled with sleep.

"Julia needs him." George left the boy putting on his boots and went back to Julia shaking over the steaming bowl of water. George held her, not knowing what else to do. Thomas passed through the kitchen, standing, for a moment, uncertain in the doorway. George glanced up at him. "Go, fast. Take Arrow."

Thomas nodded, his eyes as wide and dark as the Arizona sky outside of the window. He tripped on the step as he went out. George listened for Arrow's hoofbeats, and as they faded he held Julia tighter, leaning his cheek on her dampened hair and closing his eyes. He held her and listened to the second-hand of the clock tick in time with the crickets singing in the yard, listened to the familiar sighs of the house, their home, listened to the sound of a breeze scattering leaves across the front step, listened to each nearly imperceptible breath Julia gave, and waited for the sound of hooves again. He held her, because that's all he knew to do, all he could do. She stopped breathing before the doctor arrived.

It rained. It was the kind of dripping rain that leaves one feeling cold and damp, and no matter how hard you try you just can't seem to get warm. Rain fell from sparse clouds that seemed too thin to hold water. Rain slid across sand, too thirsty to soak it in, and ran in miniature rivers, creating a whole new world. Rain streaked down dust-covered mesquite, making them look surreal, bark polished red like the red of the vermilion flycatchers that sang with perpetual brightness even on cloudy days.

The rain dribbled on George's hat and ran around the brim before it dripped off, soaking the shoulders of his overcoat. He held Samuel close against him. Samuel's brown eyes were big with uncertainty, rain flattening his hair and dripping from his nose. George held him tight with a grip that said he just might never let go. Thomas stood beside them clasping his hands together behind his back. Rain soaked his shirt where he had left his coat unbuttoned.

"Ashes to ashes, dust to dust." The priest spoke the words slowly. It seemed to George they were spoken too slowly, as though a continuous echo of the times he had heard those words spoken before. He remembered the first time he'd heard them as he clung young and uncertain to the black skirts of his aunt. He didn't know then what they meant, but they frightened him, and he knew they were changing his world. "Ashes to ashes, dust to dust." The words echoed again, reminding him of standing with a silver watch heavy in his hand, a hammer ringing against a nail and a pair of boots on a tree. "Ashes to ashes, dust to dust." Unbelievable, uncertain words. He imagined they were said over the grave of a man shot in an alley, the young widow Soule standing with her eyes cast down in the dust. He imagined they were said over a grave in Illinois after the coffin had traveled for days by train, while the whole country stood in black.

Now he stood, as the young widow must have, but instead of dust, rain tried to hide him. George felt the words drive through him like a railroad spike perfectly placed and sunken into position, leaving an open wound. These words changed lives. "Ashes to ashes, dust to dust." Did the priest say them again? They were too familiar, and yet he felt as though this was the first time he had heard them. They struck into the emptiness of his chest and he held Samuel even tighter.

Thomas stared, his eyes fixed on the coffin. The coffin jerked as it lowered, thumping the sides of the hole, creaking and swinging. The fresh dirt was mounded at the side of the grave in rich redness, the color too bright, too clean, and George almost resented it. He watched Thomas's hands twitch with every uneven drop of the ropes.

"We commit the body back to the earth. In the name of the father, the son, and the holy ghost," the priest said, crossing himself, the people surrounding the grave following his motions, except for George, and Thomas, and Samuel, who was too small to understand the motion. "Amen."

Charlie laid his hand on George's shoulder. "I'm sorry," he said. George knew he should nod and acknowledge Charlie's condolences, but somehow he couldn't. The rest of the people who had stood clustered opposite George, across the crater of the grave, began to move by, murmuring words of sympathy. George continued to stand, rain dribbling from the brim of his hat, holding Samuel closer to his overcoat. The coffin was being covered with the fresh red dirt, dirt that hadn't been turned long enough to fade.

"Should the boys come home with us?" Mrs. Connely, an elderly woman with fluttering hands and an iron-clad constitution, whispered to her husband. The words came through George's trance, and he shook his head. "The boys stay with me," he said. Hal Connely nodded and turned his wife away. George watched them leave, wondering why they had been given the odds to live together to their elder years, and why God had deemed it fit to keep that life from him.

Kathy stopped in front of Thomas and reached to button his coat. He pushed her hands away. She looked up at George and gave a whisper of a smile, a sympathy smile. He knew she wanted to say something, maybe even offer to take the boys back, but the boys were his, his and Julia's, even if their blood ran with Kathy's. He wouldn't give them up, not now, not ever.

"Thank you," he said in acknowledgment of her smile, and to his relief she walked on. George grasped Thomas's hand. Thomas let him. A shovel of smooth red dirt thumped onto the last part of the coffin; George felt it and knew Thomas had as well, by the way that his fingers tensed against George's palm. George noticed how cold Thomas's hand was and realized that he should get the boys out of the rain. "Come," he said, and they walked away, leaving the gravediggers to pile the red Arizona dirt on the grave as the rain turned it into mud. Ashes to ashes, dust to dust, dirt to dirt, mud to mud, and all that those poetic words were saying was "She's gone, and now you have to live without her."

The house had stopped breathing, its heart stilled within its walls. George leaned back in his chair in front of the fire and listened to the silence. He could feel it. It soaked into and covered him. His hands hung limply at his sides, and he gazed unseeingly at the grate. George hardly breathed, his heart the only thing that wasn't quiet, and he nearly resented it. The fire died, leaving a bed of blackening coals and gray ash. A shutter banged. George looked toward the noise, but he didn't move, letting himself fall backward in his mind.

*There Julia stood, arms stretched out, head thrown back. She pulled the hair pins from her long blonde hair and it streamed behind her in the wind. The curls unwound and wound back, tangling across each other. She closed her eyes and smiled. George folded his arms across his chest and watched her. They stood on top of a mesa above the river, the land around them rippling in heat waves. Tumbleweeds blew, rolling toward Mexico. The sky was bluer than the bluest of robin's eggs, and everything seemed in place. Everything fit together. They fit together.*

Now a piece had fallen from that puzzle; everything was falling in broken pieces like shards of pottery too small to put back together. No longer did it all fit. George clenched his hands against the sanded arms of his chair, the wood cold on his skin. The shutter banged again, followed by the quiet pat of bare feet in the hall. Samuel appeared in the doorway. He stopped in the frame, his nightdress too big in the shoulders, his black hair messy from sleep, his bare feet curled, protesting the cold floorboards.

"There's a noise," he said.

George motioned him over. "It's just a shutter," he said, "unlatched by the wind."

Samuel came and crawled into George's lap. "The fire," Samuel said, waving his round fingers at the grate.

"Yes," George said.

Samuel snuggled into George's wool vest and closed his eyes. "I miss her," he said in five-year-old honesty that didn't know why she wouldn't be talked about.

George swallowed. He put his arms around the little boy and lay his cheek atop Samuel's head, his hair velvety, almost soothing.

"Do you?" Samuel asked.

George tightened his hold and didn't answer. The shutter banged in a new gust of wind. Samuel stiffened for a moment, then relaxed and snuggled deeper. He sighed, soon breathing the peaceful, even breaths of sleep. George closed his eyes and listened to the wind as it rushed around the house, drying the land back to dust. Then it settled, and the air grew quiet. George listened to Samuel's breathing, waiting for the wind to come back. He fell asleep before it did, the first sleep he'd had since that night.

# Chapter 34

"Y ou need to eat, Thomas," George said quietly.

Thomas stared at the bowl of lumpy porridge drizzled over in dark ribbons of molasses, in front of him. His spoon lay silent beside the bowl. "No tengo hambre," he said in a faint voice.

George nodded, "I know son, I know, but we need to stay strong."

Thomas touched his spoon. He tilted it toward his bowl. The grains of wood reflected in the tarnishing silver. Samuel contentedly plowed into his porridge, eating it with vigor despite the lumps. Molasses claimed the corners of his mouth and dribbled down his chin. George wiped the boy's face with a dishtowel, conscious that it was a motion Julia would have made. Samuel spooned another bite into his mouth, molasses ran down his chin again, landing on the collar of his shirt. George almost smiled watching him, even as his throat constricted with a lump. He turned to the window, staring at the sky until the lump went down. When he turned back Thomas had stood, pushing aside his porridge.

"No puedes hacerme," Thomas said, his face stoic, as if etched of stone. He pushed past George, slamming open the door and running across the barnyard. George watched him go, thinking how quickly things could move backward. He and Thomas had come so far, only to begin again. Maybe they hadn't come as far as George thought. Everything was coming untied, and he couldn't seem to tie it back together, the strings slipping through his fingers, beads scattering across the floor. George couldn't catch them and panic rose from his stomach into his chest, the stitching sensation that came every time Sand Creek came to his mind, tightening through his ribs.

Samuel wiped his mouth on the back of his hand, his lips sticky with molasses. "More?" he asked.

A stream of relief running through his veins, George scraped the contents of Thomas's bowl into Samuel's, grateful that Samuel could eat, a bit of normalcy in a world undone. Samuel smiled, spooning the porridge into his mouth, eating it so quickly that it dribbled from his lips. George had never realized how messily Samuel ate and wondered if Julia had constantly wiped his face during meals. He tried to recall mealtimes, but he couldn't seem to control his memories.

*Sarah laughed at something his father said and leaned down to give John a peck on the cheek, the only affection she showed in front of people. Aurora played as a young girl, her red hair loose and alight in the firelight, arranging paper cutouts for a dinner party on a rug in front of the fire. John carefully weighed amounts of sand, clay, and straw to mix and pack into the brick molds, his large hands moving in a way that always seemed unbelievably delicate. Jack, as a teenager, took careful aim at a bottle set on a stump, shooting with such precision that the rim was the only thing that shattered, then turning to grin and spin the pistol on his index finger. Julia...*

Julia wouldn't come into his mind's view, and the lump in his throat rose again.

Hooves sounded in the yard, and George went to the door, seeing Hal riding up. He met him at the hitching rail. Hal pulled his horse to a halt. "Mornin'," he said, "how are ya?"

George nodded in greeting, but didn't answer the question. Instead he said, "What brings you out here?"

"Votes are in," he said. "The count finished last night and ya did it. Ya won, George."

George rubbed the back of his neck. He should have been happy over the news, but he didn't feel anything, the news didn't bring any spark of emotion to the surface, as if nothing mattered without Julia. The lack of any kind of emotion surprised him, but he couldn't even seem to hold onto that feeling, and ambivalence slid back into the space. Samuel came down the steps and pulled on George's pants with his molasses sticky fingers. George smoothed the boy's hair. "Julia said I would," he said finally, his voice dry. It seemed to him that he had spoken too loudly, but Hal had leaned toward him as he spoke, suggesting he spoke quietly.

He looked beyond Hal, toward the barn and the river. A covey of a dozen quail scratched in some spilled grain just beyond the corner of the barn. Not two weeks ago, he'd shot a few and Julia roasted them for dinner with squash, except for the two specimens he sent to Tucson. The birds had been tender, the skin crisp, and the dinner table had been cheerful that night, with Thomas talking more than he ever had, and Samuel insisting that he was big enough to have his own horse now. George caught Julia's eyes across the table and something had passed between them that told him this was all she had ever wanted, and he realized it had been what he'd wanted, too. Oh, how he loved her, loved the two boys; this was his family, was supposed to have been his family forever.

Hal shifted in his saddle, and the creak of it brought George back to the present moment. Hal's horse lifted his head and flicked his ears. "You'll have to come to town," Hal said, "an' accept the position." He stammered a little. "Ya can delay the acceptance. After what you've gone through, people will understand. Will ya still accept the position?"

George breathed deeply. "Yes," he said. Julia would want him to.

"Good," Hal said. "Get back on yer feet. Come to town end of the week and take your position."

"End of the week," George said as though he were agreeing, but in reality he was thinking how he could possibly be ready by then. How could he be county supervisor, run the ranch and brickyard, and take care of the boys? The boys surely couldn't come with him to meetings, could they? He was alone now, alone to raise them; how could he? He'd questioned his ability to connect with them, but he'd never questioned his ability to care for them. With Julia it had been possible; without her, he just didn't know. This wasn't what he'd wanted. He could no longer see the future.

"Good, good," Hal said, cutting into the haze that blocked George's mind. "We'll finally get some good representation 'round here." George thought he heard a slight bitterness in Hal's tone, but he shook it off, too tired to question Hal. And where was Thomas? He looked toward the barn, hoping to see him there watching from the door, but the doorway was empty, yawning open and dark.

George watched Hal leave and then turned back toward the house, seeing, as he did so, the hole in the chicken yard and another scattering of chicken feathers. He should have fixed it days ago. The remaining five chickens milled around the hole, scratching and clucking to each other as they searched for grain and insects. Samuel chased the chickens, laughing when they squawked and beat wings that barely lifted them off the ground. He then settled in the shade of the coop, drawing in the dirt. The wire and hammer were still there nearby where George had left them, and he took them up, putting all his concentration into patching the hole. Unbidden, the memories came.

*Julia shook a blue-checked tablecloth and lay it down on a patch of ground made soft by tufts of grass. She spread a picnic of cold meats and cheese and melon the color of a sunset, calling to George and the boys to come get it before the flies did, her voice lilting, just on the edge of a laugh. Samuel let melon juice run down his arms to his elbows, and Thomas spit seeds at an anthill, watching the ants hurry to carry them away. George reached to squeeze Julia's hand, leaning back in the sun of a Sunday afternoon when time slowed almost to a stop.*

*"Did you ever see the stone cities?" he asked.*

*Julia shook her head, a smile tugging at her lips, and George knew he had told her about it before, but he started the story anyway, pulling Jimmy's words and his own memory of the place together until it sounded like some kind of enchanted realm.*

*"Can we go?" Thomas asked, drawn into the story like he'd never been before.*

*"Someday," George said. "We'll all go. Take a picnic."*

*Julia laughed. "This place is enchanted, too," she said.*

*"How?" Samuel asked, a piece of melon squeezed in his hand.*

*"By us," Julia said. "By the sand, the plants, the sky, the river, this picnic." She paused, her eyes sparkling. "Enchantment is love," she said.*

George shivered, even though the sun was bright and near the middle of the sky. She was perfect, there was no denying it. She knew just what to say and when to say it. If only she could tell him what to say to Thomas and Samuel now. How did one get over losing two mothers? George glanced to make certain Samuel was still playing in the shade of the chicken coop, relieved to see him there arranging stones into fortresses. George had no idea how long he'd stood, caught in memory, with the hammer and wire to repair the run in his hands. He set them down. It was time to scrounge something for dinner, time to find Thomas, and try to start putting the pieces back together. After all, he loved them, and Julia would say that counted for something. It had to count for something, didn't it?

# Chapter 35

Magdalena's stall door swung and banged against the wall. It made a hollow sound like memories gone cold. Grooves in the dirt showed she had been spurred from a stand to a gallop, a halter and a set of reins straying across the floor spoke, too, of an urgency to leave the barn. George took it all in, his heart beating so that he could feel it hitting his ribs as if it were trying to break free. How much could a heart take? At some point wouldn't it reach the end of its resilience?

He snatched Wet Blanket's bridle from its hook, even as he whistled for the sturdy bay. Wet Blanket met him at the gate and received the bit easily, standing quietly as George pulled himself onto the dusty withers of the tall horse. George pressed his spur into Wet Blanket's left side and the gelding whirled on his haunches, drilling into the sand, before springing forward into a long-strided lope. They had passed the furthest edge of the paddock, before George remembered Samuel left alone in the kitchen and pulled Wet Blanket up so short that the horse fell jerkily onto his haunches, sliding and pushing up clouds of dirt. George couldn't leave Samuel alone, but he had to go after Thomas. For the first time in the years of living on the ranch, George wished he were closer to town or a neighbor. Then he would have someone to watch Samuel while he went after Thomas.

"I can't do this," he shouted at the sky where mare's tails chased each other across a periwinkle blue the same color as the dress they'd buried Julia in. "I can't do this alone. How could you leave me on my own?"

Wet Blanket danced, nervous now and uncertain of what was being asked of him. George held the reins tight out of habit. He should have insisted she see a doctor sooner, he should have taken better care of her. She wasn't cut out for the work of a ranch, and he should have helped her. But did she really have to leave him? Hot tears ran down his cheeks, the first that had fallen since Julia's death, the first that had truly fallen since Jimmy's death. He closed his eyes tightly and the tears came in cascades, until he bit his lip and forced it to stop. Opening his eyes, he saw Samuel standing in the kitchen door frame. Samuel stood there, his eyes wide and dark, sucking his right thumb and clutching a cloth in his left. George turned Wet Blanket, sliding from the horse's back when reaching the house and gathering Samuel into his arms. He hugged the boy tightly and kissed the top of his head, before setting him down inside the kitchen.

"You have to stay here," George told him. "I have to go, go find Thomas. I need you to stay here, inside, until I get back. Can you do that?"

Samuel nodded soberly, still sucking his thumb.

George quickly cut two slices of bread, tossing them on a plate with a lump of butter. "This'll tide you," he said. "I'll be vuelva pronto. Stay inside. Permanecer en el interior."

Samuel nodded a second time and climbed onto a chair. George kissed his head again and left before he could second-guess his decision. Once more straddling Wet Blanket's broad back, George pushed the horse into a hard gallop, following a single set of horse hoofprints that led toward Mexico.

Sand rose around them in clouds, and George pulled his silk to cover his nose and mouth. He could feel Wet Blanket beginning to sweat, hot and damp beneath his thighs. His eyes stung and Wet Blanket stumbled, snorting as he found his footing again. George dug his spurs against the bay's belly, and Wet Blanket responded by lengthening his stride. Palo verde, cholla, mesquite, and manzanita bushes, grass, and sand blurred around them and George focused between the black tipped ears, numbing himself to the whirring landscape. All he could feel was Wet Blanket clamping the bit through the reins, which he had wrapped around his left hand. George knew he should unwind them, but he didn't.

The mare's tails began to come together in a brood, but they were high and the wind would soon blow them out of the sky all together. Tomorrow there might be rain, but not today. Grass crackled as the wind pushed it to the ground, and Wet Blanket flattened his ears, sweat running down his neck, staining his coat as it gathered on his chest and dripped from his withers. He faltered, then lengthened out on a stretch of desert as empty as a watering hole at the end of summer. George let the horse pick his own path across the expanse, until they topped a small rise. Then he pulled Wet Blanket to a halt, Wet Blanket rearing this time to stop his momentum. He pranced, the bit clanking against his teeth as he chewed in anticipation, while George scanned the ground for the hoofprints they followed. The prints curved down the other side of the rise, turning west at the bottom. George loosened the reins, and Wet Blanket pounded down the hill. How far had Thomas made it? Magdalena had to be wearing down.

And just like that memories flooded his mind.

"Sometimes," Jimmy said, "I feel sorry for us."

"What?" George laughed a little, unsure if Jimmy was being sarcastic or not. He fed Abe a handful of oats, glancing over his shoulder at Jimmy brushing his brown gelding vigorously. "I'll take that brush when you're done," George said.

Jimmy gave his horse one final hard brush, then tossed the brush to George. "I feel sorry for us," Jimmy repeated. "We get shifted 'cross horses so fast we never get calluses for their gaits. Instead we just keep gettin' sore in new places."

George laughed, fully this time. "Thank you, Jimmy."

"For what?" Jimmy asked.

"For being cheerful, keeping spirits up."

*Jimmy laughed, a laugh that said he didn't believe George and turned to check his saddle one last time. George gently brushed Abe's long face and the horse closed his eyes, his ears relaxing.*

Branches of a manzanita scratched George's face as Wet Blanket passed by too close. George pulled the horse away from the tree only to get cholla spines in his pant leg, but he ignored the spines and looked again to the horizon, as a vision of another horizon came into his mind.

*Light scrawled across the horizon, white and unexciting for a sunrise. George tried to pull his hands inside his coat sleeves to warm them, and when he couldn't, he blew on his knuckles. Beside him, Jack lit a pipe and puffed smoke into the frozen air. The tobacco smelled sour, and George coughed, even as he wanted to take the pipe from Jack and suck the smoke in.*

*"Two days," Jack said, "and we'll be home. We did it, George."*

*George wanted to ask what they'd done. Instead he said in a voice just above a whisper, "It seems strange."*

*"How's that?"*

*George shook his head and stood, his joints aching as he uncurled himself. A few other rangers stirred, but the camp was still mainly quiet. George blew on his hands again and Jack offered him the pipe. "No," George said; the moment for a smoke had passed.*

*The sentry came stumbling through the brush, calling the rangers to arms. "Indians along the other edge of the meadow," he panted, "painted, painted for war."*

*Rangers snapped to attention, fatigue forgotten in the habits formed from months of living and breathing as rangers. Even George jumped to action, tying his pistol to his leg and pulling his rifle from its scabbard. He passed Jack's rifle to him, as Jack fumbled with tying his pistol, then together they fell in with the others. The rangers ran, staying low along the edge of the trees around the meadow, aiming to intercept the warriors. George forgot his aching joints in the concentration of keeping low, of moving as quietly as the morning itself.*

*Jack coughed, the sound sharp in the cold, and the Indians brought their ponies around as if they, too, had heard the sharpness of it and become aware of the rangers bearing down on their position. But they grouped together, and then a laugh came to the rangers across the small piece of meadow left between them and the Indians. As Tyler gave the command to aim and each ranger sighted along their rifle barrels, the Indians swatted their ponies across their muscled rumps and pounded away in the opposite direction, disappearing from sight before a shot was fired.*

Wet Blanket's hooves pounded through the sandy soil of the desert, the tracks in front of them blurring in George's eyes from the speed. The trail had angled to the south now, following the route he took to Nogales. A gateway to Mexico. He sucked in his breath when another memory caught him, Julia's face as clear as if she stood before him.

*"Look at this," Julia said. She pointed to an ad in the newspaper. "Shortest route to the World's Fair," the ad read.*

*"The World's Fair," George said. "You'd like to see that?"*

*Julia shrugged. "Sure," she said, "who wouldn't? But I meant the claim that the shortest route is through Santa Fe. Have the advertisers even looked at a map? Chicago is over here." Julia made marks on the newspaper with a piece of charcoal to indicate Santa Fe and Chicago. "It'd make no sense to go from here, over to Santa Fe and then across to Chicago; a body'd be doing an awful lot of backtracking."*

*George laughed, and Julia smiled a smile that told George she was pleased she'd made him laugh. "There it is," she said.*

*"What?" he asked.*

*"Your laugh. You hadn't laughed in a while."*

This memory bled into another, an earlier memory, a memory he hadn't known he'd had, and yet it fit together with the previous as if from the same puzzle.

*George unfolded the cloth from around the biscuits Sarah had pressed into his hands as he rushed from the house in Colorado. A piece of paper fluttered to the ground, landing like a feather in a fragrant silver sage. George plucked it from the bush's branches. "Don't you ever forget laughter," looped across it in Sarah's clear and unapologetic hand.*

Coming around the edge of a hill, George's eyes landed on the bronze hips of Magdalena tethered to a straggling, browning bush. She dripped with sweat, and her saddle had slipped to the right, so far that one more step would send it under her belly. Thomas stood off from her, holding a horseshoe in his hand and staring at it. He didn't look up as George approached.

George slid from Wet Blanket's back before the bay had even stopped moving and dropped the reins to the ground. They burned his hand as they uncoiled from it, and he could hear his heartbeat in his ears and feel it in every inch of his body. Thomas still hadn't looked up. Magdalena whinnied at Wet Blanket and Thomas startled, dropping the horseshoe and running to the filly's side.

George rushed to cover the ground between them, thinking Thomas would mount and kick Magdalena on, but Thomas turned, pointing George's six-shooter at George and shouting, "Dejame solo. Leave me alone."

George halted, then took a step back. In all his years, he felt he had always known exactly what to do when a barrel was aimed at his heart, but now he didn't. "Thomas," he said, the name coming out chokingly.

"No te acerques." Thomas clenched his jaw, every muscle in his face drawing together in hard lines that made him years older than he was. "Stay away. Let me go."

"Thomas, no, I don't understand," George faltered.

"Todo es mi culpa! It's all my fault!" Thomas shouted.

"Thomas," George said the boy's name again, unsure of what else to say. Somehow he felt that saying it would help, but he didn't know why or what he would do if it did.

Thomas cocked the pistol. "No te acerques. Stay away."

"Why?" George said, raising his hands in bewilderment. What did Thomas think he'd done?

"It's my fault." Thomas choked on his words, then recovered himself. "I killed her."

George's knees went weak and the tears he thought he'd dispelled clouded his vision once again. "No, no, Thomas, no," he said. "It wasn't your fault. No es tu culpa."

"I took too largo getting el doctor. El could have la salvado. I was too lento."

"No, he couldn't have saved her. You did all you could." Even as he said these words, he felt their inadequacy, realizing he, too, held the same guilt in his chest. He could have saved her if he'd only been more attentive, just as he could have saved Jimmy. He should have saved them. Wasn't that what a husband, a friend was supposed to do? He suddenly knew that was why he left Colorado. He couldn't face the guilt, and now here it was staring him down in the form of a near nine-year-old boy holding a pistol on him. He knew now that he had to let it go, or else it would keep eating away at him until there was nothing left. It was time to face it all, all the memories, and his life now. It could be a good life, even with Jimmy gone, even with Julia gone. Samuel and Thomas were still here, he was still here. He shifted toward Thomas, shaking and reaching out to the boy, no longer afraid of the pistol going off, knowing even more surely that he never had and never would need a gun.

The pistol discharged. The shot reverberated in his mind long after the sound ceased. The bullet met his body, throwing George against the ground. Both horses snorted and Magdalena tore from the bush, running, limping away into the brush.

# Chapter 36

"Choose a side!" Jack's voice rose, but he kept it carefully even and just below a shout. He pinned George against the barn wall. George had an urge to spit in his brother's face, but he swallowed and kept his gaze locked on Jack.

"Why?" George asked finally.

"You can't not. You can't hide forever."

"I'm not hiding."

"Aren't you? Only cowards won't choose a side." Jack slammed George tighter against the wall and something in George snapped. He kicked Jack in the shin and Jack loosened his hold. George took advantage of Jack's surprise and knocked his body into Jack's, and getting his arms free, he swung and hit Jack in the jaw. The sound of bone contacting bone reverberated in the silent barn, and Jack stumbled, then straightened and swung. George ducked, his brother's fist missing him by a mere centimeter as Jack hit the wall, unable to halt the momentum. He cursed, shaking his hand, and George stood back, unclenching his fists and wiping his palms on his pants.

"What if there isn't a right side?" George asked. There was a difference between being careful and being a coward. Jack should know that by now. Maybe he did.

*Maybe Jack didn't mean what he'd said. Deep down, George worried he really was a coward.*

*"Are you crazy?" Jack turned to face George again, but his arms had fallen to his sides, his fists, too, unclenching.*

*"No," George said. He wanted to continue, to ask Jack what happened if you chose a side and it was the wrong one, what happened if you chose a side and someone you know chose the other, and you have to face each other across rifle barrels? But that connection with Jack had been lost long ago. Something had slid between them, as thin and transparent as a sheet of ice, but as impenetrable as stone, and George didn't know how to dislodge it.*

*Jack stared at George, then shook his head. "I hope you'll be able to live with yourself when you are the only one to stay behind and the rest of us are ensuring our families' safety," Jack said. "Father was right: you're still a boy and you'll always be one, tied to Sarah's apron strings. Just know, one day you'll regret it. You'll regret staying here and letting the rest of us do the fighting."*

*"Do ya ever wonder how you'll react when faced with shootin' someone?" Jimmy asked, breaking the icy silence of the afternoon. They'd been riding all morning without conversation, their horses complacent with the pace set by the company.*

*George rode in a comfortable blankness and Jimmy's words brought him startling back, his thoughts rearranging. "What?" he asked.*

*"Do ya ever wonder how you'll live with yourself when you have to shoot someone?" Jimmy rephrased his question, speaking slowly as if trying to simplify it. "I just don't know if I'd be able to, ya know," Jimmy continued, not waiting for an answer. "Just don't seem like somethin' you'd get over."*

*George stayed silent, not trusting himself to say the correct thing. He scanned the rangers until his eyes fell on the straight shoulders of his brother, riding as if he'd never done anything except ride the cavalry issued gray. Jack, so certain that they were doing their duty, that if they'd stayed home they'd forever regret it. And now Jimmy suggesting forever regretting leaving home.*

*"Why'd I join the rangers?" Jimmy spoke again.*

*George let the question sit in the air between them, aware of the weight of his pistol strapped to his side and the rifle scabbard chafing his leg. "It wouldn't be your fault," he said, shivering and turning up his coat collar against the wind. It rubbed, burning his already wind-burned cheeks, but it kept him warmer, so he ignored the irritating pain. George wanted to say something more, say that they were soldiers, they were doing their duty, but he didn't know if he believed it, so the words wouldn't come. He didn't know what he'd do. He didn't know if he could actually pull the trigger. "I don't know, Jimmy," he said. Jimmy turned his own collar up and stared ahead.*

*Shots popped the air and the whiz of arrows answered. The Indians stayed mounted, and from where George hunkered in the brush, he stared in awe at the way they guided their ponies with just their knees, leaving both arms free to send arrows arching toward the rangers.*

*"Take aim," Jack hissed beside him.*

*George sighted along his rifle barrel, even while aware that Jack hadn't taken aim either. The Indians were in perfect range, but somehow they seemed too far away to accurately aim, and the movement of the horses confused George. He lowered his rifle and glanced at his brother, who still wasn't sighting. An arrow passed by so close to his ear, he felt the wind of it. Jack cried out, the arrow sinking into his arm. George jerked his rifle to his shoulder and before he could think himself out of it, took aim and fired. The patched Indian horse reared as its rider fell into its matted mane. Another rider pulled the body from the horse onto his own horse's withers and turned away. Arrows arched through the air, looking for a moment like a flock of birds, before falling to the ground. A few shots fired in answer. Then, as suddenly as they had come, the Indians disappeared as if they were apparitions in the sagebrush. George dropped his rifle, breathless and shaking.*

*As he pulled the arrow from Jack's arm, George wondered if the Indian he shot had died, the thought pestering him long into the night, haunting him with every subsequent shot fired in the following days.*

"Papa, puedes escucharme? Puedes escucharme? Por favor papa, habla por favor." Thomas's voice broke urgently through the swirling memories, and George came to himself, feeling the sand beneath his body, a sharp rock under his head, and a strange warmth seeping from his shoulder down to his fingers. His head pounded with a painful, quick heartbeat.

"Papa, puedes escucharme?" Thomas pleaded again, and George opened his eyes to see Thomas leaning over him, tears running in rivers over his cheeks to join the mucus dripping from his nose. "Papa, papa! Lo siento. Lo siento mucho. No quise. Puedes escucharme? Lo siento mucho."

George couldn't tell if what he felt was real, as if somehow his brain and his body had been disconnected. It took all his concentration, but finally he lifted his head, seeing the blood on his shoulder and the shreds of his shirt. With that sight he took stock of the situation, suddenly knowing what he needed to do. Thomas continued to prattle in Spanish, repeating words over and over. George knew he should know what the words meant, but they landed scrambled in his mind, and he couldn't pull them apart to any meaning. He rolled to his good side and pushed himself up, concentrating on the action and trying to push the pain away. "Magdalena, get, bring," he said, his words slurring, and he knew they weren't coming out in full sentences. He just couldn't think of how to form a sentence at the moment. Thomas stood, sobbing, and ran, stumbling.

George succeeded in getting himself to almost a seated position just as Thomas came back, leading the filly. "Saddle," George said, "off. Behind, behind me."

Thomas struggled with the buckles, his distress making his fingers clumsy. Magdalena nervously moved away from him. George didn't know if he could stay sitting long enough for Thomas to get the saddle behind him for support. He looked for Wet Blanket, but all he saw were the twisted trunks of manzanita, the brown bark peeling away to show the unweathered red of the wood beneath. He hoped Wet Blanket hadn't gone too far away. Magdalena whinnied, the uncertain shrill cry of a young horse. Her right front hoof hovered above the ground, shoeless. Thomas shoved the saddle against George's back, and he leaned on it with relief, closing his eyes and letting the pulsing in his head take over, for how long he didn't know. He tried counting each pulse, but stopped when he reached one hundred. A canteen pressed his lips and he pulled himself back, drinking the cool water as Thomas tipped the canteen.

"Good, good," he said, his brain and his body seaming together again. He noticed the sun making its descent, the rays getting close to the ridges in the distance. He knew that somehow he had to bind his wound, somehow they had to find and catch Wet Blanket, somehow they had to get home. Samuel. The thought of Samuel alone, waiting, pushed George into action. He could see the little boy at the kitchen door, watching for dust signaling a horse and rider, his dark eyes round and liquid like obsidian stones just under water.

George motioned to Thomas, saying, "Wet Blanket, close by?"

Thomas nodded. He'd stopped crying, the tear trails drying on his cheeks, his face stoic and red in the aftermath of his sobs.

"Go, get him."

Thomas hurried away. He whistled, a high note, then a low, then a high; Wet Blanket's call. George hadn't known Thomas knew it, and his eyes pricked with tears as he realized how much Thomas must have been paying attention to him; he hadn't returned half of it. Wind swept along the ground, picking up dust and sounding like a mother shushing a child. Thomas whistled again, a high note, then a low, then a high. A nicker answered his call, relieving George, as he ripped the rest of his shirt from his wounded arm and roughly wrapped the wound. But he couldn't get it tied without help. When Thomas returned with the gelding, George instructed him to tie the cloth tightly. Thomas did, asking quietly, "Estaras bien, no?"

George clenched his jaw against the pain, then nodded. "Si." He looked directly at the boy. "Si," he said again, then, "Help me up." Thomas's strength surprised George, and soon George was standing, Thomas remaining sturdy beside him. They could do this; they could make it home. He instructed Thomas to put the saddle on Wet Blanket. "He'll take us home," he said. He focused his mind on watching Thomas's movements as the boy did as instructed, to take his thoughts away from the pain and the urge to sink back onto the ground and close his eyes. His eyelids were so heavy, but every time they closed, all he could see was the young Cheyenne falling back on the hill at Sand Creek. He couldn't help but think that maybe now this was him paying his dues. But there was something else, something deeper...

It was as if he suddenly understood now why he had fired that shot, as if he finally could see the events of his younger life more clearly. Now he could forgive himself and promise to live from those mistakes, teaching his sons that life could be lived better if you looked to keep peace at every turn. Maybe his sons wouldn't repeat his mistakes and maybe, someday, those he'd wronged would forgive him. He hoped they would, and as he stood there in the coming evening, he prayed that they would. He prayed to any and all spirits that might be out there circling in the air, watching over him, giving him another chance. He wouldn't fail them this time.

The sun hit the horizon, catching on the few clouds left in the sky, which were angel wings now, as they started their slow journey, both riding Wet Blanket. Thomas sat in front guiding the horse north, although he needed little direction, and George sat behind, feeling each step of the horse, acutely aware that each one got them that much closer to home. Magdalena's reins were tied off to the saddle horn and she limped alongside. George closed his eyes, hoping to subside the throbbing.

"The gun," Thomas said suddenly. "La deje, I left it."

"Esta bien," George answered. He didn't care about the gun. He'd always known it would bring trouble; he'd known it the moment he'd bought it. He should have returned it, should never have brought it into his home.

"No quise." Thomas choked the words out. "Acaba...acaba de disparar. It just fired. Why did it fire?"

George squeezed the boy's shoulder, not knowing what to say.

"I didn't mean to," Thomas said, his voice desperate. "You have to believe me. No quise."

"I know," George said. "It's okay, Thomas. Estare bien."

"Lo siento. Lo siento mucho."

"Lo se." George almost forgot the pulse of his own pain at the pain of Thomas's voice. "Everything will be okay," he said, wanting to believe it as much as he wanted Thomas to.

They arrived at the ranch as midnight darkened the sky, reminding George of all the midnights he had seen come and go. The cold, quiet ridge above Sand Creek, the dank barracks at Fort Lyons, the crystaled mud of Denver alleyways, the steamy kitchen gone suddenly silent, the wind banging shutters on a house hollow from death. This one, though, was different: this midnight brought him home, and he knew he and the boys would survive. The memories of past midnights settled into what they were, memories to learn from and not be haunted by.

Jimmy'd once asked how someone could leave a place they had worked so hard to build and make home, and now George found himself wondering the same thing. He could never leave no matter what happened, no matter how hard things got. This was home, and it always would be home, more than any place had ever been.

# Epilogue

*D*<sup>*ear George,*</sup>
> *Losing someone is never an easy part of life. Losing a friend can cut you deeply; I know, I've been there, and I should have told you. I shouldn't have expected you to talk when I, myself, wouldn't talk. Losing a wife is something else entirely, something that you don't fully heal from, but, believe me, you can still love. Love your boys, love your home, and in time the wound will become a scar. I'm not going to tell you it is going to be easy. I'm not going to tell you that everything is okay, because it's not. It won't be easy, things aren't okay and won't be for a long time; I know. Losing your mother was the hardest thing I've ever experienced in life. Life has this funny way of carrying on though, and you can either carry on with it or let it carry on without you. It is a choice, and I hope you will choose to carry on.*

> *I've not said this enough, but I love you, son. I'm proud of you, of the man you are.*
> *Your father,*
> *John*

George placed the letter, with almost reverence, on his bedside table. And then he cried; he let all the tears that he'd been holding inside for so long come flooding to the surface and down his face. When there were no more to be cried, he felt as though a weight had been lifted. The wounds in his heart were raw, still bleeding, but two small sets of footsteps in the hall told him that life was continuing. He turned to join it.

The sun rose over the broken plains of red sand and silhouettes of the sharp rocks that were the Tumacacori Mountains in a brilliance that only came after a dark storm. It spread gold, red, and orange into the sky as though it were an eagle opening its wings and catching fire. George watched it, sitting on the kitchen step and sipping coffee as he had for so many years, so many years now that he'd lost count. He'd been in Tucson the week before, meeting with other county supervisors and lawyers, discussing at length the lawsuit and claim of the Baca's on this land, and it had tired him. But today he was going to put it from his mind. It felt good to be home, to sit on his own step and watch the sun rise over the barnyard.

Thomas, a young man now, although with the same smooth dark hair and serious eyes he had as a child, came to the doorway. "Papa," he said, "I've been thinking." He paused as a hawk swooped into view, diving close to the ground and then spiraling back into the sky, circling around and around until lost in the colors of the sunrise. George waited for Thomas to continue and after a deep breath he did. "I'd like to change my name, to, to Atkinson."

George hid his smile by taking a long sip of coffee. "I'd like that, too," he said finally. He stood and turned to take his cup inside. As he passed Thomas, he squeezed the young man's shoulder, surprised, as always, at how tall he'd gotten. Thomas met his father's eyes and smiled. "Next week," George said, "we'll go into Tucson."

Thomas nodded, then finished his own coffee and set the mug on the counter, and even though his face remained as thoughtful as ever, George knew he was pleased and excited about a trip to Tucson. The last time he had taken the boys to Tucson had been nearly a year ago, when John and Sarah had at long last journeyed to visit them. It had been awkward at first, with John and George not quite knowing how to respond to the other, and Thomas shyly hanging back. But then Samuel had come laughing around the corner of the hotel after tethering the horses, and the ice shattered. Samuel flung himself at Sarah, engulfing her in all his boyish exuberance, hugging his grandfather in a similar manner, and soon they were all talking, trying to tell the news of their lives all at once. It was a memory that strung itself onto the chain of memories as one that would be there indefinitely, even though George couldn't recall the exact words spoken.

Samuel burst into the kitchen from the hallway, half bent over, strapping his spurs on as he went. The rowels alternately jingled and scraped on the floor, and dirt fell from the soles of his boots, which George decided to ignore for the time being. There would be time for cleaning the dirt up on another day.

"What's the hurry?" George asked the flustered boy, hair still disarrayed from sleep, his shirt only partially buttoned.

"Thought you'd left without me," Samuel said, blustering and laughing.

"We're not leaving without you, Samu," Thomas said, and although he didn't laugh, amusement shone clearly in his eyes.

George took a silver watch from his pocket and checked the time. "Get a move on though," he said. "Cows won't muster themselves."

"Yes sir, Papa." Samuel poured coffee, taking it and following the steady strides of his brother in a whirlwind to the barn, calling, "Tomi, Tomi! Wait until you hear the dream I had."

"Samu, don't you know dreams are only interesting to those who dream them? Now, memories, memories are the things to tell," Thomas called back.

Their voices faded out of earshot and George shut the watch, squeezing it in his hand before slipping it back in his pocket. He remembered when he'd received it back, eight years ago now, after sending it to Lizzie along with a long letter about his and Jimmy's time as rangers.

*He was the best friend anyone could ever have had,* he'd written. *I hope one day I'll live up to his friendship. He thought the world of you. Talked about you every day and called you sunshine. He always made me laugh and could make me forget fear, discomfort. I'll forever be grateful to him. I don't think I would have survived that time without him.*

A month later, the watch returned, accompanied by a letter in a delicate hand befitting every description of Lizzie Jimmy ever gave. *I want you to keep the watch,* she wrote. *Jimmy would want you to, I know. Just knowing he had such a friend as you at the end is enough. He was sunshine. Remember him that way, won't you?*

Recalling the words, George breathed deeply. Yes, he'd always remember Jimmy as sunshine. "Look up at the sky," Jimmy used to say. "Clouds don't last forever. Blue'll always shine through." Julia had a similar saying on a cloudy day. "Look," she'd say, "enough blue sky to make a pair of men's trousers," meaning no storm lasts forever.

George closed the door and started for the barn to join his boys, the memories making him smile. They were old friends, and he was glad of their company.

# Acknowledgements

Thank you to my family, especially my parents, who have continually supported me in my writing, from reading early drafts to traveling with me on research trips and being as excited as I was to dig into historical archives. Thank you for being there for all the ups and downs.

Thank you to my mentors who read, critiqued, and edited the story, pushing me to embrace my writing, develop my writing voice, and above all believe in the story I was telling. Thank you for your belief in my story, and that someday it would reach the world. To Burt Bradley, who saw the very first handwritten portion of the novel; Bill Hoagland, who helped me craft that handwritten piece into a short story; Robert Stubblefield, who pushed me to expand that story into a novel and who has been unfailing in his support; Deirdre McNamer, who read draft after draft and always offered encouraging and insightful critiques; Jeff Wiltse, who gave a historical perspective; Deborah Koelling, who always believed in me; and many others who have been influential along the way.

Thank you to the museum and archive curators who helped track down historical records with excitement and interest in the novel. Thank you especially to Dan at the Rio Rico Historical Society, who not only knew of George as "the brick king of Arizona," but gathered together the research he had done for me to borrow and gave me a brick made by George for me to take home. Thank you also to the bellhop at the Hotel Teatro in Denver, who's name I do not know, but whom I will always remember for the double door entrance into the hotel to show the photograph of the brick house George, Jack, and John built for Governor Evans.

Thank you to everyone at Spellbound Publishing for believing in *The George Story* and making publication a reality. I am grateful to everyone who has invested their time and effort into the novel, from the fabulous cover art, to the formatting, and everything in between. A special thank you to Alexa Nichols, who has worked tirelessly as my editor. I am beyond lucky to have her as my editor. She is a joy to work with and has been unbelievably careful with George's story. Thank you.

Finally, thank you to the real-life George Atkinson. Without him having lived, this story never would have been possible. Thank you for living an inspiring life, and I hope that within these pages I have done you justice.

# About the author

*Picture of Callie*

Growing up on a small farm in Belfry, Montana, Callie Ann Atkinson spent her childhood outdoors, deeply influenced by her biologist parents. Family trips often involved field surveys and visits to Yellowstone, which nurtured her love for nature. Farm life instilled in her the delicate balance of joy and heartache—a theme that frequently emerges in her writing. Fascinated by the magic of words from a young age, Callie has always dreamed of becoming an author, finding writing to be an essential part of her life.

As the middle of three sisters, family plays a pivotal role in Callie's life. After college, she returned to the family farm, where she built a tiny house next to her parents. She shares her home with two English Shepherds, Missy and Brydie, and a cat named Dingle. On the farm, Callie raises Paint and Quarter Horses, Galloway cattle, and is constantly followed by her nosy Dutch Belted milk cow, Zyzy. Hiking and running are two of her passions, and she is a semi-competitive ultramarathoner. Additionally, she loves experimenting with new recipes in the kitchen.

Callie holds an MFA in Poetry from Spalding University and an MFA in Fiction from the University of Montana. Currently, she teaches English at Joliet

High School in Montana. Her work has been published in *Farming Magazine*, *The Small Farmers Journal*, *The Whitefish Review*, *The Best Emerging Poets* (Z Publishing), and *The Louisville Review*.

Follow Callie on social media:

Instagram: @CallieAnnAtkinson

Facebook: Callie Ann Atkinson Author

Printed in the USA
CPSIA information can be obtained
at www.ICGtesting.com
LVHW030828271024
794827LV00002B/3

9 798891 230828